TED TAYLER

WHISPERED TRUTHS

BOOKS

By Ted Tayler

The Freeman Files

Red Herring Season
Gathering Clouds
Still Standing

Vinci Books

vinci-books.com

Published by Vinci Books Ltd in 2025

1

A CIP catalogue record for this book is available from the British Library.
Paperback ISBN: 9781036705053

Chapter One

Tuesday, 2 October 2018

GUS TOOK a deep breath as the lift doors opened. He and Lydia stepped into the office.

"Welcome back, you two," said Neil.

"You look worried, guv," said Blessing. "We hoped you might be the bearer of good news."

"Have you heard from Grace and Alex yet?" asked Lydia. "We thought they would be here by now."

"Alex texted me thirty minutes ago," said Neil. "He reckoned it was a wasted journey. He said you would be happy that Amazing Grace asked the right questions, but Anna Cromwell's answers didn't advance our cause. Alex didn't believe they were closer to finding Katherine Alford's killer."

"It was unlikely they would find the answer in Dorchester," said Gus. "Unless DI Packenham ignored my assertion there was only one car on the housing estate when Bert Harris walked Biggles."

"You've learned there was another car?" asked Blessing. "Who saw it?"

"Grace and Alex are on their way home," said Gus. "They should be here in the next half-hour. Lydia and I will update the Freeman Files with the information we gathered during our two interviews this morning. I suggest you and Neil get your records straight, too. What were the headlines?"

"We visited Bert Harris, guv," said Neil. "He was having one of his vague days. Because our last visit wasn't in the newspapers, Bert needed reminding who we were and what we'd asked him last time. Blessing got Bert on track after a few minutes, and we went over what happened as he returned home from Coldharbour Lane. We were careful not to put words in his mouth."

"I asked Mr Harris to close his eyes and see Katherine's red car," said Blessing.

"Bert repeated what he told us the other day, guv," said Neil. "The Peugeot drove across the junction at the top of the road, travelling from left to right."

"I asked him whether he'd heard any other cars nearby," said Blessing. "Either before or after he saw the red car."

"Bert said it was the sound that made him look up," said Neil. "He'd been enjoying a quiet stroll with Biggles. They'd stopped by a lamppost, and when he glanced up, he spotted a car he recognised and then carried on walking home."

"I asked Mr Harris to keep his eyes closed, guv," said Blessing, "and describe what he saw next. He told us he had to wait for another car to pass him before crossing the road. I asked if he could remember what colour it was and whether he had seen the driver. He told us the car was dark, perhaps grey, and the driver was female."

"We believe it was a Honda Civic," said Gus.

"Not a Jazz then, guv?" asked Lydia. She looked puzzled.

"What aren't you telling us, guv?" asked Neil.

"They didn't start making the Jazz in Swindon until 2009, Lydia," said Gus. "My guess is Amy Gray switched to the Jazz later, but back in 2008, the Civic was a readily available model for the good doctor. We can ask Wayne Barnett to check."

"Are you going to tell Neil and Blessing what we know, guv?" asked Lydia.

"I haven't heard everything they have to tell me yet. What did Bert say happened next?"

"He made his way home and went to bed," said Blessing. "Mr Harris confirmed he had never seen the second car on the estate before."

"We have to remember how Bert came to respond to the TV appeal, guv," said Neil. "The police wanted to hear from anyone who saw Katherine's Peugeot on Saturday night. Bert remembered he had, and that was the only car he told them about."

"How does Amy Gray connect to the sighting of the cars, guv?" asked Blessing.

"All in good time, Blessing," said Gus. "What was the other task you two handled?"

"We dug into Amy's background, guv," said Neil. "She lived closer to Dominic Gray in Marlborough than Katherine Alford, but Amy fell somewhere between the two age-wise. All four children went to the same local schools. So, they would have been aware of one another but moved in different circles because of their age."

"Katherine and Alice were great friends," added Blessing, "but we found nothing to suggest Amy was ever close to the two younger girls. I spoke with several former sixth-form pupils from St John's who were in Amy's year. They remembered her as the quiet, studious type, but they all agreed Amy had a crush on the dashing Dominic. A couple of those former students are still registered as patients of Amy Gray at the town surgery."

"Did any of those women have anything to add?" asked Gus.

"Amy's reputation as a man-eater was well-founded, guv," said Neil. "Nobody suggested she has ever carried on with one of her patients."

"Is that it?" asked Gus.

"Pretty much, guv," said Neil. "We started updating our files before you got back. Give us fifteen minutes, and we'll be finished."

Neil looked towards Blessing, and she nodded.

"I'll get the coffee," she said. "I wish Grace and Alex would hurry. I want to know what's going on."

"I'll come with you, Blessing," said Lydia. "Believe me. I was in the same situation ninety minutes ago."

The files were soon done and dusted, and the coffee mugs were back on the shelf beside the Gaggia. Ten minutes later, Gus heard the lift descend to the ground floor and prepared for the ice storm that was sure to follow.

Neil dispensed with his customary cheery quip when Grace and Alex arrived in the office.

"Welcome back," he said.

"I hope the rest of you had more joy than we did," groaned Alex.

"It sounds like a quick debrief is in order before updating your files," said Gus. "I'm sure you asked the right questions, Grace, so why didn't ACC Cromwell provide you with telling answers?"

"Anna treated us very well, Gus," said Grace, flopping

into her chair like a petulant teenager. "She was polite and eager to assist in our cold case review but didn't tell us much we didn't already know."

"I doubt Wayne Barnett ever received a Christmas card from her, guv," said Alex. "The ACC took great pleasure in listing the number of black marks against Wayne during their investigation. However, we sensed the story Callum Brady told us was true. Wayne made a pass at Anna Cromwell, and she rejected his advances."

"Wayne's an idiot," said Gus. "However, all was not what it seemed at George Street."

Grace turned her head towards Gus at that remark.

"If you picked up gossip, or fresh facts this morning, it could have helped," she said. "Why didn't you update us?"

"Meetings with witnesses and potential suspects have a habit of moving at a snail's pace for ages, then suddenly racing at one hundred miles an hour, ma'am," said Lydia, "as you well know."

"I can't think of much we learned this morning that might have helped you, Grace," said Gus. "Neil and Blessing arrived here just after you left the car park en route to Dorchester. As it turned out, hearing Neil's background on Amy Winters and how she fitted into the scheme of things would have been vital. But, unfortunately, we weren't to know that until we'd started interviewing her husband."

"Lydia looks like the cat that got the cream, guv," said Alex. "It strikes me we're several steps behind you in this investigation."

"Lydia was right about a missing piece of the jigsaw producing a sudden acceleration in progress," said Gus. "What I thought would be a brief social conversation with Eve Northwood turned the case on its head."

"Are you telling us you've found Katherine Alford's killer?" asked Grace.

"That's only half of what we learned this morning," said Lydia.

"I must admit to an error," said Gus. "It didn't seem likely another vehicle was involved when Katherine died. My head told me Katherine met her killer soon after leaving home, and they stayed in the car throughout, except for a brief stop at The Roebuck. We knew Katherine worked at Savernake, and however brief the time their careers over-lapped, she and Dominic Gray could have known one another. But, unfortunately, I didn't give that snippet of information sufficient thought."

"It was Dominic Gray who found the body," said Grace.

"Yet when the uniformed officers took his statement, he didn't tell them he recognised the deceased," said Gus.

"Dominic Gray was at Savernake Hospital the evening of the murder, guv," said Alex. "His wife said he arrived home not long after eleven. How could he have been with Katherine that evening at all, let alone at West Woods after midnight? Why would Katherine rush out to meet Dominic, anyway?"

"You'll have to fill in the gaps, guv," said Lydia. "They don't have the missing pieces of the jigsaw."

"They're still looking at the wrong picture on the box, like the rest of us, guv," said Blessing.

"I'm more in the dark now than I was on Monday morning," sighed Grace.

"Wayne Barnett has plenty to do yet to determine when it all started," said Gus. "It's easy to understand how Dominic Gray's views on end-of-life suffering evolved after losing his only sister to leukaemia. We had learned Katherine and Alice were the best of friends. I didn't realise how those facts connected until we spoke to Dominic Gray. Once the first domino fell, the cascade continued until the full picture was revealed. There was no time to consider whether to call the office or text Alex to keep you two in the loop. I'm sorry, but we kept watching the dominos falling."

"If there was any hesitation," said Lydia. "Gus gave a slight nudge that encouraged Dominic and Amy Gray to tell us the full story," said Lydia.

"You think Dominic killed Katherine and Amy helped him cover it up?" asked Grace. "What possible motive did he have? Why would his wife stand by him, anyway?"

"We need to go back further than the night of the murder, I'm afraid," said Gus. "Trefor Davies's wife may not have been the first when she died of bone cancer at Savernake Hospital. But Dominic Gray handled her palliative care while she was there. We learned that Amy Gray was Megan's doctor. The Alford family had been registered with the same practice for many years. When we read the statements from West Woods in the murder file, there was nothing to indicate the two cyclists were so closely connected to our victim."

"Remind me again how Katherine's mother died, guv," said Alex.

"Cancer, Alex," said Gus. "Amy Gray referred her to the Great Western Hospital in Swindon. The aggressive treatment she received there only delayed the inevitable, and Mary transferred to Savernake."

"Where Dominic Gray tended to her in her final weeks," said Lydia.

"The mists are clearing," said Grace. "When did Katherine realise Dominic Gray was responsible for her mother's death?"

"Don't jump to conclusions, ma'am," said Blessing. "We don't have enough information yet."

"When we left Trefor's office to speak to Wayne Barnett, I asked Trefor why he put Wayne Barnett in charge of the Alford murder case," said Gus. "Trefor told us he thought it was the right thing to do. After listening to the other conversations that morning, it made perfect sense. When we went to speak to Wayne, Eve Northwood was in his office, so we waited in the corridor. I was surprised to see Eve so far from Gablecross, but it appears she's Wayne's aunt. I have no idea why she was visiting him, but Eve told me Dominic Gray had performed a similar role to her in the past. Dominic Gray had been on standby to perform post mortems if the regular pathologist was absent."

"How did that impact the Alford case?" asked Grace.

"The regular coroner had flown home to South Africa for his father's funeral at the time of the murder," said Gus.

"If Dominic Gray did the post-mortem, that opens up several possibilities," said Alex.

"Go on," said Gus.

"The coroner's role is to establish the time and cause of death, guv. If Dominic Gray and Katherine were in a relationship, and she died after an argument, he could manipulate the facts to give him an alibi."

"Surely, Anna Cromwell and Wayne Barnett would have recognised him when they attended the post-mortem?" said Grace.

"I asked Wayne why they didn't notice, and he shrugged and said they all looked alike in a mask and scrubs. Wayne reminded me it was Anna's first post-mortem, so she had her eyes closed for most of it. When they were at West Woods two days earlier, her focus was on the Peugeot. Wayne Barnett was hungover and paid scant attention to the uniformed officers taking statements from the two cyclists."

"Why didn't Trefor Davies get Barnett and Cromwell to do a follow-up interview, guv?" asked Alex.

"Trefor Davies guided them in another direction," said Grace. "He realised Dr Gray had brought his wife's suffering to a premature end and didn't want anyone to probe too deeply."

"Right," said Alex. "So that's what was going on. Even if Katherine realised something similar had occurred with her mother, it doesn't explain why Dominic Gray called her that night or why she dropped everything to meet him. What was the nature of their relationship?"

"When I studied Katherine's bank account, there was just one anomaly," said Grace. "Katherine didn't always need to withdraw cash. So we reckoned someone was paying her for services rendered. Was Katherine black-mailing Dominic Gray?"

"A moot point, Grace," said Gus. "This case should be a lesson learned. How was Katherine portrayed in the murder file? What was it you said, Blessing?"

"Katherine was a devoted mother-of-two, guv," said Blessing. "Nobody had a bad word to say about her, whether members of her family, friends, or neighbours. So I queried how a woman who appeared to be a saint could anger someone so much they strangled her."

"Why *was* Dominic Gray paying Katherine cash then, guv?" asked Alex.

"As with other aspects of this case, you need to analyse the distant past, Alex," said Gus. "Alice and Katherine were best friends as kids. They spent a lot of time playing together, often at Alice's home. Dominic remembered Katherine had an unusual skill. She could reproduce a copy of anyone's handwriting, apparently at will. So when they met at Savernake Hospital, Dominic realised he could contact Katherine whenever he needed a signature forged. Katherine needed the extra cash after Daniel Matravers walked away from their marriage. We may never know how often Dominic Gray shortened the suffering of a dying patient in his care, but I suspect the cost of a signature rose steeply from 2000 onwards."

"Katherine wasn't as saintly as I believed, guv," said Blessing.

"I've just remembered something," said Grace. "A footnote attached to the post-mortem referred to the IUD, and the coroner said he'd discussed the matter with the victim's GP. We did not know that signified Dominic Gray had spoken to his wife."

"We followed the threads from the initial investigation and concentrated on the relationships between Daniel and Katherine, Katherine and Emily, and even Emily and Paul," said Gus. "Both investigations sought a lover, a casual employer, anything to explain who Katherine had dashed out to meet and why."

"It was a person Katherine thought of as being like a brother," said Lydia. "As thick as thieves one minute and at arm's length the next, but never on intimate terms."

"Or so we thought," said Gus. "We'll get to that in a minute. But first, I want to explain how my insistence there was never a second car kept us from asking the right questions earlier in the piece. Bert Harris said Katherine's car sped past him, travelling left to right, as he walked towards the junction. Callum Brady conceded that Anna had concentrated on the actual sighting of the Peugeot, even though they both knew half a dozen boy racers were reported to be causing a nuisance until midnight around the town. Callum Brady said Bert Harris might have noticed another car, but Anna discounted it as irrelevant as he didn't recognise it."

"So, who was driving the other car?" asked Grace.

"Amy Gray," said Gus.

"She must have known what her husband was up to and followed him," said Grace.

"We interviewed Dominic Gray first," said Gus. "Everything followed the familiar path of events we had read in the murder file. The hospital rang that evening to tell him his patient was dying. Dominic Gray went to Savernake in a vain attempt to save him. He completed the necessary documentation and then returned home, where he spoke to his wife just after eleven o'clock."

"Dominic and Amy drank wine with their evening meal," said Lydia. "He took a taxi to Savernake. When we asked how he got home, he claimed he'd called Amy and told her what had happened. Someone happened to be travelling his way and gave him a lift."

"That sounds convenient," said Neil. "With slight variations to the statement in the murder file."

"Dominic stuck to the story he and his wife rehearsed for what happened on Sunday morning," said Lydia.

"When I asked why Amy didn't recognise the car, Dominic was screwed," said Gus. "He tried to bluff his way out of trouble, but it didn't make sense that Amy wouldn't have seen the red Peugeot at the doctor's surgery. He was further on the back foot when I suggested he must have been shocked to find the victim was Katherine, someone he'd known since childhood."

"Dominic said he'd realised it was Katherine after working inside the car for several minutes," said Lydia, "but he still didn't tell the uniformed officers he knew the victim."

"He tried to fob us off by saying he hardly met Katherine when they worked at the same hospital and couldn't recall the last time they'd spoken," said Gus. "I couldn't get my head around Katherine's random cash deposits. Nor could I accept it was acceptable for him to do the post-mortem despite Eve Northwood saying it made sense to maintain continuity from the crime scene."

"Dominic Gray had ample opportunity to mislead the original investigation," said Grace. "When did the murder take place?"

"An hour earlier than reported," said Gus. "We didn't get confirmation of that until we interviewed Amy Gray. By that time, I'd unpicked Dominic Gray's version of events on Saturday night and Sunday morning, and she suspected I had the upper hand."

"I imagine you presented Amy Gray with a modified version that suggested you knew far more than you did," said Grace. "She fell for it."

"Amy was a far weaker opponent," said Gus.

"Gus sat back and let Amy tell us the full story," said Lydia. "My overall impression was Amy was relieved it was over."

"Amy would have done anything for Dominic," said Gus. "They both wanted children, but it didn't happen for whatever reason. Dominic didn't object when his wife slept with other men in the hope of conceiving. As far as Amy was concerned, Dominic never looked at another woman until Katherine took Paul into the surgery one day."

"Katherine and Dominic *were* having an affair," said Grace. "How did they keep it under wraps for so long? Lily never suspected a thing, nor did Katherine's daughter, Emily."

"Did Amy mention to Dominic that Katherine had asked for her coil to be removed, guv?" asked Alex.

"Amy Gray confirmed she had, Alex," said Gus. "That was wrong, but she couldn't have known what would follow. Katherine and Daniel's marriage was falling apart for obvious reasons, and she had never had feelings for Dominic. But, unfortunately, the same couldn't be said for him. Dominic had pursued her ever since they met again at Savernake. We can only guess at Katherine's motives, but the one occasion she relented and they had sex resulted in her getting pregnant."

"No wonder Daniel left," said Grace. "What did happen on Saturday night? I can't quite put the pieces together."

"The medical emergency was genuine," said Gus. "Dominic had made a fatal mistake on drug dosage. He needed Katherine to forge another document to stop his illustrious career from disappearing down the drain."

"Katherine thought she was helping him with another cancer patient," said Lydia. "Dominic had watched his sister dying and refused to let anyone suffer longer than necessary."

"Amy drove into town on her way to the hospital to collect Dominic," said Gus. "She saw Katherine and Dominic talking outside the pub, waited, and followed Katherine's car when they left. That was the grey car Bert Harris had to wait for until he could cross the road."

"So, Katherine and Dominic argued on the way to West Woods, and then he killed her," said Grace.

"No, Dominic was guilty of many things, but not Katherine's murder," said Gus. "He told us he'd called Amy to explain what had happened to his patient. That was a lie.

She didn't know a thing; therefore, he didn't know she wasn't home. Katherine dropped him at their house in Clench Common and headed for Bath Road to make her way home. Amy chased the Peugeot through the lanes and forced Katherine to stop at the car park at West Woods. When she joined Katherine in the car, Amy told her she'd known Paul was Dominic's child for years. She accused them of having an affair. Katherine put her straight. She had slept with Dominic once, and he meant nothing to her. He was just a means to an end."

"Gosh," said Grace.

"Amy couldn't listen to Katherine laughing at her," said Lydia.

"Amy strangled her, not Dominic," said Grace. "I didn't see that coming."

"Trefor Davies didn't come out of things too well, guv," said Alex.

"He's asked DS Mercer if he can retire earlier than planned," said Gus.

"You look puzzled, ma'am," said Lydia.

"I don't see how you explain the white cotton gloves," said Grace.

"Did Amy Gray wear them, Lydia?" asked Alex. "Were they lightweight driving gloves?"

"Perhaps the time of death wasn't the only misdirection Dominic Gray included in the post-mortem report," said Gus. "Time to update these files and then get off home."

Gus switched his attention to his keyboard. Perhaps he could avoid any further interrogation.

"Is it always like this?" Grace asked Neil.

"Pretty much," said Neil. "Have you ever played volleyball?"

Neil realised it was a daft question by how Grace shook

her head. However, he ploughed on regardless with his sporting metaphor.

"You must have seen the game on TV," said Neil. "Six players on each side, five whose main role is to stop the opposition from scoring. They then set up an unreturnable smash from the team's superstar within a couple of moves. Gus is our player who suddenly leaps above the height of the net when you least expect it to deliver a killing blow."

"Is it genius or luck?" asked Grace.

"Do you think the other five members of the volleyball team care? It's the win that's important."

Neil could tell Amazing Grace remained unconvinced. Unless you worked with Gus Freeman's team, you can't win them all.

At five o'clock, the office was already empty. Team members left after updating their files and reading through their colleagues' contributions. But, as far as Alex, Lydia, Blessing, and Neil were concerned, it had been a good day.

Gus scanned the Katherine Alford folder to check nothing essential was missing. He was happy that an early call to London Road would see him sitting in Kenneth's office later in the day.

Gus wondered whether he could still catch Geoff Mercer tonight to put in a good word for Trefor Davies. As his hand hovered over the phone, Grace Packenham emerged from the restroom.

"I thought everyone had gone home," said Gus.

"I wanted to congratulate you on another successful case," said Grace.

"I sense there's a 'but' on its way," said Gus. "You think keeping you out of the loop while in Dorchester was deliberate? I can assure you it wasn't. When Lydia and I reached Marlborough this morning, I had no idea we were close to solving the case. I thought we were light-years away. These things happen. This morning, meeting Eve Northwood at the George Street police station was a huge slice of luck. I can't explain why Barnett and Cromwell didn't check who the person was performing the post-mortem. Perhaps Trefor Davies unduly influenced how they then approached the investigation. We know now why that might have been. For the two young officers involved, they regarded Trefor as an experienced hand who knew the right path to follow."

"After a few weeks searching in vain for the mystery man Katherine dashed off to meet, they switched to different cases," said Grace. "They moved on, while the murder file remained open until the Chief Constable selected it for review. If Anna knew Dr Gray had discovered the body and carried out the post-mortem, she would have insisted on a follow-up interview."

"You spoke to Anna this morning," said Gus, "and I've read the report you and Alex included in the files. Why didn't you press her on how Trefor Davies monitored the initial investigation? It was the most significant case Wayne Barnett had handled to date, plus it was Anna's first murder case. Trefor should have given them far more guidance and support than he did."

"Anna didn't criticise her old boss," said Grace. "Her target was Wayne Barnett. She thought he should have been sacked by now, and as for Callum Brady, she dismissed him as a workhorse who never had an original thought in his life."

"Wayne warned us Anna didn't recognise the term 'team' and would always look after her reputation," said Gus. "I don't follow that approach. Our team discussed their concerns about the investigation before you left for Dorchester. For instance, did Anna ever wonder about the similarities in the statements provided by Dominic and Amy Gray?"

"Once you spoke to people in Marlborough this morning, you were in a position to question those statements," said Grace. "Hindsight is a wonderful thing. Anna couldn't have deduced much from their replies to the questions asked by the uniformed officers. Not with the evidence she had at her disposal ten years ago."

"Perhaps," said Gus, "but humour me, and reread them before leaving the office. Dominic and Amy didn't bat an eyelid when I said they rehearsed the evidence they provided on Sunday morning. The white cotton gloves were a clever ruse, and that threw me when Kenneth quoted details from the post-mortem. However, it stopped me from thinking about what they didn't say when questioned. The murder file successfully relegated them to a minor role of two cyclists who just happened upon a murder scene."

"Dominic Gray admitted he was a doctor working at Savernake Hospital," said Grace. "That's why the police accepted his assertion the victim had been strangled."

"Dominic and Amy knew the victim but never said a word," Gus said.

"We know why now," said Grace.

"Right. When interviewing an eyewitness, the standard procedure is to ask questions beginning with words such as Who, What, Where, When, Why, and How. We ask open-ended questions to allow the witness to provide their own answer. When you've reread those statements, I bet you'll see that Gray didn't allow the officers the opportunity to ask supplementary questions. Because of his background as a deputy coroner, he ensured the basics were covered when they prepared their statements on Saturday night. The uniformed officers got everything they needed, or so they thought. When the detectives and the forensic team arrived, the patrol car returned to the station, ready to respond to the next emergency call. If you need further proof, when Wayne Barnett glanced towards the lycra-clad cyclists, the couple were standing together. That suggests the uniforms didn't keep the witnesses separate. Amy listened as Dominic told the officers what he wanted them to hear."

"Then Amy told her story, using almost the same words," said Grace.

Gus grabbed his jacket, checked he had his car keys, and walked to the lift.

Grace sighed and opened her copy of the Freeman Files.

Chapter Two

AS GUS THREADED his way through early evening traffic on the outskirts of Devizes, he wondered how long it would be before Grace went running to Geoff Mercer.

Why worry? The best way for the Crime Review Team to survive until Kenneth Truelove was packing his suitcases for the cruises his wife had planned was to solve cases. The clues had fallen in their lap today; they might not be so lucky next time. But, as Blessing proved only weeks ago, any team member can deliver the coup de grâce. Grace would get her chance in time.

Gus couldn't deny he'd sent Grace to Dorchester because he didn't want to upset ACC Cromwell. But, sure as eggs were eggs, he would have asked a question that would have ruffled her fine feathers.

First, why didn't she suss that Dominic and Amy Gray had included too many specifics in their statement? Most eyewitnesses remember one fact they would swear to in court and a few vague recollections. But, on closer inspection, a rising star like Anna should have spotted the subtle misdirects even without hindsight.

Gus swung the Ford Focus through the gateway of the bungalow and parked under the rambling roses. He should have spent an hour at the weekend tidying those beauties. After a couple of summers, where he despaired that Tess's favourites were on their last legs, they were thriving but untidy.

He wasn't surprised to see Suzie's Golf parked to his right. Grace had delayed his departure from the office by ten minutes. Roadworks in Seend added a further five.

"The wanderer returns," said Suzie when Gus threw open the front door.

"A happy wanderer," said Gus. "My cup runneth over."

"Psalms," said Suzie, emerging from the kitchen. "You stopped at the allotment and bumped into the Reverend."

"No, I came straight from work," said Gus. "Lydia and I wrapped up the Katherine Alford case today. DI Barnett should have her killer in custody this evening. As for her husband, he faces a tricky time explaining the assisted deaths of several patients. But, on the other hand, Wayne Barnett can improve his reputation by defining the exact number."

"Doctor Gray? Are you serious?" asked Suzie.

"I won't ask which doctor," said Gus. "I'll leave Neil to attempt to make a joke out of that before the week's out. The wife strangled Katherine Alford because she succeeded where Amy failed."

"Paul was Dominic's son."

"Daniel knew it couldn't have been his because he'd had a vasectomy. His lover left in a huff, and Daniel calmly got his financial affairs in order and then walked out. Katherine was not as innocent as everyone thought. She made a tidy sum from forging documents for Dominic Gray to cover his drug prescriptions. His cause might appear noble to a jury. It wouldn't surprise me if he got away with the more serious charges the CPS will bring against him. Nevertheless, he won't work again. Even if he escapes a custodial sentence, the cosy retirement they planned together is finished."

"I heard a rumour this afternoon at London Road," said Suzie. "Was Trefor Davies involved in the fallout from the Alford case?"

"His first wife, Megan, was one of Dominic's first mercy killings," said Gus. "Trefor will retire earlier than planned, but I hope Geoff Mercer can find a way to limit the damage."

"Trefor's not firing on all four cylinders," said Suzie.

"The future's not bright," said Gus. "Right. Time to shower and change. Then I want to discover what smells so delicious in the kitchen."

"Brain food," said Suzie. "Sweet chilli grilled chicken, bean sprouts, carrots, radish, sesame seeds and mixed greens."

"A meal that will taste even better because I grew a third of the ingredients," said Gus.

Wednesday, 3 October 2018

GUS AND SUZIE left the bungalow at eight-thirty and joined a slow procession towards London Road. The Water Board was carrying out essential improvements for the next eight weeks. So when Suzie negotiated the right-turn into the Wiltshire Police Headquarters car park, Gus sat in the Focus four cars back from the not-so-temporary red light.

It allowed him to consider alternative routes to the Old Police Station office.

Thirty minutes later, he parked in the final space assigned to the team. Unfortunately, there was nothing for it. If he wished to get to work before nine o'clock, he needed to leave home earlier and travel to Devizes via Nursteed Road.

Gus travelled up in the lift, thinking this wasn't the positive start to the day he'd anticipated.

"Morning, guv," said Alex. "Road works at Seend again?"

"No, a nightmare on London Road threatens to last until Christmas. I've learned to take completion dates from utility companies with a pinch of salt. Eight weeks will be a minimum. They're bound to uncover another stretch of Victorian engineering in danger of imminent collapse that ramps up the inconvenience."

"I spoke to my father last night," said Lydia. "We fly out to join him and Rosa in Dubai on Saturday the thirteenth. My mother will join us on Sunday."

"We did mention it, guv," said Alex.

"I remember passing the details to Vera Butler at the time, Alex," said Gus. "I'm sure DS Mercer would have contacted me if there was a problem with you being out of the country for two weeks."

"You had forgotten, hadn't you, guv?" said Lydia.

"We've been busy," said Gus. "I made a mental note to ask DS Mercer for a helping hand. October has crept up on us sooner than I thought. We coped with just the four of us when we started. No doubt we can handle matters if nobody can be spared to join us at short notice."

"Rick Chalmers would jump at the chance to work with us again," said Neil.

"I'll test the waters when I visit London Road later today," said Gus. "That reminds me, I must call Vera to request an audience with the Chief Constable."

"We'll start clearing the decks ready for the next case, guv," said Lydia.

Gus watched the team swing into action, removing crime scene photos from the wallboards and returning the maps of Marlborough and the surrounding district to the cupboard. He wondered where they would go next.

One person was still seated at her desk, working on her computer. Grace Packenham didn't think maintaining a tidy ship was part of her remit. Gus picked up the phone.

"Good morning, Vera Butler speaking. How may I help you?"

"Vera, it's Gus here. When can I meet with Kenneth?"

"Don't tell me you've ticked another of his cold cases off the list?" said Vera. "Give me ten minutes, and I'll get back to you. He's not with the PCC today. I believe I saw him disappear into Geoff's office as soon as he arrived this morning."

"I think I know what that's about," said Gus. "I can be in his office in thirty minutes if I catch the traffic lights just right."

"I'll let Kenneth know as soon as he's finished with Geoff," said Vera. "I'm sure he'll want to see you. I'll call you back."

Vera ended the call, and Gus realised Amazing Grace was hovering at his shoulder.

"May I go through this report with you, Gus?" she asked.

"I take it this won't be included in the Freeman Files," said Gus.

If this was the first draft of a complaint to HR, Gus

thought it was decent of Grace to show him the details. He nodded towards the chair beside him.

"I took your advice and reread those two witness statements," said Grace. "I agree there were opportunities missed early in the investigation. For example, the uniformed officers should have split up to question Dominic and Amy Gray. Although our current procedures are detailed and comprehensive, everything can benefit from a periodic review. I've compiled a list of questions for DS Mercer to consider."

Grace pointed to an item in the main body of the four-page text.

Did you know the deceased? If No, move to the next question; if Yes, ask these follow-up questions.

"How late did you stay last night?" asked Gus. "You've put a lot of thought into this."

"It's what I do," said Grace. "I left here before half-past five and worked on it at home. I don't have a busy social life. Do you think it has merit?"

"It can't do any harm," said Gus. "I'll pass it to DS Mercer later if you wish. Unless you have something that you need to discuss face-to-face?"

"Not at present," said Grace. "I'd be grateful if you would hand it in. If your journey from Urchfont via London Road will be troublesome for the next couple of months, I could always collect you. I'm renting a two-bedroomed terraced house in Easterton from Monty Jennings. I don't know if you're familiar with the name. Vera put us in touch. Mr Jennings also found a place for Rhys Evans in Worton when he arrived from South Wales."

"Vera was married to Monty for over twenty years," said Gus. "Yes, our paths have crossed."

"Well. What do you say?" asked Grace.

"Monty's one of those people who's a prince one minute and a pauper the next. As a landlord, though. I've never heard anyone say anything detrimental."

"Not about Monty. Would you like me to bring you to work each day?"

"I appreciate the offer, Grace," said Gus. "It's early days yet. I'll get back to you if the situation doesn't improve. Some days, I drive Suzie into London Road, and over the next couple of months, those occasions could increase."

Grace was still seated beside him when his phone rang.

"Gus?" said Vera. "Kenneth's in his office now. Geoff will join you when you get here."

"Thank you, Vera," said Gus. "I'll leave straight away."

"I'll put this report with the Katherine Alford folder, Gus," said Grace. "Is there anything you need me to do while you're gone?"

"The others appear to have finished tidying the office, Grace," said Gus. "They might appreciate a coffee."

He grabbed the folders and headed for the lift.

When he reached his Focus, he shivered. Spending an extra hour every weekday trapped in that Smart car with Grace Packenham would be too much to bear.

His journey to London Road was uneventful, except for the final three hundred yards. Since he and Suzie had passed this way earlier this morning, the Water Board had shifted several tons of earth and stone. Most of which seemed to block the entrance to the car park until they could transfer it to a waiting lorry.

Gus threaded the Focus through the narrow gap and hunted for spare space. Finally, after his customary brief delay at Reception, he trotted upstairs to the mezzanine. He found Vera Butler seated at her desk in the Administration area.

"Your phone call was perfectly timed, Vera," said Gus. "Amazing Grace was trying to persuade me to travel to work in her ghastly vehicle."

"Very cosy," said Vera. "You're still talking then? That's progress."

"Grace tells me she's another of Monty's flock. Are you getting a commission on these tenants you send his way?"

Vera laughed.

"As long as Monty keeps clear of get-rich-quick schemes and can earn an honest wage from his properties, he won't try squeezing any more money out of my parents and me."

"How much does Grace know?" asked Gus.

"About Monty or us?"

"Both, I guess," said Gus.

"Very little about Monty because I don't think Grace mixes with the locals in Easterton. We're ancient history now, and I don't think anyone has mentioned it here at London Road. So why do you ask?"

"I'm sure Grace has a plan. She's been in the office for one whole day, had a trip to Dorchester with Alex, and everything has gone too smoothly. It makes me nervous."

Vera chuckled.

"You don't think maybe you've misjudged her, Gus? Kassie and I watched Grace deliver her report on the support staff to Geoff Mercer last Friday. Over the weekend, everyone was on edge, wondering how many people Grace proposed should receive a redundancy notice. If the rumours are correct, we're losing a Detective Inspector and gaining two support staff."

"I bet Grace didn't offer to fall on her sword," scoffed Gus. "Don't tell me she's targeted Suzie because she's an all-rounder and on maternity leave five months from now."

"Don't worry, Suzie's name wasn't mentioned. John

Carpenter is eighteen months from retirement. He won't see out his time at London Road now. I've heard there's a spot closer to where he lives that's more his style."

"Where does he live?" asked Gus.

"Avebury," said Vera.

"Eight minutes of driving time saved each day," said Gus. In addition, Geoff Mercer had solved the problem of replacing Trefor Davies with no one asking questions.

"Don't keep Kenneth waiting," said Vera. "Kassie will do the rounds with lunch later. I asked her to add your usual chicken wrap to the order."

Chicken again, thought Gus, as he crossed the mezzanine to Kenneth's door. If they visited the pub tonight, he would have beef or lamb, whatever happened.

Gus knocked, waited for the customary single-word invitation to enter, and found Geoff Mercer had arrived before him.

"Trust you to embellish your work again, Freeman," said the Chief Constable. "Why can't you solve a case and leave it at that?"

Gus placed the Katherine Alford folder on Kenneth's desk.

"I could have left this in the office if you know its contents, sir," he said. "We use the information we're handed at the outset, add to our knowledge, and the cards fall as they will. Nobody suspected Dominic Gray had been carrying on a personal crusade for over a quarter of a century when Katherine Alford died. It remains to be seen whether he found an alternative method of hiding his work in the subsequent years."

Gus handed Geoff Mercer the second folder from Grace Packenham.

"Grace has ideas on how we might improve our interview techniques for witnesses at a crime scene," he said. "I hope it shows we offer more than a mere crime-solving service."

Kenneth stood and walked to the window. Of course, he didn't have the same view he had when he was in his old office, but Gus knew from experience that old habits die hard.

"I had no idea people would stop telling me things when I took this job," said Kenneth. "When I was still an ACC, I would have heard the concerns about Trefor Davies's mental health. I've known Trefor since he moved here from South Wales. My wife and I met his first wife, Megan. We attended her funeral."

"I'm sorry, sir," said Gus. "I didn't realise."

"We're not good at dealing with feelings," said Kenneth. "Far too many officers suffer in silence. Trefor remarried, we lost touch, and as he was tucked away in a station scheduled for closure, his condition was never monitored."

"I'll do what I can to let Trefor leave with his dignity intact," said Geoff. "We couldn't have known what was going on at Savernake. Dominic Gray was known to be arrogant, but everyone regarded him as a respected physician. There were no rumours of wrongdoing."

"I've already reminded the team," said Gus. "This case proved that nothing you hear should ever be taken at face value. Nobody had a bad word to say about Katherine Alford, yet she helped Dominic Gray end the lives of an unknown number of people. She accepted money for her services, and the amounts she demanded possibly increased after Daniel Matravers left and they divorced. Various explanations were offered for Katherine keeping her daughter at arm's length after she gave birth to Sophia. We couldn't fathom why Katherine couldn't look after her grandchild during the school holidays. Rather than it being inconvenient, as she claimed, Katherine just couldn't be bothered. These are hardly the actions of a devoted mother. I believe she knew Daniel was involved with Guy Faulkner, and the baby was a deliberate ploy to drive Daniel away for good. Dominic Gray had stalked her for years. She knew she could have him whenever she wished. Unfortunately for Katherine, Amy Gray wasn't a forgiving sort. One look at Paul in her surgery, and she knew Daniel had cheated on her."

"Why did she wait so long to take her revenge?" said Kenneth.

"Dominic probably told Amy it was a mistake. One night of madness," said Gus. "Then, ten years later, after her husband went to Savernake that night, Amy drove into town to collect him, expecting to find him alone at the hospital. Instead, he was chatting to Katherine outside The Roebuck. The red mist descended, and Amy followed Katherine's car to Clench Common. Little did she know the couple argued throughout the time they were together."

"Your team did well to put the whole mess together, Freeman," said Kenneth. "Grace Packenham contributed more than a questionnaire, I hope?"

"Grace is still finding her feet, sir," said Gus. "This was her first murder case, and she's new to working in a team. It's not Wednesday lunchtime yet. I'm sure Grace will have her views on how her first few days have gone. Let's see how she feels after working together for a couple of months."

"Quite," said Kenneth. "Anything else before we move on to the next case?"

"DS Hardy and Ms Logan Barre have booked a holiday simultaneously, sir," said Gus, crossing his fingers. "They reminded me this morning. Is that okay?"

"I've sanctioned that holiday, Gus," said Geoff. "They're off for two weeks from the end of next week."

"That could prove tricky," said Kenneth. "Will you have the resources to cope, Freeman?"

"We've previously handled several cases with a small team, sir."

"I can't spare anyone to help," said Geoff.

"In that case, I suggest the entire Crime Review Team takes a break together."

Kenneth checked his calendar.

"Shut the office from the close of play on Friday the twelfth and start back to work on Monday the twenty-ninth. How does that sound?"

"Terrific," said Gus. "I hope the next file on your list won't be as taxing as the last."

"I've not handed you a double murder before," said Kenneth. "The luck of the draw, I'm afraid. So the first task is to determine whether it was a double murder or a murder followed by a suicide."

"Where are we off to this time?" asked Gus.

"Kington Langley, a village two miles north of Chippenham," said Kenneth. "Mark Fennell was shot at his home in April 2005. At ten-fifteen, he answered his door, and someone shot him with a twelve-gauge shotgun. Fennell was forty-eight years old and said to have no criminal connections and no known enemies. Although considering what you said earlier, perhaps we should ignore that and assume he was a rogue who mixed with the wrong crowd."

"Who was in charge of this one thirteen years ago, sir?" asked Gus.

"Detective Inspector Jim Francis from Chippenham," said Kenneth. "Jim was in his early fifties at the time. He's playing golf in Spain these days. His Detective Sergeant was

Henry Gibbs, who has moved to Avon & Somerset since then and been promoted. A young Detective Constable, Annie Drew, was Family Liaison Officer on the case. She spent time with Helen Roker. Roker was Fennell's partner, three years his junior."

"I suppose DC Drew has moved on, too," said Gus.

"There's no sign of the name on the present staff roster," said Geoff. "Annie's married with children, perhaps."

"The only pub in the village closed in 2015, too," said Kenneth. "Two weeks before the murder, the landlord was awaiting his first evening customer when a man walked in and asked for Mark Fennell. The landlord, Marcus Weston, knew who he meant but told the man Fennell hadn't lived in the village long, and he was far from being a regular. The man was tall, well-dressed, wearing a charcoal-grey three-piece suit. Weston thought he was in his late thirties, early forties, with a mop of unruly blond hair."

"Mr Weston noticed more than most witnesses," said Gus. "What about distinguishing marks or jewellery? Did he get the guy's collar size?"

"No tattoos visible," said Kenneth, "but Weston spotted an expensive gold wristwatch."

"What's Kington Langley like?" asked Gus. "It's another Wiltshire village I've never had cause to visit."

"You would have to go out of your way," said Geoff. "Most traffic stays on the A350 en route to the M4. The village is less populated than Urchfont, at around eight hundred."

"Mark Fennell lived half a mile from the pub," said Kenneth. "He moved to Kington Langley six months earlier with Helen Roker. They planned to get married. Roker had never married, but Fennell was in the process of divorcing his second wife. On the day of the murder, Fennell had worked on his car in the garage. When he returned indoors at around six o'clock, the couple ate a meal and decided to spend the evening at home watching TV. At ten o'clock, Helen Roker went upstairs to bed. She wanted to read a few chapters of Dan Brown's Da Vinci Code. Mark Fennell was half-asleep in the chair. Helen nudged him as she left the room, and Mark said he'd be up in a few minutes."

"He didn't make it," said Gus.

"Fennell made it upstairs," said Kenneth. "He visited the bathroom and was crossing the landing to their bedroom when he heard a knock at the door. He cursed and went back downstairs. Helen Roker got out of bed, went to the window, and saw a white BMW parked across the entrance to their driveway. She couldn't see the driver as he was on the doorstep, and nobody else was in the car. The police asked whether more than one person had come to the door, but she couldn't say."

"Helen Roker didn't go downstairs to check what was happening?" asked Gus.

"No, nor did she go back to bed. Instead, she stood on the landing trying to hear any conversation," said Kenneth. "The only raised voice she could identify was Mark's. Then there was a loud bang and a shout. As Helen ran downstairs, Mark staggered through the front door, bleeding from the chest, and collapsed on the floor. Helen dialled 999 from the landline in the hallway, but Mark Fennell died before the ambulance reached them."

"Did Helen Roker venture outside?" asked Gus.

The Chief Constable shook his head.

"No, she stayed with her partner throughout. Helen heard the BMW pull away at speed but couldn't tell the police anything about Mark's attacker or whether he had an accomplice."

"How long before Jim Francis arrived?" asked Geoff Mercer.

"Uniformed officers responded first," said Kenneth. "They received the call at the same time as the paramedics. Then, DI Francis arrived with DS Gibbs just before eleven o'clock. After that, the uniformed officers were sent door-to-door, hoping to find someone who saw the gunman or the BMW."

"I bet the locals appreciated that," said Gus.

"You know there can be gaps between properties in a village, Gus," said Geoff. "Kington Langley is one and a half miles long and stands on a hilltop. So a gun going off in the countryside isn't as big a shock as it would be in the centre of Devizes. Of course, the nearest neighbouring properties might have heard a noise. But with triple-glazing and wide-screen television with full surround sound, even that isn't certain. The uniforms got to those closest houses quickly. DI Francis continued the door-to-door around the rest of the village in the morning."

"Did the police establish a motive?" asked Gus.

"DI Francis had a few ideas but suspected Fennell was an innocent victim."

"A case of mistaken identity?" asked Gus. "That doesn't fit with the actions of our suited and booted visitor at the pub. He asked for Mark Fennell by name."

"Unfortunately, Mark Fennell is not uncommon, " Kenneth said. "Anyway, the two events may not have been connected."

"I'm flicking through Facebook," said Geoff Mercer. "Not something I do very often, I can assure you. Facebook was in its infancy in 2005. My search today suggests a minimum of fifty people with the same name in the country."

"Did the door-to-door bring results?" asked Gus.

"Mrs Ruth Redman lived three doors from Fennell and Roker," said Kenneth. "She told police she saw a white BMW 3-series driving through the village earlier in the evening."

"What time?" asked Gus. "She knew the make and model. What about a number plate?"

"Afraid not," said Kenneth. "Mrs Redman was watching TV in her lounge at half-past seven when sounds of a commotion caused her to go to the window and look outside. Her words, not mine."

"I take it Ruth Redman was an elderly lady?" asked Gus.

"If you consider sixty-one elderly."

"Point taken."

"Kington Langley doesn't trouble the crime statistics often, but they have their share of anti-social behaviour. One family who lived on the outskirts of the village was the main contributor in 2005. Kyle Harding was the fifteen-year-old son of parents frequently in trouble with the law. Ruth Redman recognised Kyle, even in the semi-darkness."

"The village still had street lighting back then," said Geoff Mercer.

"Kyle was standing on the pedals of his mountain bike, kicking over the wheelie-bins that householders had placed on the edge of the pavement ahead of the following morning's waste collection. Ruth Redman waited for the young hooligan to cycle off before going outside to pick up the stricken bins. While she righted hers and that of her closest neighbours, the white BMW drove past. Mrs Redman said the car looked brand new and had only one occupant."

"The number plate would have been a big help," said Geoff Mercer. "Over forty-five thousand of that model were sold in the UK in 2005. Of course, Jim Francis knew the colour, which would have reduced the number, but needle and haystack still spring to mind."

"Why did Ruth Redman remember the car?" asked Gus.

"Mrs Redman hadn't seen it in the village before," said Kenneth. "Then, as she walked from the pavement to her front door, the car drove past again. The driver didn't appear to be in a hurry. She wondered if he was lost or looking for someone. When she got indoors, Mrs Redman drew back her curtains and settled to watch TV with the light off. She wanted to keep an eye out for Kyle Harding in case he was still intent on causing trouble. Kyle must have cycled home, but headlights soon loomed in her lounge window, and Mrs Redman confirmed it was the BMW yet again. She reckoned the car continued driving up and down through the village for at least two hours."

"Did Mark Weston tell the blond-haired man where Mark Fennell lived?" asked Gus.

"No," said Kenneth, "Weston didn't think it was his place to do so. He didn't know the man from Adam, and although he considered Fennell was only a casual customer, he didn't want to get involved."

"Something about the man raised alarm bells," said Gus. "Did Fennell or Roker learn someone was hunting for Mark Fennell that night?"

"DC Annie Drew spoke to Helen Roker the morning after the murder," said Kenneth. "Drew was acting as Family Liaison, but she still encouraged Roker to think of a motive for the shooting. Annie pressed her for the name of someone with a grievance against her partner. Roker remembered an incident where the couple had spent the weekend in Burnham-on-Sea at a caravan park, and she spent Monday evening catching up with the laundry. Mark was in the garage, working on the car. It had been troublesome on the return journey, and Mark moaned that he might need a new gearbox."

"Does that sound familiar, Gus?" said Geoff.

"Not a bit," said Gus. "I hope I haven't tempted fate. Whatever ailed Fennell's car, he hadn't solved the problem two weeks later. He spent the day working on the car on the day he died."

"Anyway, Roker told Annie Drew that friends from Chippenham had dropped by," said Kenneth. "Sam and Mary Webber told Helen they passed a car parked a short distance up the road towards Chippenham. They got a good view of the driver, who wore a dark suit and had long blond hair. Sam Webber thought he was a few years younger than Mark, and although sitting in the driver's seat, he reckoned the guy was above average height."

"When was this?" asked Gus.

"Eight-thirty on the same night the man visited the pub," said Kenneth. "Helen said Sam and Mary were renting their caravan for a midweek break and came to collect the keys."

"Who owned the caravan?" asked Gus.

"Mark Fennell bought it in 2003, shortly after meeting his second wife, Jessie."

"Did Mark hear what Sam and Mary Webber told Helen?"

"No, Helen said that Mark was in the garage with the doors closed. Their friends collected the keys and drove home to Chippenham. Helen went to bed at ten, just before Mark returned indoors, but forgot to mention the car Sam and Mary spotted. It hadn't registered with her that it might be important. Annie's questions jogged her memory, but Helen didn't recognise the driver's description. It might have been someone Mark knew, but he must have met him before they got together."

"All the sightings so far have been for the first recorded visit of the BMW driver," said Gus. "Did nobody catch a glimpse the night Mark Fennell died?"

"The police received a phone call a week after the murder," said Kenneth. "George Miles lives in the last house on the road leaving Kington Langley at a place they call Lower Common. George had cycled home from the village hall, where he had attended a skittles evening. As he got close to his gateway, a car sped past, almost knocking him off his bicycle. George thought it was a foreign white car. He couldn't be certain of the time because he admitted having had a couple of pints during the evening. George thought it was half-past ten, give or take."

"A speeding car, possibly a BMW, heading towards the Stanton St Quinton roundabout," said Geoff Mercer. "In a few minutes, it could join the M4 at Junction 17 and head east or west. Take your pick between London and South Wales."

"The simple option is often the best, Geoff," said Gus. "Swindon's the nearest big town where criminals who carry guns hang out. However, we need to know more about Mark Fennell and Helen Roker. Where did they live before moving to Kington Langley? What did they do for a living? I want to take this murder file back to the office to learn about Fennell's brief second marriage and his first. Unless they've upset somebody, people don't get blasted in the chest with a shotgun."

Chapter Three

"YOU'VE ONLY HEARD HALF the story, Freeman," said Kenneth. "Of course, you must delve deeper into the lives of the people involved. I assume you listened when I started giving you the headline report?"

"I was hanging on your every word, sir," said Gus.

"Jim Francis is long retired, and although I'm happy for you to ring him in Spain, he might be uncooperative."

"DI Francis had a reputation for cutting corners," said Geoff Mercer.

"Hence his suggestion it was a case of mistaken identity," said Gus. "The odds against solving that class of murder are high. If Jim Francis wanted to get away for a golfing weekend, he could have used it as an excuse to close the investigation early."

"I can't see a problem with getting in touch with DI Henry Gibbs in Taunton," said Geoff. "However, tracking down Annie Drew could prove tricky."

"I told you about the gentleman who cycled home from the village hall," said Kenneth. "It's the only place you can get a drink in the village these days since the last pub closed."

"I'm not sure they should be able to call Kington Langley a village, sir," said Gus. "The last time I checked, there were three thousand villages in England. It's difficult to imagine one without an imposing country church. A building that has stood on the same patch of ground since the Middle Ages."

"St Peter's was built in 1855," said Geoff. "The vicar looks after four or five other churches in the area."

"The Reverend Clemency Bentham performs a similar role at Urchfont," said Gus. "So, Kington Langley has a church, but the public house is essential in village life. No matter how many pretty cottages are built with the local stone they still have, the heart of the community has been ripped out."

"You'll be waxing lyrical about cricket on the village green next, Freeman," said Kenneth. "Kington Langley has at least three sizeable areas of common land, so it scores another point towards village status. Times have changed, Freeman. People can get their beer, wine, and spirits from the supermarket."

"I can't deny that Suzie and I buy alcohol as part of our weekly shop," said Gus. "I still believe everyone should have a choice. However, I can tell you're keen to continue the headline report, sir."

"Helen Roker left the village soon after Mark Fennell's funeral."

"That sounds callous, sir," said Gus.

"I told you Fennell was in the process of divorcing his second wife, Jessie," said Kenneth. "Mark and Jessie were separated but still legally married."

"I imagine Fennell hadn't had time to provide for Roker in his will," said Gus.

"At least he had one," said Geoff. "Many blokes of his age haven't got around to it."

"You can speak to Robert Rideout, the solicitor who handled probate," said Kenneth. "Things were complicated in Fennell's life. He married young, had two children, and his wife got fed up with the affairs and threw him out. Fennell met Jessie North, a whirlwind romance followed, and they married at Christmas 2003 on a beach in St Lucia."

"Eleven months later, Fennell was up to his old tricks again," said Geoff. "He left Jessie in October 2004. He had met Helen Roker in a pub in Chippenham in July. The day after he walked out, Fennell and Roker moved into the rented house in Kington Langley."

"Where did Helen Roker move to after learning the contents of the will?" asked Gus.

"Back to Chippenham," said Kenneth. "Helen rented a property on Foundry Lane. Joe Morgan, a forty-one-year-old delivery driver, was her latest boyfriend. Morgan found Helen's body when he got home from work in January 2006."

"Cause of death?" asked Gus.

"Morgan discovered Helen Roker dead in the bath," said Kenneth. "Police found two empty bottles of Chardonnay in the living room, a half-empty wine glass in the bathroom, and a selection of pills. Morgan told police that since Mark Fennell's murder, his partner had been depressed. Most of the pills were anti-depressants prescribed by her doctor, but Helen had also taken sixteen paracetamol caplets."

"Who handled the investigation into this case?" asked Gus.

"DI Dave Perry and DS Frankie Price from Chippenham," said Kenneth.

"Mark Fennell died in Helen's arms nine months earlier," said Gus. "Helen was receiving treatment for depression, and although she appeared to have moved on with a new relationship, she was a troubled soul. Was there any indication Helen wanted to take her life?"

"Joe Morgan didn't think so," said Kenneth. "He thought Helen was responding to treatment. Dave Perry asked if Helen was a heavy drinker. Morgan reminded Perry he hadn't known Helen that long. He insisted there were never empty wine bottles lying around when he got home. They both enjoyed a drink when they went out in the evenings, particularly at weekends, but that was it."

"Was Helen working?" asked Gus.

"Yes, as a care worker, supporting people with all aspects of their day-to-day living, including social and physical activities, personal care, mobility, and meals."

"I take it Perry and Price left you a leaflet in that headline report," said Gus.

Kenneth nodded.

"You know how it is, Gus," said Geoff Mercer, "people in that role can work in a care home or people's houses. Helen would have met with many people, not just the elderly but also adults with learning and physical disabilities."

"Care workers come into contact with adults with substance misuse issues and mental health conditions, too," said Gus. "Was that the right job for someone like Helen struggling with life after a tragic bereavement?"

"DI Perry soon made the connection with Mark Fennell's death in Kington Langley," said Kenneth. "He had to consider whether Helen might have been murdered because of her close connection to Fennell. Helen Roker had told DC Annie Drew she didn't go outside and hadn't seen the killer, but perhaps she lied. Whether she could identify him or not, the killer might have viewed Helen Roker as a loose end."

"So, the initial thoughts were Helen Roker had committed suicide," said Gus. "With DI Perry keeping a second murder on the table, just in case."

"That sums things up," said Geoff Mercer, "given the information available before the post-mortem."

"The coroner in Chippenham in 2006 was a chap called Conrad Alderslade," said Kenneth. "Alderslade was old school and had been in the job for over thirty years. He was past his retirement date, but they couldn't convince him to retire."

"Had he become incompetent?" asked Gus.

"No, Alderslade was a capable, thorough practitioner," said Kenneth. "Perry wanted a clear-cut verdict and no messing, but Alderslade was non-committal."

"Everything at the scene pointed to it being suicide," said Geoff Mercer.

"The bath was filled to overflowing," said Kenneth. "The water was tepid when Joe Morgan returned home, but he could tell Helen had used bubble bath. That seemed odd because Helen favoured a shower over a bath since they'd been together. He couldn't recall when she'd pampered herself in that manner, even though she had the ingredients available."

"What time did Joe arrive home?" asked Gus.

"Seven o'clock," said Kenneth. "He didn't work regular hours."

"Even if Helen filled the bath with water hot enough to scald her, it wouldn't take longer than two hours to cool down," said Geoff.

"Had Helen worked that day?" asked Gus.

"She completed several regular home visits and finished her shift at two o'clock."

"How long to get back to Foundry Lane?"

"No more than fifteen minutes," said Kenneth.

"We need to speak to the care staff she worked with that morning," said Gus. "The people Helen visited too, if possible. Something major had to have happened to make her go home, drink two bottles of wine and swallow a cocktail of drugs designed to end her life. Joe Morgan thought the pills her doctor prescribed were working. It strikes me that Helen didn't need the bath to finish the job."

"When Conrad Alderslade carried out the autopsy, he determined that Helen had hit her head on the edge of the bath," said Kenneth. "He found bruising to the occipital bone."

"At the base of the skull," said Geoff.

"I know where it is, Geoff," said Gus.

"Alderslade also found marks around the face and mouth," said Kenneth, "but wouldn't commit to saying how or when they occurred."

"What final verdict did he arrive at?" asked Gus.

"Alderslade provided a narrative verdict," said Kenneth. "because there was no single identifiable cause of death, he couldn't determine whether one individual was responsible. Instead, he maintained multiple factors, uncertainties, and complex issues surrounding the death meant a narrative verdict enabled him to describe the circumstances leading to the death. I doubt whether it helped Joe Morgan or Helen's only sister, Becky Hood."

"Based on what he found during the autopsy, Alderslade couldn't declare Helen's death was suicide, nor could he say she was unlawfully killed," said Geoff.

"A narrative verdict sounds better than an open verdict," said Gus. "I can't say I suffered many instances of dealing with a narrative verdict in any murder cases I handled."

"Around thirty thousand coroner's inquests held in England and Wales conclude with a verdict each year," said Kenneth. "Accident, misadventure, natural causes, suicide, and homicide make up most of all verdict conclusions. Narrative verdicts have been more widely used since the turn of the century. I read in one of those never-ending reports I receive that the increase in the use of narrative verdicts by coroners has not had a statistically significant impact on published suicide rates in England and Wales."

"Becky Hood?" asked Gus. "Was she Helen's only living relative?"

"According to this report, yes," said Kenneth.

"When did Becky last see her sister?" asked Gus,

"They spent New Year's Eve together at a party in town. Becky lives with her husband, Ian, in a detached bungalow in The Tinings."

"That's a street beyond Monkton Park north of the town," said Geoff. "Becky lived less than three miles from her sister when she lived in Kington Langley."

"How did Becky describe her sister's mood that night? Was Joe Morgan there?"

"Joe and Helen went to the party together," said Kenneth. "It was the first social occasion Becky and Ian had arranged with the couple. The other guests were mutual friends, Sam Webber and his wife, Mary."

"The couple who rented Mark Fennell's caravan at

Burnham-on-Sea," said Gus. "Did Ian Hood know Mark Fennell? Chippenham has a population of over forty thousand."

"True," said Geoff Mercer, "but caravanning might have been the link they shared."

"I've got nothing in the report to confirm or deny whether Ian and Becky Hood ever rented that caravan from Mark Fennell," said Kenneth. "However, there were no problems with anyone attending the party. Everyone had a great time, according to Becky. They left her sister's home at around two o'clock and shared a taxi home with the other couple."

"That was the last time Becky saw Helen alive," said Gus. "So, there was nothing to suggest her sister was just days away from committing suicide?"

"It wasn't the last time they spoke," said Kenneth. "Becky rang Helen two days after the party. She hoped to persuade Helen to go shopping in Swindon at the weekend. Helen couldn't make it because she and Joe were booked to go to Bristol to see a show at the Hippodrome. They planned to make a weekend of it, staying overnight in the city."

"So, there was nothing to suggest problems between her and Joe Morgan, " Gus said. "Everything was sweetness and light between her and her sister. Helen had a rewarding job and a new boyfriend. No wonder Conrad Alderslade found it impossible to rule her death a suicide."

"When the press got hold of Dave Perry, they asked whether he had discovered a motive for the two killings," said Kenneth. "He had to admit to being non-plussed. One reporter had heard a rumour the two murders had been contract killings, but Perry insisted there was no suggestion Fennell and Roker had ever been involved in criminality."

"Did Perry have the same silly thoughts as Jim Francis?" asked Gus. "It had to be a case of mistaken identity?"

"DS Frankie Price was present at the same press conference," said Kenneth. "She told reporters Helen Roker was popular with her colleagues and everyone she came into contact with through her work."

"Which echoed what Henry Gibbs said about Mark Fennell nine months earlier," said Geoff Mercer. "Fennell was a good bloke, salt of the earth, straight as a die, and nothing was too much trouble."

"Another saint," said Gus. "Like Katherine Alford, and look how that turned out."

"Careful, Freeman," said Kenneth. "You don't want to become cynical in your old age."

"Our last case left a bitter taste in the mouth, sir," said Gus. "I wonder who tipped off the press about the possibility of a contract killing? Those tend to be restricted to criminals and their associates, not innocent members of the public."

"Fennell and Roker wouldn't necessarily have needed any criminal involvement to have a hit put out on them," said Geoff Mercer. "They could have just had someone who hated them or had a reason for wanting them dead."

"A reason neither investigation uncovered," said Kenneth. "The eyewitnesses who saw the man in the white BMW in Kington Langley worked with the police to create a computer-generated picture."

"Most of those images look like what the eyewitness remembers jumbled up with their worst fears," said Geoff. "Every image I've seen looks scarier than the person eventually arrested for the crime."

"What reaction was there to the image they produced?" asked Gus.

"Almost none," said Kenneth. "One interesting addition to the case came after the local newspaper printed a story about the narrative verdict at Helen Roker's inquest. A young teacher called Jamie Munday phoned the police. At lunchtime, he'd heard a school dinner lady mention Helen Roker's name. The dinner lady, Joan Fisher, had met Helen when she visited her mother to change the dressing on her leg ulcers. When Helen returned to work after her partner Mark's murder, Joan said Helen became increasingly worried someone was following her. Joan realised Helen was still getting over the tragedy, but she didn't believe Helen was being paranoid."

"When did Helen start taking the anti-depressants?" asked Gus. "I wonder if she mentioned this concern to her doctor?"

"Dave Perry and Frankie Price spoke to Joan Fisher.," said Kenneth. "She told them Helen was convinced someone was following her. That first meeting at Joan's mother's home was in August 2005. The old lady had passed away since that time, but when the news broke about Helen's death, Joan waited for news of an arrest. She was convinced Helen had been murdered before Conrad Alderslade made his report public. Joan told Frankie Price that although she only met Helen on a handful of occasions, she was one of those people you just knew weren't the type to take their own life."

"Who do you think might have wanted Mark Fennell dead, Gus?" asked Geoff Mercer.

"I reserve judgement on the first wife. I haven't heard her name yet," said Gus. "I assume it will be in the file somewhere. Jessie North would have been my first port of call. A whirlwind romance, a beach wedding in the Caribbean, and her husband playing away less than a year later. She could be forgiven for having murderous feelings towards Mark Fennell."

"Fennell had a history of straying," said Kenneth. "Jessie North might not have been in such a rush to tie the knot with Fennell if she'd spoken to his first wife. Her name was Mandy, by the way, Freeman."

"Jessie North had an alibi, I take it?" said Gus.

"Cast-iron," said Kenneth.

"Although Mandy and Jessie might have a motive for killing Mark Fennell, surely neither wanted Helen dead?"

"I can't see why, Geoff," said Gus. "Mark Fennell's death looks more like a hit because of the choice of weapon."

"When someone turns up on your doorstep late at night with a shotgun, you know it won't end well."

"It's not subtle, is it?" asked Gus. "Which makes Helen's death more interesting. It could have been suicide, but the bruising to the base of the skull Alderslade found, plus the marks around the face and mouth, caused him to consider an alternative."

"I see where you're going, Freeman," said Kenneth. "A common criminal might use a gun to eliminate someone who crossed him. It takes thought to create the illusion Helen Roker committed suicide."

"Could Gus be looking for two killers?" asked Geoff.

"We can't discount that at this stage, Geoff," said Gus. "Walk me through what you think happened from around two-fifteen on the afternoon Helen died."

"Helen arrived home from work, changed, and... I don't know. Was there evidence to suggest she did any housework?"

"Joe Morgan left for work at eight in the morning," said

Kenneth, "after he had loaded the washing machine and set it going. Helen had gone to work at six. When Joe checked the following morning, Helen must have used the tumble dryer on much of the washing, ironed it, and put it away because he had clean underwear and a shirt to wear. That was the first time he shed tears; the shock of finding Helen dead had numbed him."

"Right, then Helen decided to take a bath at about four o'clock…," said Geoff.

"Why have you stopped, Geoff?" asked Gus.

"What level of alcohol did they find in her body?" asked Geoff.

"One hundred and forty-five milligrams per hundred millilitres," said Kenneth. "Almost twice the drink-drive limit."

"Helen must have started drinking while she waited for the tumble dryer to finish its cycle," said Geoff.

"Then she ironed Joe's shirts and the rest of the washing while consuming the second bottle," said Gus. "I can't imagine it was perfect."

"There was no suicide note," said Kenneth.

"They're not compulsory," said Gus. "However, if something significant happened during her last shift, would she have gone to the trouble to be so meticulous? Why worry if Joe didn't have clean clothes the next day? Did Joe find Helen's clothes in a damp heap beside the washing machine? Or was it neatly stacked in the airing cupboard, wardrobes, and drawers in the bedroom?"

Kenneth Truelove flicked from page to page in his report.

"That level of detail might be in the murder file," he said. "If not, you would need to ask Joe Morgan. He's still single, but now he lives in Corsham."

"Did the autopsy determine the number of pills Helen swallowed?" asked Gus.

"Thirty, give or take," said Kenneth.

"We need to check with the staff and clients who spoke with Helen in the last hours of her shift," said Gus. "We believe she went straight home, arriving at a quarter past two. That ties in with the idea she and Joe had a set routine on a designated wash day. Helen sorted out a three to five-kilogram load that needed washing; Joe did the necessary before he left for work, and Helen picked up the next stage when she arrived home in the afternoon. Many couples would recognise the system."

"Helen could relax, do whatever she liked while the clothes dried, then finish the ironing before Joe got home," said Geoff Mercer.

"Which left the evening clear for both of them to have a meal, watch TV together, or pop out for a couple of hours to socialise," said Kenneth.

"That's something the three of us recognise as a normal day in the life of two people living together," said Gus. "It didn't apply to us because just when we sat down for a meal, the balloon would go up, and we'd have to drive to a crime scene."

"I'm not seeing the trigger for suicide, Gus," said Geoff.

"Nor me," said Kenneth. "Unless something dramatic occurred that morning, why did Helen start drinking and consider taking every pill she could get her hands on? If there had been an incident at one of Helen's homes, DI Perry would have heard about it."

"You asked how many pills Helen swallowed, Gus," said Geoff, "but you changed tack and concentrated on the washing. What was it about the pills that didn't make sense?"

"The police found two empty wine bottles in the living room," said Gus, "and a half-empty glass in the bathroom. So, when did Helen start drinking? And which came first, the paracetamol or the anti-depressant? Would any of her actions be logical if she was in that state? Yes, we know Helen suffered a tragic loss nine months earlier when the man she loved died in her arms. Joe Morgan hadn't known Helen for more than a couple of months, but she told him upfront about her bouts of depression in the previous six months. Joe believed Helen was coping, thanks to the treatment provided by her doctor, and there was nothing to suggest Helen used excessive amounts of alcohol to numb her pain. Everything Joe, Becky, her colleagues, and even Joan Fisher said went against the idea of Helen being suicidal in the months leading up to her death. So, let's start from two-fifteen when Helen opened the door to the flat. What do we think might have happened considering what we've just discussed?"

"Did you disagree with my version of the first two hours, Gus?" asked Geoff.

"Not to any great degree, Geoff," said Gus. "If you ignore one item Alderslade included in his autopsy report, it made perfect sense."

"As we're still on the same page at four o'clock, Helen had to have started running the bathwater by then," said Geoff. "If it had been much later than that, the water would have been warm when Joe Morgan got home."

"The narrative report wouldn't have been necessary if everything proceeded in the fashion you're describing, Geoff," said Gus. "Alderslade would have concluded Helen Roker took her own life."

"I think you'll have to spell it out for me in words of one syllable," said Geoff.

"When I first saw the crime scene photos and listened to Kenneth reading the headline report, I thought Helen must have emptied the last of the second bottle in the living room," said Gus. "Then, carried a full glass of wine into the bathroom where police found a selection of pills. There was also discarded packaging from her prescription meds and the paracetamol in the living room. Nobody knew how many pills Helen had with her in the bathroom when she started swallowing them. Kenneth told us Alderslade reckoned what he found in her system equated to around thirty pills. So I wondered whether the deed hadn't been done until she had spent time in the bath."

"I thought you believed nothing pointed to Helen being suicidal," said Geoff Mercer.

"We still need to speak to as many people involved as possible," said Gus. "As Kenneth said a moment ago, I don't see the trigger. Perhaps we can't see it because it happened that morning, and only Helen knew its significance. But, on the other hand, maybe there was no trigger. The prescription meds were in the flat anyway. It wouldn't be unusual to discover a blister pack of paracetamol pills in a medicine cabinet. So it wasn't hard to find the tools to do the job. The couple enjoyed a drink, so it's easy to understand them having two bottles of Chardonnay in the kitchen fridge. They're designed to last until the next weekly shop in our house. Longer now that Suzie is expecting. What did you make of the bruising to the base of the skull?"

"Alderslade noticed there was bruising," said Kenneth. "He couldn't confirm whether it related to something that happened while Helen was in the bath. She could have hit her head anywhere in the flat, especially if she staggered around drunkenly."

"Fair comment," said Gus. "If we follow Geoff's interpretation of events, Helen drank six glasses of wine by half-past three. She did whatever ironing was required, despite being three sheets to the wind. Why didn't she start emptying the second bottle and use her last glasses of wine to swallow half a dozen pills at a time? Then use a hot bath to help her fall asleep and escape this mortal coil. By a quarter past four, she was ready to undress, get in the bath, and finish off the wine and a final handful of pills. Helen was drunk, thanks to the Chardonnay, by then. Helen was unsteady on her feet due to the cocktail of drugs she'd already consumed. Helen slipped, cracked her head on the bath's edge and lay there, stunned, maybe even knocked out, while the drugs did their stuff. Joe arrived home at seven and found her dead."

"Was it a cry for help?" said Kenneth. "Maybe something Helen saw or heard that morning pushed her over the edge. She drank too much and swallowed more pills than intended, thinking Joe would find her in time. But, sadly, Helen reckoned without the crack on the head."

"Death by misadventure?" said Geoff. "Are you suggesting another verdict the coroner could have chosen to use?"

"Suicide was never Helen's intention, in my view," said Gus. "For all the reasons I gave earlier. If you need further proof, why would she and Joe book a trip to Bristol Hippodrome if she planned to end it all before the middle of the week? No, I think the marks on Helen's face and mouth are significant. I appreciate Conrad Alderslade wasn't confident those marks occurred between four and six that afternoon. Still, with the damage to the occipital bone, it feels more like murder than anything else."

"You believe it *was* a double murder?" said Kenneth.

"How did Joe Morgan get into the flat when he returned from work?" asked Gus.

"Used a door key, I imagine. There were no signs of a break-in. Nothing was stolen. They'd lived together for a couple of months, and Joe would have had a key."

"Which means Helen Roker opened the door to her killer," said Geoff Mercer.

"Bingo," said Gus. "I don't know where that reporter got the idea someone ordered the killing of Mark Fennell and Helen Roker, but once they blasted Fennell with the shotgun, her days were numbered."

"Why didn't they kill Helen Roker in Kington Langley?" asked Kenneth.

"The man who visited the pub asked if the landlord knew Mark Fennell. He didn't ask if he knew where Mark Fennell and Helen Roker lived. Helen hadn't been in Mark's life that long. Maybe the killer didn't know about her, let alone know she might be in the house. Helen remained upstairs while the conversation on the doorstep took place."

"The killer learned Helen was in the house from media reports on the murder," said Geoff. "Then, Helen moved away from the village, and he needed to trace her."

"I will describe a scenario that fits better with what Alderslade found during the autopsy," said Gus. "My guess is her killer arrived between half-past three and four. Helen had finished that ironing and stored it away. She answered the door, and the killer grabbed her face with a gloved right hand, told her not to scream, closed the door with his left hand, and shoved her backwards into the living room. Helen stumbled and fell, hitting her head on a hard surface. Alderslade recorded bruising but no mention of blood, so the coffee table or another hard surface could have been the culprit. Helen was stunned, possibly knocked out, giving the killer ample time to restrain her."

"What about the Chardonnay bottle and the wine glass?" asked Geoff. "Police didn't find signs of damage resulting from a struggle or any marks on her wrists."

"The wine was still in the fridge, Geoff," said Gus. "Or it was, if I'm right. I don't believe Helen had a drink before four. She occupied herself while the tumble drier did its job, and then she ironed clothes while watching TV. Everything was put away when Joe got home. The iron and ironing board were back in their usual place. I'm sure you'd agree those are not actions one would expect an hour before committing suicide. The killer gathered the tools necessary to confuse the police. It didn't take longer than a couple of minutes. He could reasonably expect to find everything he needed. Don't forget; he'd followed Helen for weeks, knew her routine and understood the timeframe he had to work with. When we learn his identity, we'll discover he's a size-able physical specimen. While the water was running for the bath, he used the two bottles of Chardonnay to get the anti-depressants and paracetamol into Helen's system. His large hand left impressions on Helen's face and mouth, where he ensured that little escaped its target. As time passed, she would have become easier to handle. He removed her clothing and lowered her into the water. Police found her clothes lying on the bathroom floor in a manner that didn't arouse suspicion. They found dry towels on the heated towel rail and a dressing gown hung on the back of the door. Why not? They would have been there anyway.

"The killer thought of everything," said Geoff.

"He moved the bottles and empty blister packs to the living room table to create the impression everything started there," said Kenneth.

"How could he be certain Helen would die?" asked Geoff.

"If he's as clinical an operator as I think, he stayed until Helen took her last breath. Then, if necessary, he was on hand to push her unconscious body under the water. Alderslade would have recorded it if he found water in her lungs. So, Helen died where she lay. He knew Joe Morgan worked irregular hours. It might have been as late as six o'clock before he slipped out of the flat, closed the door behind him, and disappeared."

"Clever," said Geoff.

"I've got a completed jigsaw that fits the facts as I've interpreted them," said Gus. "The tough part will be finding out why someone wanted Mark Fennell and Helen Roker dead."

Chapter Four

"I HADN'T EXPECTED this morning's meeting to follow this pattern," said Kenneth Truelove. "Do you think the narrative verdict played a part, Freeman?"

"Is Conrad Alderslade around to question further?" asked Gus.

"Unfortunately not," said Kenneth. "He passed away last year."

"He would have been guessing if he declared the marks on Helen's face significant," said Gus. "They seemed odd enough for him to ensure they appeared in his narrative. We should be thankful he went that far."

"Although DI Perry didn't follow that thread in his investigation as far as I can tell," said Kenneth.

"Perry couldn't pin down a motive," said Gus. "We'll speak to him. Maybe hearing the words 'contract killings' from that reporter sounded too fanciful to follow up on. But on the other hand, the crime scene indicated suicide as the most likely verdict. I wonder whether Perry checked with Jim Francis to see what they'd discovered about Fennell?"

"We know Francis and Gibbs still believed Fennell had no criminal connections," said Kenneth.

"I can't deny things appear very differently in your version of events, Gus," said Geoff Mercer. "The killer arrived after Helen had removed the evidence of ironing those clothes. Joe Morgan told the police he didn't think Helen was depressed enough to take her own life and that she had never taken a long, soaking bath while he'd known her, yet they didn't act upon it."

"Helen had known Joe for three months," said Kenneth. "Perry and Francis would have wondered whether Joe knew Helen well enough to be certain. So they carried out the usual checks, found nothing that didn't ring true, and moved on to a new case."

"I'd like to think my interpretations have merit," said Gus.

"The best way to prove whether they do or not will be to determine a motive for the killings," said Kenneth.

"Where do you start?" asked Geoff.

"Mandy, the first wife," said Gus.

"I wish you luck, Freeman," said Kenneth. "Is that the Tattooed Lady I can hear outside?"

"Lunchtime is upon us, sir," said Geoff Mercer.

"None too soon, Geoff," said Gus. "I can see your bones starting to poke through."

A sharp knock on the Chief Constable's door heralded the arrival of Kassie Trotter and her goodies.

Gus could never guess which Kassie would appear next. The style or colour of her hair would have changed since he saw her last, or the young girl had paid another visit to the tattoo parlour. As for her clothing, it could never be described as dull.

Gus recalled the first occasion he met Kassie in Kenneth's old office. A sleeveless black vest made it easy to see her full-sleeve tattoo in all its glory. Her black jeans fitted where they touched on the teenager's well-rounded body.

Gus wondered why he bothered to chastise Lydia over her choice of office wear when Geoff Mercer didn't impose a sombre regime in the Administration area at London Road.

Kassie's eyebrows were thick and black and stencilled higher than nature intended, a modern craze that produced a look of being permanently frightened. But, even on that first afternoon, Kassie's saving grace was her penchant for baking. Gus had lost count of the different varieties of delicious cake he'd enjoyed in the months since.

This morning, he was in for another surprise. There was no sign of the sleeve tattoo today, as Kassie had discovered a tailored white shirt in her wardrobe. The charcoal grey and white pinstriped suit looked new, too. Gus was glad to see Kassie's rebellious streak live on. She still wore her black Doc Marten leather ankle boots.

"What have you done with Miss Trotter?" asked Kenneth.

"Do you like it, sir?" asked Kassie, giving Kenneth a twirl before handing him his cup of coffee. "I'm trying a different approach to finding my soulmate."

"Brilliant, Kassie," said Geoff.

"I spent all my money on new clothes last weekend," said Kassie as she put the rest of their orders on the desk. "So, you'll have to get used to my hair being the same way for a while. I might just let it grow back. That shaved look has had its day. Before you ask, Mr Mercer, my mood had perked up enough for me to resume baking on Sunday."

"What goodies do we have on offer today?" asked Gus.

"A Dorset apple traybake, Mr Freeman. I made one big enough to cut into sixteen slices. So, Mr Mercer can have one slice now, and I'll bring him another with his cuppa this afternoon."

"You're too good to us, Kassie," said Geoff.

"Life's a little easier since you-know-who left the building," said Kassie. "I don't need to be so secretive about what I've got on offer."

Gus smiled to himself. Kassie always had a way with words. They often gave the wrong impression, but she was too naïve to realise it.

"Grace will be back at London Road before you know it," said Gus. "Don't lower your defences just yet."

"Vera and I hoped you would have talked sense into her before Christmas, Mr Freeman."

"Don't you have other offices to deliver food to, Kassie?" asked Geoff.

"That's me told," said Kassie. "I'll pop back for your empty cups and plates later. Enjoy your lunch."

With that, Kassie turned on her heel and headed for the door.

Geoff Mercer had finished his bacon bap and was already eyeing the slice of apple cake.

"Vera and Kassie will have to get used to seeing Grace Packenham around the place again sooner than she thinks," said Kenneth.

"Won't Grace Packenham take a break along with Gus and the team, sir?" asked Geoff, wiping grease from his chin with a serviette.

"Grace won't have accrued as many days' leave as the rest of the team," said Kenneth. "She hasn't been with us long. Grace took time off when she moved into her place in Easterton and a long weekend soon after leaving the Portishead HQ."

"I'll break it to Grace gently when I get back to the office," said Gus. "What's the damage?"

"We can allow her to take a week," said Kenneth, "then Mercer can make good use of her from Monday the twenty-second before DI Packenham returns to work with the rest of you on the twenty-ninth."

"I'm sure I'll think of something, sir," said Geoff, preparing to devour his second bap.

"Will there be anything else, sir?" asked Gus.

He'd finished his chicken wrap, but the apple slice would keep until his coffee break later. Gus wrapped it in his serviette and collected the two folders from Kenneth's desk.

"I can't think of anything, Freeman," said Kenneth. "I haven't heard from the PCC for almost thirty-six hours. It tends to make one nervous. I hope he isn't working on another cost-cutting initiative."

"Keep calm and carry on," suggested Gus.

Geoff Mercer had polished off his second bap and was ready to return to his office.

"You can't beat Wiltshire pork sausages," he said when he joined Gus by Kenneth's doorway.

"Lost in space," said Gus, giving Geoff a nudge and nodding towards their boss.

Kenneth Truelove had forgotten them already and was gazing out of his window.

The pair walked to the top of the stairs leading from the mezzanine to Reception.

"Good hunting, Gus," said Geoff. "I fancy you'll be covering some ground on this case."

"I've heard the North Somerset coast is a great place to visit this time of year," said Gus.

He trotted down the stairs to the car park to retrieve the Focus.

Thirty minutes later, he was in the lift to the first floor of the Old Police Station.

"Welcome back, Gus," said Grace.

That was a first, thought Gus. Neil and Lydia will get an inferiority complex.

He draped his jacket over the back of his chair and dropped the two folders onto Alex's desk.

"Where are we off to this time, guv?" asked Alex.

"Kington Langley, a village two miles north of Chippenham," said Gus.

"I think we've got maps to cover that part of the county, guv," said Lydia. "We can place the one we used for Alan Duncan's murder in Biddestone beside one of the Swindon maps we've collected."

"They're not the same scale," said Grace. "I checked our stock this morning while Gus was at London Road. It would be more professional to ask the Hub to provide a new one."

"Quite right," said Gus. "We've earned the right to have the correct tools at our disposal. This case covers a wider area than the village, anyway. We also need street maps for Chippenham, a rough guide to the layout of Corsham, and a list of caravan sites at Burnham-on-Sea in Somerset. Depending on what we find in the coming days, other towns could get added to the list."

"Got it, guv," said Alex. "I'll ring Divya Yadav at once."

"One piece of admin before I give you the details of our new case," said Gus. "The Chief Constable has asked me to try putting this one to bed by Friday week. So when Lydia and Alex fly to Dubai, this office will also take a break. I know it's short notice, and it might not be possible to get away as far as our colleagues, but the boss thinks we deserve a rest."

"Melody will find plenty for me to do at home," said Neil. "I'd put the finishing touches to the nursery earlier this year, so there's little to do there. But, no doubt Melody will have another room that needs decorating."

"We hope everything goes well this time, Neil," said Lydia.

"I echo that," said Gus.

"Did the Chief Constable mention me?" asked Grace.

Gus walked over to Grace's desk and quietly relayed Kenneth's message.

"I'm sorry, Grace," he said. "Perhaps you can pay your family a visit?"

Grace scowled, and Blessing wondered whether Jamie had any leave due.

"Right, let's make a start," said Gus. "Mark Fennell died in Kington Langley in April 2005. He answered his door at a quarter past ten at night and was shot with a twelve-gauge shotgun. Fennell was forty-eight years old and had no criminal connections or known enemies."

"Who carried out the original investigation, guv?" asked Neil.

"DI Jim Francis," said Gus. "Francis has since retired to Spain. DI Henry Gibbs from Avon & Somerset Police was a DS in those days and was Francis's right-hand man on the case. DC Annie Drew was Family Liaison Officer because our victim had a girlfriend, Helen Roker, who was in the house when Fennell got shot. All three officers were operating out of Chippenham police station."

"Is Annie Drew still there, guv?" asked Neil.

"DC Drew was young and single thirteen years ago, Neil," said Gus. "DS Mercer couldn't find the name among the current crop of Chippenham's personnel."

"I'll start digging," said Alex. "Divya sends everyone her love. The maps we need will be with us tomorrow morning."

"Thanks, Alex," said Gus. "Locating the detective team who handled the case won't be our only problem. A man seen two weeks before the murder by several eyewitnesses visited the local pub and asked for Mark Fennell. That pub closed three years ago. The landlord, Marcus Weston, whereabouts unknown, knew Fennell had only lived in the village for six months and didn't visit his pub often. Weston gave DS Gibbs a decent description of the man. He was tall, around forty, with blond hair. On that occasion, our possible suspect wore a charcoal-grey three-piece suit. Weston didn't remember any other jewellery, scars, or tattoos apart from a gold wristwatch. In the murder file, you'll find a photofit image of the suspect. As you would expect, it bears a vague resemblance to the man I just described, but no more."

"Who were the other eyewitnesses, guv?" asked Neil.

"Mrs Ruth Redman lived three doors from Fennell and Roker," said Gus. "She saw a white BMW 3-series driving through the village at seven-thirty. Weston said the man came into the pub not long after six. A noise outside had caused Mrs Redman to look out of her lounge window. She spotted a local juvenile delinquent messing around. His name was Kyle Harding. I don't believe he had anything to do with Fennell's murder. Mrs Redman noticed the BMW slowly driving past. She thought it was new, and the driver was alone."

"The registration would have helped," said Neil.

"Mrs Redman didn't get it, Neil," said Gus, "but she did see the BMW again as the man continued driving through the village for two hours."

"Did anyone else see this man and his BMW that night, guv?" asked Blessing.

"Fennell owned a caravan at a site in Burnham-on-Sea," said Gus. "DC Drew asked Helen Roker whether she could think of someone with a grievance against her partner. Roker couldn't, but she did recall an evening when Sam and Mary Webber, friends from Chippenham, called to collect a set of keys. The couple told Helen they passed a white BMW parked a short distance up the road from the house. The driver wore a dark suit and had longish blond hair. When DC Drew pushed Roker for the time and date, it turned out to be eight-thirty on the same night the mystery man visited the pub."

"So, he hung around the village from six o'clock until half-past ten or thereabouts," said Neil. "I can't imagine there was much to do in Kington Langley."

"Even less now; the last pub has closed," said Gus.

"You suggested we needed a map of Burnham, Gus," said Grace Packenham. "Do you think a caravan site is significant?"

"We won't know until we investigate further, Grace," said Gus. "it could well be that Fennell bought the caravan in 2003, shortly after meeting his second wife, Jessie."

"In 2003, guv?" asked Lydia. "That marriage didn't last long."

"Exactly, Lydia," said Gus. "Jessie North was one of a long line of women who Mark Fennell charmed into an affair or a marriage. I'm afraid Fennell was a serial offender, which increases the suspect pool. Unfortunately, we might not get some of his victims to come forward. Two women we *can* speak to are his first wife, Mandy and Jessie."

"You're forgetting his girlfriend, Helen Roker, guv," said Neil.

Gus shook his head.

"Now I know why you brought two folders from London Road," said Alex.

"Sam and Mary Webber were renting the caravan, something we might find they often did," said Gus. "They could have known Mark Fennell before he got together with Helen Roker, but the couple didn't hang about to speak to Fennell as their sole purpose was to collect the keys. Fennell was working on his car in the garage. Roker told DC Drew that when she told Fennell the following day the couple had collected the caravan keys, she forgot to mention the man in the BMW."

"So, we have no idea who this BMW driver was or where he came from," said Alex.

"We know he was desperate to find Mark Fennell," said Neil.

"Two weeks later, Fennell had spent the day tinkering with his car in the garage at the side of the house. He and Helen enjoyed a quiet evening at home, and she went to bed at ten. Fennell followed shortly after and returned downstairs when he heard someone knock at the door. Roker got out of bed, and from the bedroom window, she saw a white BMW parked across the driveway. Someone was on the doorstep because she could hear talking, but Helen couldn't tell whether more than one person had come to the door."

"Did Helen go downstairs, guv?" asked Lydia.

"No, she kept quiet and tried to make out what was said," said Gus. "The only voice she could identify was

Mark's, and he was shouting. The next thing that happened was someone shot him with a twelve-gauge shotgun."

"At that range, it had to make a mess," said Alex. "Fennell didn't stand a chance."

"Mark Fennell staggered into the hallway, bleeding from the chest, and collapsed on the floor," said Gus. "Roker called the emergency services, but Mark Fennell died in her arms before the ambulance arrived. She heard the BMW accelerate away but couldn't describe the attacker or whether he had an accomplice."

"Was there any doubt the killer was the man in the BMW, Gus?" asked Grace.

"He had to be connected, Grace," said Gus. "The police didn't find any neighbours who saw or heard a thing that night. When you study the map, you'll find Kington Langley is a typical country village. It takes forever to get from the first building to the last. One and a half miles, to be exact."

"The main road is the central spine," said Neil, "with an occasional branch road to a group of houses."

"The gap between the houses gets bigger the further you get from the centre," said Lydia.

"It could explain why nobody heard anything, I suppose," said Grace. "Why was Mark Fennell killed? What lines of enquiry did the detective team pursue?"

"DI Francis suspected Fennell could have been an innocent victim," said Gus. "He'd never been in trouble with the police. He questioned his neighbours, current partner, and ex-wives but couldn't establish a motive. The idea it was a case of mistaken identity became a stronger contender as each day passed."

"That doesn't explain the BMW driver," said Blessing. "Unless he was searching for another Mark Fennell. Did anyone see the driver in Kington Langley on the night Mark Fennell died?"

"A chap called George Miles cycled home from the village hall after a skittles match," said Gus. "He lives in a place they call Lower Common. You pass it as you leave the village before heading towards the Stanton St Quinton roundabout. He slowed to turn into his gateway, and what could have been a BMW sped past, almost knocking George off his bicycle."

"What time, guv?" asked Alex.

"George Miles reckoned it was around half-past ten or a little later," said Gus.

"The timing fits with Helen Roker's account of the shooting, guv," said Alex.

"What did happen to her, guv?" asked Blessing.

"Let's concentrate on one case at a time, Blessing," said Gus. "Right, you know the drill. Extract whatever we need from the murder file, get the crime scene photos on the board, and prepare a list of interviews. I want to start with Fennell's first wife, Mandy."

"Where does Mandy live these days, guv?" asked Alex.

"Pass," said Gus. "Search for Mark Fennell's first wedding. It will be in the mid-Seventies, and nobody mentioned Fennell as being from outside the county. Their two children will be between thirty and forty years old now. A cursory check should eliminate them from having any connection to their father's murder. Mandy will be most useful for learning about Mark's background. Where did he grow up? How did he earn a living?"

"Was there no mention of it in the murder file?" asked Grace.

"The Chief Constable prefers to give me the highlights, Grace. You might find the answer hidden deep in the murder file. Either way, I want to hear about Mark from the woman who lived with him the longest."

"Where did you say DI Gibbs went after he left Chippenham, guv?" asked Alex.

"If memory serves, he's in Taunton with the Avon & Somerset Police," said Gus.

"I've found a number for him, guv," said Alex. "Henry Gibbs might be able to tell us what happened to DC Annie Drew."

"Good idea," said Gus.

"Which of us do you want to contact DI Francis, guv?" asked Grace.

"Whatever we do must be over the phone, Grace," said Gus. "DS Mercer won't sanction a trip to Spain. If you're volunteering to talk to Jim, I should warn you the Chief Constable said he's a prickly specimen."

"I've had to deal with plenty of those, Gus," said Grace. "Was he a senior officer who didn't think women should rise above the level of police constable?"

"I never met him," said Gus. "Your best bet is to take great care over how you frame the questions you wish to ask. We need to understand how the team handled the investigation, but try to avoid accusing him of making mistakes."

"I think I can manage that, Gus," said Grace. "We'll have a friendly chat, one Detective Inspector to another."

Gus couldn't wait to hear how that went.

"I've found Marcus Weston, guv," said Neil. "He's on Facebook and still has photographs taken while he was a pub landlord. He lives on the other side of the motorway now in Great Somerford, and he's retired from the hospitality trade."

"Pass his details to Alex, and we can add him to the

list," said Gus. "Jessie, the second wife, should be higher in the pecking order. Her maiden name was North when she married Fennell in 2003. We need to check whether she reverted to her maiden name. Maybe Jessie decided to risk getting married again. Who wants to tackle that search?"

"I've started already, guv," said Blessing.

"How do we find the other women in Fennell's life?" asked Lydia.

"I'd start with the two ex-wives," said Neil. "People say they're always the last to know. Once they discovered Fennell cheated on them, they learned everything they could about them."

"I can't comment on that," said Gus, "but it's a starting point."

"I've trawled through the murder file, guv," said Alex. "Ruth Redman died in 2013, and George Miles is in a hospice in Wroughton, near Swindon."

"It can't be helped," said Gus. "Add Sam and Mary Webber to the interview list. They were friends of Mark Fennell and Helen Roker. Until we speak to them, we won't know whether they'd known Mark before he met Helen."

"I can tell you're avoiding the Helen Roker folder, Gus," said Grace. "When did Helen die?"

"Nine months after Mark Fennell," said Gus.

"Was she still living in the rented house in Kington Langley?"

"No, a solicitor called Robert Rideout contacted Helen as soon as he learned of Mark Fennell's death in the media. According to the terms of the will, Fennell's ex-wife, Jessie, was the sole beneficiary. Fennell and North were still legally married, even though he'd walked out six months before, and they were getting divorced. So Helen Roker left the village and rented a place near the railway station in Chippenham."

"I can't remember having so few people on our interview list before, guv," said Alex. "It wasn't like this when Luke worked here."

"Where do you think we've got the best chance of unearthing fresh clues?" asked Gus. "Anyone?"

"If we speak to the detectives who handled the case, we might get a thread to follow," said Lydia.

"Something they discarded as unlikely to produce a positive result?" asked Gus. "We're looking into this murder thirteen years from when it happened. The murder file will tell whether other detectives gave it another go every five years. They didn't make a better fist of it than Jim Francis and his team. Does anyone else have any bright ideas?"

"If we could have spoken to Mrs Redman, she couldn't tell us much more than she told police at the time," said Neil. "She saw a BMW creeping through the village throughout the evening, but we'd have little chance of tracing that car and its driver now without a registration number."

"If the driver was a criminal, the car could have been stolen," said Blessing. "Criminals aren't known for taxing and insuring their vehicles, and often drive while disqualified."

"The eyewitnesses provided descriptions of the driver," said Grace, "so we do have something for the Hub to use. Also, if there's a link between Fennell and the caravan site in Burnham, it might be possible to find someone who matches that photo who lived there in 2005."

"We can't be sure the killer came from Burnham," said Alex.

"How could Marcus Weston help us, guv?" asked Neil.

"I've read his statement, which didn't add anything to your brief highlights. The guy wandered into the pub, asked for Fennell by name, and when the landlord told him he wasn't there and wasn't expecting him that evening, the guy left."

"Marcus Weston knew where Mark Fennell lived," said Gus. "Fennell and Roker had only been in the village for six months. The couple didn't use the pub that often, so what was it about Mark Fennell that caused Weston to know his name? We've come across this situation before. The land-lady of a pub in town told us she knew dozens of her regulars and considered them friends. She only knew them by their first name or their nickname. She didn't need to know their surname, where they lived, what car they drove, or what they did for a living. The only thing that concerned her was remembering what they ordered, so she could start pouring a pint of lager or a Guinness as soon as they stepped into the bar. It makes the customer feel welcome and encourages them to return."

"I wonder if it had something to do with cars, guv," said Blessing.

"Fennell was working on his car while the man was cruising around the village," said Lydia.

"He also worked on the car the evening he died," said Grace.

"We need to know what make and model of car it was," said Gus. "Maybe that was what piqued Marcus Weston's interest. Helen Roker told Annie Drew they had spent the weekend before the BMW driver was seen in the village at the caravan in Burnham. Mark worked on the car until late on Monday night, which was why he missed seeing Sam and Mary Webber when they called to collect the keys. Sam and Mary planned to use the caravan for a midweek break. Maybe they drove to Burnham on Tuesday evening to spend two nights away. The Chief Constable mentioned that Helen Roker had told Annie Drew the car had caused problems when they drove home from Burnham, and Mark thought he might need a new gearbox."

"Was his car off the road for the fortnight, guv?" asked Neil.

"Good question, Neil," said Gus. "I think we need to talk to Marcus Weston, though, don't you? Was Mark Fennell one of those drivers who love tinkering under the bonnet of his car, or was he involved in the business full-time?"

"The fact that the BMW driver first appeared in Kington Langley the day after Fennell and Roker had returned from the caravan site has to be significant," said Grace.

"DI Francis was convinced neither Fennell nor Roker was involved in criminal activity," said Blessing. "So that only leaves one possible motive for the killings."

"The couple saw, heard, or did something while they stayed in Burnham-on-Sea, which led to their deaths," said Lydia.

"We don't have to wait until our scheduled holiday to take a trip to the seaside," said Neil.

"I suggest we call it a day," said Gus. "Divya will be here first thing tomorrow to deliver our maps. After that, we can ask her to hunt through the members of criminal gangs in North Somerset using the photofit image from the file."

"Why are you still keeping us from learning what happened to Helen Roker, guv?" asked Alex.

"We're still scratching the surface on Mark Fennell's murder, Alex," said Gus. "Lydia might be right; Mark and Helen could have bumped into a gang up to no good that weekend. But Mark bought the caravan two years earlier when he was with Jessie North. So they must have spent time there together. Let's hear what she has to say first."

"Burnham-on-Sea sounds a nice place to visit," said Blessing.

"Everywhere has its dark sides, Blessing," said Grace. "We immediately thought of the cities when someone mentioned organised crime twenty years ago. Now the idyllic English countryside is every bit as much their hunting ground as anywhere else."

Chapter Five

GUS WASN'T FAR behind everyone else when he left the office. It was another early finish for the team, but it didn't mean they were slacking. On the contrary, he knew they had a mountain to climb to get a successful conclusion and helped him hand two completed folders to the Chief Constable by next Friday.

He considered Grace's words as he drove past the roundabout to Crook's Way. Could they be looking at a criminal gang operating in the seaside town? He hadn't admitted it to the others, but he didn't have a clue how to find the resort on a map. When he and Tess lived in Downton, it was quicker to drive to the New Forest or head directly to the coast for a weekend getaway.

What did he have to look forward to tonight? He and Suzie planned to visit The Lamb later for a meal and an evening with friends. Gus spotted the serviette on the passenger seat. He'd forgotten to take it upstairs to the office, and although Lydia had brought him a cup of black coffee halfway through the afternoon, he hadn't given his apple slice another thought.

Gus waited until he reached the bungalow before sitting in the car and enjoying the fruits of Kassie's labours. Then, he went inside and dropped the serviette into the waste bin in the kitchen and looked at the clock. It was just five o'clock; Suzie wouldn't be home for another twenty-five minutes.

Gus tried to place the variety of apples Kassie had used as he showered. The cinnamon flavouring had been very welcome, but it made his task difficult. Did it matter? Not really, but Gus worried it might be the first of a string of defeats.

He would have loved to interview Conrad Alderslade. Unfortunately, that wouldn't be possible now, but perhaps he could give Eve Northwood a ring. He always enjoyed their conversations, and she might offer valuable insight into the Helen Roker case.

Gus dried himself and walked into the bedroom. He selected a fresh shirt from the wardrobe and thought of Joe Morgan. The van driver had shed a tear when he discovered the last thing his partner had done was to iron his shirt.

Gus had shed tears after Tess died, but ironing wasn't the exclusive domain of his late wife. Gus had often ironed his uniform while at home with his parents and saw no good reason not to continue doing it when he and Tess married. Over the years, household duties became split between them. Tess would argue whether the split was equal, but the hours they worked demanded that 'whoever was nearest' should cook a meal, do the ironing, or mow the lawn.

Gus sat on the end of the bed and thought about Friday week. What would Suzie want him to do with his enforced leisure time? Since they met, they hadn't holidayed together, but he remembered Suzie having time off when her rugby-playing ex-boyfriend arrived back in Devizes. What was his name? Gus couldn't remember. Nor could Suzie when it mattered, but Gus made a mental note not to remind her of the incident.

As he daydreamed, he heard the rattle of stones in the driveway. Suzie was home.

"Another half-day, darling?" she asked when Gus met her in the hallway.

"We got as far as we were going to get with our new case," said Gus.

"First-day blues?" asked Suzie. "While I shower and change, why don't you get us a coffee, and you can tell me all about it."

Gus strolled to the kitchen; resistance was futile. Twenty minutes later, Suzie joined him, looking radiant.

"Are you a little cheerier than when I got home?" asked Suzie.

"The gloom descended before Kenneth handed us a double murder file," said Gus.

"When was it?" asked Suzie.

"Thirteen years ago," said Gus. "You were hardly out of school. Mark Fennell and Helen Roker were the victims."

"Flattery will get you nowhere," said Suzie. "Mark Fennell, did you say? That was a nasty shooting at Kington Langley, wasn't it?"

Gus nodded.

"I hadn't realised it had become a double murder."

"Nor did several others until today," said Gus. "I believe Fennell's killer found Roker, stalked her, and tried to make her death look like suicide."

"I remember her case now," said Suzie. "The coroner was an old stick working in Chippenham since World War

Two. He refused to go with the flow and call it suicide, despite bags of evidence to the contrary."

"It was a matter of interpretation," said Gus. "I think I'm right, but I will check before getting too deep into the detail. Anyway, that's for another day. I'm more interested in what Kenneth decided this morning."

"I'm all ears," said Suzie. "I know, but you still love me."

"I do, but don't blame me; blame Alex and Lydia. They had an invitation to visit Dubai."

"I know. Lydia told us all about it at the pub the other night. Her father takes a holiday in Dubai after a busy summer in Rotterdam. How does that affect you?"

"Kenneth decided London Road can't provide cover for those two being on leave simultaneously. I said we'd cope, but he decided the office should close next Friday for two weeks. Grace Packenham won't be so lucky because she hasn't accrued enough leave. She'll be helping Geoff on a special project for a week and have one week free."

"I can't take time off at the drop of a hat," said Suzie.

"I hoped Geoff might jump in and save me," said Gus. "But he wanted Kenneth to move on to the new case."

"To avoid you answering awkward questions about Alex and Lydia," said Suzie.

"Exactly," said Gus. "Kenneth assumed they just happened to want their holiday the same week. Not so they could fly out to Dubai together for two weeks with Lydia's father."

"I'm sure Bert Penman would have several ideas of how you should spend the time," said Suzie. "You don't spend as long at the allotment as you once did."

"I had nobody to come home to then, sweetheart," said Gus.

"Sorry, that was crass of me. Perhaps we can make plans at the weekend?"

"I thought we would work on turning the second bedroom into the nursery together," said Gus. "I need a project you're happy with me handling alone."

"Unsupervised, you mean?" asked Suzie. "Will it involve power tools?"

"If it does, I'll need to start ringing around for quotes. The whole point of moving here five years ago was because it promised a low-maintenance future."

"I'll give the matter thought while you're spoiling me at The Lamb tonight," said Suzie. "I'm about halfway through my second trimester, and my necessary calorie intake has changed drastically. I need to consume at least three hundred and fifty extra calories daily. It will result in weight gain, but that's normal during pregnancy. The extra calories should ideally be coming from protein and calcium sources. So, chicken parmesan with sweet potato chips with salad would be terrific. You had better pray the chef hasn't changed the menu."

Gus wasn't about to complain. He needn't feel guilty about his steak tonight now.

They walked along the lane to The Lamb at eight o'clock. Bert Penman was sat in his usual place by the bar. Gus noticed the lack of cider in his old friend's glass.

"I see you're almost ready for another pint, Bert. Timed to perfection again."

"Years of practice, Mr Freeman, Gus," said Bert. "I won't say no. Irene has gone to stay with her sister in Horton for a couple of days. Beryl's a few years older than Irene. She was coming downstairs, thought she'd reached the last step, but had one more to go and ended in a heap by the front door. Twisted her ankle and gave herself a nasty bump on the forehead."

"Have you eaten today, Bert?" asked Suzie as Gus ordered their drinks.

"I lived alone for years after Cora died, Miss Ferris," said Bert. "Keeping myself fed and watered has never been a problem. I cooked myself a meal before I visited the allotment for a last tidy-up ahead of the rain forecast for the weekend."

"We're meeting Clemency and Brett in a few minutes," said Suzie. "I thought you could join us, but if you're sure?"

"I'm sure," said Bert. "I'll finish this pint of cider your intended has just kindly bought me and get off home. Irene will ring later to check I'm not taking advantage and staying in the pub until closing."

Gus smiled to himself as he and Suzie found a table for four. If Bert Penman couldn't take advantage of eighty-five, what hope was there for the rest of us?

"He never gives up, does he?" said Suzie.

"I should hope not," said Gus. "Bert's enjoying every second of life while he can."

"So he should," said Suzie, "but I meant him referring to you as my intended."

"Are you happy with things as they are?" asked Gus.

"Very happy," said Suzie.

"Enough said," said Gus.

Suzie checked the menu and punched the air.

"Someone's excited," said Brett Penman.

The Reverend and Brett had crept into the bar through the back door. Their bicycles were undoubtedly propped against the low stone wall surrounding the beer garden.

"Suzie has a favourite dish in the specials section, Brett," Gus explained. "I left money behind the bar for you two to get drinks. We can order food when you're ready."

"You're a gentleman, Gus," said Brett.

"We haven't seen you at the allotment lately," said Clemency. "Bert was only saying earlier that he misses the stimulating conversation."

"I hoped to put in an appearance at the weekend," said Gus. "Nobody can be in two places at once. The Chief Constable has been keeping me busy."

Brett returned with his pint of lager and a soft drink for The Reverend. Everyone ordered food, and the conversation got into full swing. Clemency told them about the last film they'd seen in Devizes, while Brett reported an increase in cat owners visiting his veterinary practice in Royal Wootton Bassett.

"We've chipped cats for years," he said. "A quick injection between the shoulder blades should last the cat's lifetime. A scanner can then read the unique number, and if a missing cat is found and handed in to a rescue centre or us, the cat can be scanned, the microchip database accessed online, and the owner's details retrieved."

"Why the sudden increase in activity?" asked Gus. "I appreciate dogs get stolen to order, but there can't be many cat breeds that command a sum worth the effort."

"You will have noticed the increased level of security that owners have installed over the years," said Brett. "CCTV cameras, proximity lighting, doorbell cameras and the rest. Although the cat flap isn't the simplest way to break into a house, there are other unwelcome visitors people wish to keep out."

"Feral cats, the urban fox, and Rover, the neighbour's black Labrador," said Suzie.

"Exactly," said Brett. "The microchip cat flap uses radio

frequency identification technology that allows your cat to come and go freely. However, it remains locked and denies access to unprogrammed cats, wild animals, pets, and strays."

"Just when you thought you'd heard everything," said Gus.

"You're not a cat lover, Gus," said Clemency.

"I'm an admirer of people who dream up different ways for people to spend their hard-earned cash. Life was simpler when I was a child. My parents wouldn't recognise what people regard as essentials these days."

Their food arrived from the kitchen, and conversation stopped while they ate.

"That was delicious," said Suzie.

"It looked it," said Clemency. "My constant battle with the bathroom scales means I have to cut down on the calories. I'm going to have dessert as we're cycling home. I convince myself one balances the other."

Brett went to fetch another round of drinks and order their four desserts.

"Cats make a change from horses," said Gus. "His bosses like to keep Brett on his toes."

"I think Brett enjoyed treating those racehorses," said Clemency. "He asked the stable owner to let him know if an opportunity arose for more work in that area. So far, he's heard nothing. A large animal to specialise in would suit him better than handling a wide variety of small domestic pets."

Brett returned to the table with a tray of drinks.

"Are you getting itchy feet, Brett," asked Suzie. "Clemency told us how much you enjoyed working with the horses at Lambourn."

"In Canada, I dealt with cattle, sheep, and horses. Large

animals in a vast country. The novelty of guinea pigs and budgerigars is wearing thin here in Wiltshire. I shan't be in a hurry to move away, though. I have too much to keep me here."

"While Bert's still around, you mean," said Gus, grinning at The Reverend. She blushed a deep crimson and dug into her chocolate brownie.

Brett and Gus settled the bill at closing time while Suzie and Clemency visited the Ladies.

"Will you be here at the weekend?" asked Brett.

"I'll give you a ring," said Gus. "Perhaps we could visit the Fox and Hounds on Saturday night. Suzie and I enjoy it there; change is as good as rest."

Brett nodded.

"I can see Clemency waiting by the back door. We'll fetch our bikes and meet you in the lane."

Suzie joined Gus, and they walked outside.

"I wish I'd worn a jacket," she said. "The nights are getting colder."

"I sense rain in the air, too," said Gus.

Brett and Clemency emerged from the pub car park pushing their bicycles.

"Goodnight, you two," called The Reverend as she cycled towards the Rectory.

Brett gave a wave as he hurried to catch her.

"I wonder if Bert thinks of Clemency as Brett's intended?" asked Suzie.

"He'll still call her Reverend even when she becomes his, whatever it will be. Is there such a thing as a grand-daughter-in-law?"

"I think so," said Suzie.

What a strange Wednesday evening, thought Gus as they walked home in a light drizzle.

Thursday, 4 October 2018

THE WEATHER HADN'T IMPROVED in the morning, making the diversionary route into Devizes seem greyer and more depressing than ever. Roll on Christmas! Suzie gave a wave and joined the queue of traffic trying to reach London Road.

Gus continued through the town centre, heading for Caen Hill. He pulled into the Old Police Station car park with five minutes to spare. Somehow he'd managed to arrive before Amazing Grace.

When he reached the first-floor office, he realised what was going on. Grace had contacted Divya Yadav and arranged to collect the maps from London Road, saving Divya the trip from Devizes. The lift returned to the ground floor as Gus sat at his desk.

The lift doors opened, and Grace emerged carrying the maps.

"Divya has agreed to start a couple of searches for us, Gus," said Grace. "We'll have an address for the former Mandy Fennell before your mid-morning coffee. The hunt for the BMW driver will take longer, but Divya has strong links with her counterparts at Portishead. The computer geeks hope to put a name to the face by the end of today."

"That's good," said Gus. "I'm sure you left the rest of the team something to do."

Grace laid the maps on the table at the back of the office. Lydia and Blessing started getting them onto the walls.

"We've got ninety minutes, guv," said Alex. "Who do you want to handle each of these interviews?"

"Grace volunteered to contact Jim Francis," said Gus. "I'll leave it to her to decide when the best time might be."

"You won't find him at home now, ma'am," said Neil. "If Jim's an avid golfer, he'll get eighteen holes in well before the noonday sun. I bet Jim has a tee-off time as close to eight o'clock as possible. So, he's five or six holes into his round now. I'd leave it until one o'clock this afternoon before giving him a try."

"If he's spent an hour in the club bar, that conversation could be fun," said Alex.

"I researched Jim Francis last night," said Grace. "He had a drink problem during his last few years at Chippenham. He's coping one day at a time, and I understand he's been teetotal for three and a half years."

"Perhaps it won't be so bad after all," said Alex.

"She researched him," whispered Lydia. "Well, she would, wouldn't she?"

"I'll leave DI Henry Gibbs to you, Alex," said Gus. "Get hold of him as soon as you can. But first, find out what he knows about his former colleague, Annie Drew. Then, if you can get a phone number or an address, Lydia and I will visit her."

"I'll drive out to Great Somerford to chat with Marcus Weston, guv," said Neil. "I'll ring him now and insist he stays put until I get there."

"Thanks, Neil," said Gus.

Gus searched for Eve Northwood's number and gave her a call.

Eve was at her surgery when she answered her mobile.

"Gosh, I didn't expect a call from you, Gus," she said. "I can't talk now. My next patient will be outside my door in less than a minute."

"Can you spare me thirty minutes at lunchtime?" asked Gus.

"It's a long time since anyone asked me that," said Eve. "If you plan to drive into Swindon, we'd better meet somewhere to get a drink and a bite to eat."

"Why don't we split the difference? I'll meet you in Marlborough. We can park in Hillier's Yard and take our pick of the cafés on the High Street. Shall we say one o'clock?"

"That sounds fine. I'm intrigued to learn what it is you want of me."

"Before I make a complete fool of myself, I want your professional opinion on a narrative verdict from 2006."

"I'll do my best," said Eve. "Ah, there's the knock on my door. See you later."

Gus ended the call as Neil was heading for the lift.

"Marcus Weston was happy to oblige, guv," said Neil. "I'll get there in time for coffee at ten."

"Marcus retired from hospitality, Neil," said Gus. "Don't expect to get any Hobnobs."

Gus spotted Blessing hovering beside his desk.

"Something amiss, Blessing?"

"You didn't mention my name when you allocated the interviews, guv. What can I do to help? I've got an hour's work on Jessie North, and then I'll have everything we need."

"Well done," said Gus. "Liaise with Grace. Then, as soon as she's spoken to Jim Francis, you two can arrange to meet Mark Fennell's second wife."

Gus wondered whether he had time to access the Freeman Files and prepare for the reports on the meetings that lay ahead. He'd no sooner opened a new file when

Grace Packenham dragged her chair across to sit beside him.

"Divya Yadav came through with the information we required on Mandy Fennell, Gus," she said. "She was born Amanda Jane Moth, in June 1958, in Malmesbury. Today, the town's main employer is Dyson, which has a site on the edge of the town where it employs around four thousand. James Dyson is a research, development, and design organisation with manufacturing carried out in Malaysia. There have been rumours that many current operations will move to the Far East. At the beginning of WWII, the electronics company EKCO moved to the town from the south coast to avoid the danger of bombing. They produced radar equipment which was then a new technology. The factory continued manufacturing a range of products after the war. Various international companies took over the EKCO factory, and the site had reverted to housing by 2004. Amanda left school at sixteen and worked at the factory from 1974 until 1980. She met Mark Fennell at a dance held at the firm's social club in 1978. The couple married in 1979 in Malmesbury Abbey."

"Why have I heard of that place?" asked Gus.

"I saw a reference to it in the files on Clive Palmer's murder, Gus," said Grace.

"That's it. It was to do with the derivation of the name of Purton."

"The Abbey has a continuous history back to the seventh century," said Grace. "It was the site of an early attempt at human flight in the eleventh century. The monk Eilmer attached wings to his body and jumped from a tower. He flew over two hundred yards before landing, breaking both legs. Eilmer reckoned he didn't fly further because his glider lacked a tail."

"Fascinating," said Gus, "what else did you learn about Mandy Fennell?"

"She had two children in quick succession," said Grace. "Philippa and Graham, at the beginning of 1980 and the end of 1981. Mark and Mandy lived in Chippenham after the wedding. The kids went to local schools, found work in the town, and are married with children."

"Does Mandy still live in Chippenham?" asked Gus.

"No, Amanda Jane, as she prefers to be called these days, moved to Calne after the couple divorced and lives on Lickhill Road, just off the A3102. She reverted to her maiden name and recently retired at sixty. After leaving the factory in Malmesbury and having her family, Amanda Jane retrained and has worked in local government since 1982."

"Amanda Jane fared better than her ex-husband," said Gus. "Right. When can we see her?"

"I heard you on the phone earlier," said Grace. "I can take Blessing with me after catching up with Jim Francis if you wish."

"I'm leaving here at a quarter past twelve to drive to Marlborough," said Gus. "I'd prefer to leave Ms Moth until this afternoon. Two o'clock would be best. Give me the address, and I'll meet Blessing there. You'll have your hands full with Jim Francis. We'll stick to what I told Blessing about Jessie North. You two can fix up a meeting with her. Get the lowdown on her brief marriage to Mark Fennell, the affairs, and the caravan site."

"Those subjects could be pivotal to us solving this case," said Grace.

"Don't worry. I'm sure you'll manage to get the answers we need," said Gus.

Grace wheeled her chair back to her desk. Gus hoped she was happy to have a worthwhile project to get her teeth into. He could hear Alex grilling Henry Gibbs on the other side of the office. Neil would arrive in Great Somerford in ten minutes to speak with Marcus Weston. The pot was starting to simmer nicely.

"Coffee, guv?" asked Lydia.

Gus gave up trying to set up his digital files. His head was spinning,

He decided to drink his coffee while touring the office and studying the maps Divya had provided. Burnham-on-Sea is notable for its beach and mudflats, the danger they pose to individuals and shipping, and the efforts locals have made to defend their town and prevent loss of life. Burnham is close to the estuary of the River Parrett, which flows into the Bristol Channel, and has the second-highest tidal range in the world. The parish includes the neighbouring small market town of Highbridge, which brings the population to around twenty thousand. That number swells in the summer during the holiday season.

Gus could see holiday parks carrying national brands on the Burnham map and touring sites that relied on the tourist trade. They would need to check with Jessie North, but Gus thought they needed to find a location where an owner could berth his caravan all year round. He knew the number of months a static caravan could be occupied per year was restricted on specific sites. Mark Fennell must have bought his holiday home at a residential caravan park. That narrowed the field somewhat.

As Gus returned to his desk, Blessing Umeh called out.

"I've finished compiling the report on Jessie North, guv."

"Let's go through it with Grace," said Gus.

"We'll stay at this end of the office to not disturb Alex and Lydia," said Blessing.

Grace joined them, and they stood under the map of Corsham.

"Is this relevant?" asked Grace. "Did Jessie move just a few miles from the home she shared with Mark Fennell?"

"Jessie North moved to a three-bedroomed semi-detached dormer bungalow in Swan Road in 2005," said Blessing. "Pavel Dudek, a Polish electrician, moved in with her in 2007."

"The interlude with Fennell didn't put her off blokes for life then," said Gus.

"Jessie hasn't been tempted to get married again, though, guv," said Blessing.

"Most of the answers we need from Jessie require a face-to-face meeting, Gus," said Grace.

"I've got Jessie's contact number," said Blessing.

"Get onto it straight away then, Grace," said Gus. "Jessie could still be working, and she might not want Pavel to hear some of what we need to ask. If you can squeeze her in this afternoon, it would help."

"Jessie works part-time, guv," said Blessing. "She's a lunchtime assistant at a children's nursery."

"Didn't they call that a dinner lady when I was at school?" asked Gus.

"She should be home by two o'clock," said Blessing.

Gus returned to his desk and finished his preparations without further interruption. Finally, at a quarter past twelve, he made for the lift.

He had taken Blessing via Calne the last time he'd driven to Marlborough. Today, he opted to head for Devizes and give the Focus a chance to rattle along the Beckhampton straight. What was life without a bit of risk? He reached Avebury without the windows dropping unasked and soon slowed to enter Marlborough High Street.

Parking was a nightmare in most towns these days, but people were always on the move. So drivers had to play a waiting game, cruise slowly past the ranks of cars parked in the centre of the extra-wide street, and grab a space when it became available - regardless of how long the others had been waiting.

Gus eased the Focus alongside a large white van. He wondered whether he'd chosen market day, but a sign reassured him that it was yesterday. The van driver was making deliveries to a carpet shop opposite. Gus realised he wasn't in the best spot for Eve Northwood to spot him, so he got out, locked the Focus, and darted between two slow-moving cars to reach the pavement.

Gus looked up and down High Street. Perhaps they should have made more specific arrangements. After a green van departed, a buttercup yellow Mini Cooper turned sharply into a space on the other side of the street. Someone sounded their horn and yelled abuse at the driver of the Mini Cooper.

Seconds later, a red-faced lady scuttled across the road to join Gus.

"That was lucky," said Eve. "I thought I would have to drive around the block for ages."

"Let's duck into the nearest café," said Gus. "In case that guy you upset is on the warpath."

They didn't have to walk too far and were soon seated at a table for two near the window.

Gus studied the menu while Eve kept an eye out for anyone tampering with her precious car. The café was busy, and thirty minutes increasingly felt an optimistic assessment of how long this impromptu meeting would last.

Gus cut to the chase as soon as the server had taken their order. He explained the details of Helen Roker's death and the subsequent autopsy.

"This is all news to me, Gus," said Eve. "I didn't always have my finger on the pulse regarding crimes around the county in those days. The people at Gablecross were happy to rely on the established coroner. Although I was preparing for the eventuality that I could offer my services, they weren't required until much later."

"Conrad Alderslade saw things he wasn't happy with," said Gus. "Because the narrative verdict had only recently been available to him, perhaps he trialled it in this instance to see whether it fit the bill. I haven't checked, but this could be his only use of it. We can't ask him why he chose to report her death in the way he did. I'm concerned that I'm reading too much into the narrative verdict. Helen Roker had been treated for depression for over six months. The immediate response from police and paramedics when they reached the flat was that they were dealing with a suicide. Plain and simple. Helen Roker took her own life because she couldn't cope with losing her lover, Mark Fennell."

"Although anti-depressant medications are the backbone of moderate to severe clinical depression treatment, they also carry serious risks, Gus," said Eve. "Evidence suggests they can bring on suicidal tendencies in rare instances. Or, if the patient is already suffering from them, they can worsen the situation. For example, they might cause panic attacks and disrupt normal sleep patterns."

"We'll ask Joe Morgan if he noticed either of those changes in Helen's behaviour," said Gus. "But everyone Helen came into contact with believed she was in good spirits. Joe was closest to her, and he maintained Helen was coping well with the help of the pills her doctor prescribed. Which way do I turn?"

The arrival of their snacks and drinks cut short the conversation for several minutes.

"As much as I'm enjoying spending time with you, I must get back to work," said Eve as they savoured the last of their drinks.

"I was about to say the same thing," said Gus. "We'd better ask for the bill."

"I paid when I popped to use the loo," said Eve. "No panic. I'll claim it on expenses."

"That's a relief," said Gus. "My boss doesn't encourage the Crime Review Team to spend more than the absolute minimum. If we need to put our heads together again, any food or drink will be my shout, agreed?"

"Agreed," said Eve. "I've considered your last question. Which way should you turn? If Ms Roker's partner is adamant her medication didn't produce any unusual symptoms, I'd say that suicide was the least likely cause of death. Therefore, if natural causes and an accident can be ruled out categorically, it's reasonable to assume someone killed her."

"That's good enough for me, Eve," said Gus. "Now, let me walk you to your car in case that driver whose parking space you nicked is still suffering from road rage."

Eve laughed. Early afternoon traffic was at a standstill as they crossed the road and threaded their way through parked cars and vans until they reached Eve's bright yellow Mini.

"Unscathed," she said. "Right. I'd better go before Gablecross sends a search party."

Eve was quickly into the driving seat and reversed into oncoming traffic. Gus shook his head as several drivers stood on their brakes to avoid rear-ending the car in front. Gus waved an apology to the driver of the closest car despite the fact it wasn't his fault. Eve's Mini Cooper disappeared in the direction of Swindon, and Gus walked to his Focus.

As he made the return journey to the office, he had ample opportunity to consider his options. Whatever caused the snarl-up on Marlborough High Street was catching. When Gus arrived in the Old Police Station car park, he glanced at the single space. Neil was back. Gus wondered how he got on in Great Somerford.

Chapter Six

NEIL HAD THOUGHT there were worse places to be on a Thursday morning as he left the office and drove past the turning to Lacock. Even the drizzle that had been falling all morning was easing. By the time he reached Great Somerford in another thirty minutes, he could be bathed in sunshine.

Neil joined Cepen Way and bypassed the town of Chippenham. He followed the signs to Stanton St Quintin and thanked his lucky stars he wasn't on the M4 when he saw the constant stream of traffic below him. Neil took the second exit off the roundabout to join the A429, which delivered him to Marcus Weston's doorstep at five to ten.

Marcus must have seen Neil pull up outside his cottage on Dauntsey Road. Before Neil had time to lock his car door, the retired landlord was on his doorstep.

"DS Davis?" asked Marcus.

"That's me," said Neil. "You picked a good spot here, Mr Weston. The Volunteer Inn is a mere hundred yards away."

"I have been known to visit the place," said Marcus.

Neil could tell his host was eager to get him inside and shut the door. Word would soon spread if the neighbours suspected the local constabulary was calling on one of their own.

"Coffee?" asked Marcus when he'd closed the solid oak door behind them.

"Much obliged," said Neil.

"We'll be more comfortable in the kitchen," said Marcus, pointing to the door at the end of the short hallway.

Neil thought the directions were unnecessary as there were only two rooms on the ground floor in this style of cottage. The accommodation comprised a large country kitchen, which Neil suspected would have an Aga, and a living room.

"Do you live alone, sir?" asked Neil as they entered the kitchen.

"I can see why you made detective, DS Davis," said Marcus, searching for two clean mugs. "I haven't tidied the living room for a few days, and despite the size of this kitchen, I don't have much in the way of pots, pans, and utensils."

Neil sat on the chair nearest the Aga. He could see the recycling bin through the window. It was overflowing, and Neil recognised the empty cardboard containers poking out of the lid as the mainstay of Rick Chalmers' diet.

"I hope instant coffee will suffice," said Marcus.

"No problem," said Neil. "White, one sugar, please."

"A Rich Tea biscuit? They're my one indulgence these days."

"You're too kind," said Neil.

"I don't know what I can do to help you," said Marcus.

He placed a single biscuit beside his and Neil's coffee mug. Times are hard, thought Neil.

"DS Hardy called to say we were re-opening the Mark Fennell murder case," said Neil. "I'm sure you must have thought about what happened in 2005 in the intervening years."

"I had no idea the man who came into the pub asking for Fennell would return to shoot him in cold blood two weeks later. I would have gone to the police if I'd suspected that was his intention."

"Let's forget that night, sir," said Neil. "What can you recall when Mark Fennell moved to Kington Langley?"

"He came with a reputation," said Marcus. "The village is only a couple of miles from Chippenham, and Fennell had lived there all his life."

"Did you know him?" asked Neil.

"We had never spoken, but I'd seen him around. As soon as he left school, he worked at Westinghouse and spent time overseas on various projects the company was involved in. I'm not sure what he did for them exactly, but I'm sure his first wife or one of his many lovers will be able to join the dots."

"Mark Fennell had a reputation for cheating on his wife," said Neil.

"Exactly," said Marcus.

"So, you knew about Mandy, his first wife?"

"Not personally, but behind the bar in the village pub, you hear all manner of gossip and rumour. In those days, we had a good few regulars who drove out from town for a pint and a pie, especially at weekends."

"Was that the Royal 'we', sir?" asked Neil.

"My wife, Caroline, was with me then. She left not long after Fennell's murder. The breathalyser had started the demise of the country pub decades earlier, but the smoking ban delivered the final blow. It became harder and harder to earn a crust. Scraping along wasn't Caroline's style."

"Your old regulars let slip the occasional gossip about Mark Fennell, I take it?" asked Neil.

Marcus Weston nodded.

"Caroline?" asked Neil.

"Fennell preferred women of his age, or younger, DS Davis. My ex-wife and I are the same age. Fennell never spent any time in the pub as far as I can remember before moving to Kington Langley. I doubt that Caroline ever met him. Fennell dropped by, now and then, with his partner, or a friend, for a drink midweek. He enjoyed a Sunday roast too. But, as I told the detective who came to see me in 2005, Fennell wasn't one of our regulars."

"He rented a property on the Chippenham edge of the village," said Neil. "That's half a mile from the pub, isn't it?"

"About that, yes," said Marcus.

"Could you name the people living on either side of Fennell's property?"

"Not with any certainty. However, we knew several families in the village well. We were there for more years than I care to remember. I knew where Fennell lived because the previous tenant had been a regular customer. One morning, I returned from the nearest Cash & Carry and saw a removals van in the driveway. Another customer put a name to the new tenant that evening. It was a week before the new arrivals made their first visit."

"Let's go over the evening when the well-dressed man approached you," said Neil. "The pub was quiet, in the traditional lull between five and seven in the evening. Then, the door opens and...."

"He was tall and wore a charcoal-grey three-piece suit. I placed him in his late thirties or early forties. His long blond hair contradicted my first impression of him."

"In what way?" asked Neil.

"Caroline used to say I was a snob, but I thought he was a business person when the door first opened. Possibly a brewery rep, an estate agent, that sort of fellow. Someone used to getting suited and booted whatever their profession. The long hair threw me, and suddenly he put me in mind of the younger element we saw in the pub. Instead of the standard hoodie and jeans they usually wore, their parents forced them to wear a suit to a wedding or a funeral. They never looked comfortable."

"Yet this man didn't have tattoos, earrings, or jewellery to make the charcoal-grey suit appear incongruous?"

"No, just the Rolex on his left wrist."

"You're very observant, sir," said Neil.

"Not really. He asked if Mark Fennell was in. I said he wasn't and stressed he wasn't a regular. He seemed to lose interest and glanced at the clock on the wall behind me. He checked his watch but made no comment, and then he left."

"Your clock was several minutes fast," said Neil. "Standard practice for publicans."

"We called time a few minutes early, so what? Show me a customer who doesn't try to stretch the ten-minute drinking time as far as possible."

"Was your ex-wife with you behind the bar that evening, sir?"

"Not that early in the evening," said Marcus. "Caroline put in an appearance between eight and nine when we were the busiest. But, of course, if I needed a helping hand, I could always call her."

"You lived upstairs; I take it?" asked Neil.

"As pub accommodation goes, it was comfortable enough," said Marcus. "We never had children, so the two of us scrubbed along well enough for over a decade before things started to slide."

"Where do you think your visitor came from, sir?" asked Neil.

"How would I know? I didn't follow him outside to see what car he drove or check which direction he went when he left the car park."

"We believe he drove a white BMW Series 3, sir," said Neil. "Ruth Redman, a lady who lived half a mile from the pub on the road leading out of the village towards the M4, saw him several times that same evening."

"Mrs Redman wasn't one of our customers, but her husband was before he died. She's passed away too since the pub closed, I believe."

"We would have liked to speak to her," said Neil. "I realise you had never seen this man before, and you couldn't know where he lived, but you were so accurate on what he wore, the length of his hair, and the Rolex. Think about what he asked and the exact words he used."

"Is Mark Fennell here? He leaned forward, put both hands on the bar, looked me straight in the eye, and said those four words. A bit scary to tell the truth. Not the sort of fellow you wanted to annoy. I answered, and when he realised I didn't have anything to add, he nodded at me and left without another word."

"You haven't mentioned an accent, a lisp, or a throaty voice," said Neil. "I'm sure you would have noticed something more. He leaned forward and put his hands on the bar. You spotted he didn't have 'love' or 'hate' tattooed on his fingers and no rings. Did he have the soft hands of an office worker or the toughened hands of someone used to manual work? Did those four words give any hint as to where he was born?"

"I told you that the way he stood, staring at me as if he dared me to lie to him, unnerved me," said Marcus. "That suit fitted him like a glove. He was well-muscled. A hard man who could handle himself. Four words aren't much to place him from, but I'd say he was English and from the West Country."

"Bristol, perhaps?" asked Neil.

Marcus Weston shook his head.

"Somerset, maybe. Someone who hadn't moved far from where he was born."

"Why do you say that?" asked Neil.

"People ridicule country folk from Wiltshire, Somerset, or Gloucestershire, DS Davis. As a result, many well-educated West Country people flatten their tones to disguise their roots, but those whose circumstances determine they stay close to home never feel the need. So what did I take from the way he spoke? He'd had the bare minimum of schooling and lived a life of hard knocks."

"That's more like it, sir," said Neil. "I take it the other detectives didn't ask you that type of question?"

"Just the basics," said Marcus. "Do you think the extra embellishment can help?"

"It can't hurt, sir," said Neil. "So, you didn't see or hear from the man again?"

"Not a dicky bird. Once news of the murder swept through the village, everyone wanted to hear about what I'd seen, but the fuss died quickly, and life returned to normal."

"Not for Mark Fennell," said Neil. "Nine months later, his partner was also dead."

"I read about that poor girl in the Gazette and Herald," said Marcus.

"Helen Roker," said Neil.

"A sad case, DS Davis. She sat in the bar on half a dozen occasions, and I never knew her name. Only the reference to Fennell in the newspaper report enabled me to make the connection."

"I think that's all for now, sir," said Neil. "Thanks for the refreshments. I'll head back to the office."

Marcus Weston accompanied Neil to the door and watched him pull away from the kerb. Then, he closed the door and returned to the kitchen. Another coffee with a splash of brandy and a handful of Rich Tea biscuits would get him through to opening time at The Volunteer Inn.

GUS EXITED the lift and found the room buzzing with activity. What a satisfying sound.

"Welcome back, guv," said Lydia.

"Thank you, Lydia," said Gus. "Can I have an update, please?"

Neil Davis gave Gus the highlights of his conversation with Marcus Weston.

"It was worth the trip, guv," he said. "We've established that our man was a tough nut who could have come from Burnham-on-Sea. It's possible he was responsible for both deaths."

"If you haven't finished entering your report in the Freeman Files, Neil, then crack on with that task. Alex, how did your conversation go with Henry Gibbs?"

"Gibbs wasn't keen to comment on how Jim Francis handled the investigation, guv," said Alex. "Henry trotted out the usual stuff. They were working against the clock with limited resources."

"Who did Jim Francis think was responsible?" asked Gus.

"He wanted to check out the women in Fennell's life," said Alex. "Henry Gibbs admitted they hadn't traced everyone before the case got shunted into a siding, and the team moved on. It wasn't because DI Francis thought a woman had blasted Fennell in the chest with a shotgun. He argued one of the women could have paid someone to do the job. Gibbs couldn't find any evidence to support that theory. The next option Francis came up with was that a jealous husband, or boyfriend, had taken their revenge on Fennell. Henry Gibbs spent many wasted hours searching for a likely candidate for that eventuality. He told me some of the husbands hadn't known their wife was playing away, or if they had, they had never learned the man responsible was Mark Fennell. After DI Francis had trodden through their lives in his size twelve shoes, some of those fragile relationships were doomed."

"Didn't they visit Burnham-on-Sea to learn the attraction for Fennell and his partners?"

"Gibbs knew Fennell had a caravan on a residential site there," said Alex. "Helen Roker answered their questions on that part of their lives. There's no evidence to suggest they spoke to Jessie North, the second wife, about the caravan. DI Francis just wanted to check Jessie's alibi and confirm there were no extraordinary cash withdrawals from her bank account. When Mandy Fennell threw Mark out of the house, he'd met Jessie, and they got married only months later. Mandy didn't have a new husband, or boyfriend, who might have wanted to kill Fennell."

"It does leave one possibility," said Gus. "We believe an incident at that caravan park led to two people getting killed. Helen Roker must have known what that incident was, and by fielding the questions herself, she could down-play the caravan and the trips to Burnham. But, unfortunately, Francis firmly fixed his eyes on revenge as the motive, so he chose not to double-check with Jessie North that everything at the caravan park was above board."

"If Helen Roker had told the police everything she knew," said Blessing Umeh, "she might still be alive."

"I had assumed Helen thought she was safe because the killer didn't appear to know she was in the house," said Lydia. "If he had known, she would have died on the same night as her partner."

"But if both of them knew whatever they had seen or heard could come back to bite them, then Helen must have been petrified after Mark Fennell's murder," said Blessing. "No wonder she needed medication."

"Helen can't have confided in Joe Morgan," said Alex. "If she had, he would have been more likely to accept that she committed suicide."

"Did you manage to get anything useful from DI Gibbs, Alex?" asked Gus.

"He gave me Annie Drew's contact details, guv," said Alex.

"Has she risen above the rank of Detective Constable?"

"Annie Drew is a civilian these days, guv. We can ask if she'll agree to speak to us, but Henry Gibbs wasn't confident."

"Does Ms Drew still live in the Chippenham area?" asked Gus.

"Annie didn't move far, guv. She lives near Newton St Loe, the other side of Bath, towards Bristol."

"I know where it is, Alex," said Gus. "Call her, fix an appointment, and we'll drive out to speak to her."

"What if she's working, or turns us down, guv?" asked Lydia.

"We could tell her to get to Manvers Street Police Station for an official interview, guv," said Blessing.

"Perhaps not the best way to get a former colleague to co-operate, Blessing," said Gus. "On this occasion, Alex can discover where she works first and hint that we'll drop by uninvited. I suspect Annie won't want that, and we'll meet on neutral ground. If Alex ever listened to Luke making appointments over the past few months, he'll know which buttons to press."

"Keep pushing the person into a corner until they realise they have no option but to turn up and start talking to us," said Neil.

"A gentle nudge, rather than pushing, Neil," said Gus, "but you've got the gist."

Alex picked up the phone and dialled Annie Drew's number.

Gus thought Amazing Grace had been unusually quiet since he returned.

"Have you spoken to Jim Francis yet, Grace?" he asked.

"My initial call went to voicemail," she replied. "Jim Francis must have had his mobile with him but chose not to answer. An hour later, he texted me to say he was unavailable until five o'clock."

"Cheeky," said Gus.

"I took that to mean I could call him at four o'clock," said Grace. "I can't see the conversation lasting more than an hour. I'd rather not have to stay late tonight."

"It's important we get his side of the story, Grace. So get what you can today, and pin him down for another bash tomorrow."

"The kid-gloves approach did the trick, guv," said Alex,

putting the phone down. "Annie Drew works in the centre of Bath, a stone's throw from the Abbey. So if you want to leave now, she'll see us this afternoon."

"Happy days," said Gus. "Let's get cracking. Hang on. Weren't you planning to visit Mandy Fennell this afternoon, Grace?"

"We should call her Amanda Jane Moth, Gus," said Grace. "If Blessing and I leave now, we can get to Calne and back in time for a brief conversation with our man in Spain."

"So be it," said Gus.

"I'll drive, guv," said Alex.

"No problem. My Focus has had its exercise for today," said Gus as the four of them huddled in the lift together.

"Do you mind if we take my Nissan, ma'am?" asked Blessing.

Gus thought Grace was about to protest but had realised there would be more room in the Micra than her Smart car. Blessing was a well-padded individual.

"No, that's fine, Blessing," said Grace.

Alex led the two-car convoy out of the Church Street car park, and Blessing soon disappeared from view as she took the A3102 out of town on their twenty-minute journey to Calne.

"What's Annie Drew up to on civvy street, Alex?" asked Gus as they approached the village of Box en route to the Roman city.

"When I asked where she worked, Annie told me she was a wuss. Or at least I thought that's what she said. She explained that she worked for Wood Security Services."

"I suppose it's not unheard of for a former police officer to move into the private sector," said Gus. "It's a growth industry."

"The public doesn't see enough evidence that we can keep them safe from harm, so they employ people to guard their business properties and homes."

"Understandable," said Gus. "Surely, Annie Drew could have found a better use for her talents?"

"I believe her role in the organisation is varied, guv," said Alex. "WSS is a local firm with links to a charity helping domestic and sexual abuse victims. Another task that Annie tackles is locating missing persons."

"Just up her street as a former Family Liaison Officer," said Gus. "If she were a piece of seaside rock, I imagine she'd have empathy stamped throughout."

"I wonder why she left us in that case, guv," said Alex.

Not for the first time, Alex parked in the Manvers Street car park on a trip to Bath. He and Gus headed towards the Abbey and soon stood on the pavement outside a modern-looking office with tinted windows bearing the Wood Security Services logo.

"All very discreet," said Gus. "Nobody can see what's going on inside. Don't pick your nose, Alex. There's a camera in the top left-hand corner of the entrance. Let's get buzzed in."

"They *are* a security firm, guv," said Alex. He pressed the buzzer, and a female voice answered.

"DS Hardy and Mr Freeman?"

Alex showed his warrant card to the camera. Gus searched for his consultant's card. There was a long buzz, and Alex opened the door. They saw a short, stocky woman in her mid-thirties standing by an office door at the far end of the office when they stepped inside. She beckoned them to join her.

Gus looked to his right to check the rest of the ground floor layout. He spotted three workspaces separated by glass partitions. This afternoon, neither space was occupied, but the small firm was a hive of activity, judging by the stacks of files on the desks.

"My two male colleagues are providing personal security for a left-wing comedian whose UK tour has attracted attention in the media," explained Annie Drew as they reached her doorway. "Our other female employee is visiting a young mother at the Royal United Hospital. Last night, she walked out on her partner and asked us to get her to a woman's refuge in the city. When we arrived at the Charlotte Street car park to collect her, the partner had beaten us to it. They hope to save the sight of her right eye, but the kicking she received resulted in a suspected fractured skull and fractures of the jawbone, palate, and eye socket."

"You've chosen a worthwhile but challenging career, Annie," said Alex.

Annie gave a wry smile. She pointed to the two chairs available for visitors. She sat behind her desk and studied them for a second.

"Or perhaps it chose me, DS Hardy. So what made you come back, Mr Freeman?" she asked.

"I thought I could make a difference," said Gus. "However, I'm more interested in hearing what caused you to leave us."

"DS Hardy called me to ask for help with an old case," said Annie, ignoring Gus's question. "It seems a lifetime ago now, but the Mark Fennell murder was a nightmare from start to finish."

"Was it your first murder enquiry?" asked Alex.

"First and last, we didn't get many to deal with in Chippenham. It was my first time as a Family Liaison Officer too. DI Francis pulled strings to get me on the team. There were more senior officers at the station who had an experience in the role."

"When did you first arrive at the house?" asked Gus.

"Jim and Henry got the call at around ten-thirty. When the phone rang, I was at home, thinking of going to bed. I lived just off Pew Hill in those days and drove to Kington Langley in minutes. I found Helen Roker kneeling in the hallway next to Fennell's body, covered in her partner's blood. I helped her into the kitchen and made a brew. Henry had a word with the paramedics, and a doctor arrived perhaps fifteen minutes later to give Helen something to help her sleep. Jim entered the kitchen and whispered they were about to remove the body. The place crawled with the forensic crew, and he didn't want Helen to be left alone. I helped her upstairs to their bedroom, and Helen was asleep within minutes. I found a chair to sit on outside the bedroom door. Jim and Henry went home by midnight, but it was almost two before the others left. One of the CSIs collected Helen's bloodstained clothing and reminded me someone would be back first thing."

"They needed to eliminate Helen from having any connection to the shooting," said Alex.

"Jim, Henry, and a CSI were on the doorstep before seven o'clock," said Annie. "Helen hadn't stirred. No idea what the doctor gave her, but it did the trick. The horror hit her like a ton of bricks when she came around. It was almost ten o'clock before I could ask Helen to think of a motive for the shooting. I asked if she knew anyone with a grievance against Mark. That drew a blank. She hadn't known Mark that long, I guess. As far as she was concerned, he was as pure as the driven snow."

"Helen was concerned enough about one incident to think it worth mentioning?" said Alex.

"Yes, she and Mark had returned from their caravan in Burnham Sunday evening. The car had been playing up, something to do with the gearbox. Mark worked on the problem on Monday evening in the garage at the side of the house. Helen told me friends from Chippenham had dropped by to collect the caravan keys."

"Sam and Mary Webber," said Alex.

"That's them," said Annie. "I got the impression Mark had known Sam Webber since their schooldays. Sam told Helen they passed a car parked up the road facing Chippenham. The long-haired driver wore a dark suit. He was sitting there, waiting. They thought he looked suspicious. When I asked Helen if she knew when that was, she said two weeks ago, yesterday."

"The night the mystery driver called into the pub to speak to Marcus Weston," said Alex.

"I hadn't heard about that when I spoke to Helen. Weston came forward after the murder was reported on television that evening. Sam and Mary wanted the keys because they had been using the caravan for two nights. Helen said that wasn't unusual. Mark had bought it to be used, and several friends and acquaintances were happy to oblige."

"Mark bought the van while he was with Jessie North, his second wife," said Alex.

"Jessie's name never came up in conversation with Helen. I'm sure she knew of her existence, but she believed Mark was committed to being with her. She kept mentioning that they were planning to get married, which started the tears flowing again."

"Although Helen told her partner that Sam Webber had collected the keys when he finally finished working on the car, she forgot about the mystery car and its driver."

"It wasn't uncommon for Helen to go to bed before her partner," said Annie. "When I described the car and driver to Helen, she didn't recognise them. Helen thought the man could have been someone Mark knew before they met."

"They were together less than a year," said Gus. "Two percent of someone's life isn't long. In the subsequent enquiry, nobody's name surfaced that might have fitted the description. How much more involvement did you have with the case, Annie?"

"I visited Helen daily while Jim and Henry interviewed anyone connected to Mark Fennell. Unfortunately, it wasn't long before we lost contact."

"Jessie North's solicitors got involved," said Alex.

"The romance had moved so fast that Mark Fennell hadn't had time to erase Jessie North from his memory banks," said Annie.

"A rather callous remark," said Gus. "You learned that Mark and Helen started seeing one another six months into his marriage to Jessie. Did you have chapter and verse on why he felt the need to stray so early in the marriage?"

"Jim and Henry had uncovered a string of affairs stretching back to the early years of Fennell's marriage to Mandy. The first time was when Mandy was six months pregnant with their daughter, Philippa. Mark Fennell was a serial philanderer."

"So, the solicitor produced the will, and Jessie wanted Helen out of the house," said Gus.

"Can you blame her?" asked Annie.

"Helen left Kington Langley and returned to Chippenham to live," said Alex.

"Why didn't DI Francis ask you to stay in touch with Helen Roker? She was a material witness," said Gus.

"You would need to ask him," said Annie.

Chapter Seven

"I THINK you need to tell us the whole story, Annie," said Gus. "You've carried the weight for long enough."

"I knew I couldn't fool you by appearing not to have heard your question earlier," she said. "I was at the start of my career. Jim Francis was over twenty years older and in a position of authority. Everyone knew him, and he never missed a chance to tell you how well-connected he was in the force."

"How well did you get to know him?" asked Gus.

"Jim could be charming, especially when he was sober. I was flattered by the attention. We attended a seminar at London Road together, went for a drink in town, and one thing led to another. The affair lasted two years, on and off, but as his drinking worsened, another side of him emerged. Jim became controlling, and there were times when he would lash out. I decided to end it, but he phoned, begging me to forgive him. Finally, I threatened to report him if he didn't leave me alone. Jim laughed and said that nobody would believe me. The only reason I was on the Mark

Fennell case was so Jim could keep tabs on me. I realised my career was on the line, but I had to tell someone what was happening. A month after Fennell's murder, the investigation was stalling. Jim was fixated on finding an ex-lover or a jealous partner responsible for Fennell's death. I wasn't needed after Helen Roker moved back to Chippenham, which gave me time to think. I managed to stay out of Jim's clutches for forty-eight hours, and as soon as I entered my Federation rep's office, I burst into tears. He took me straight to another Inspector's office."

"Did they begin an investigation at once?" asked Gus.

"Yes, but you know the system. The investigation was carried out by people who knew him. People Jim had worked with for twenty years. Jim was never arrested, the CPS wouldn't bring charges, and everything dragged on for weeks. I'd sat in front of the Inspector, pouring my heart out, and it was all for nothing. My confidence and trust were shattered. Instead of Jim losing his job, he sailed on unharmed until retirement while senior officers at the station questioned my integrity. There was no point in applying for a promotion because my card was marked. The only option was to quit."

"I'm so sorry you had to experience that," said Gus. "If a member of the public acted in that manner, we would arrest them at once. The public rightly expects our standards of behaviour to be very high. Any inappropriate behaviour is inexcusable, and no officer should ever use their rank to exploit others."

"I'd like to think things have improved in the past thirteen years," said Alex. "Rescuing domestic and sexual abuse victims must be harrowing yet rewarding work. So how do you keep going when the tide of new cases never seems to stop rising?"

"I don't know who said it," said Annie, "but you have to act as though you're living in the early days of a better world."

Gus thought that was an excellent way to keep the demons at bay. He looked out of Annie's window and tried to get his bearings. There was something familiar about the rooftops at the rear of the property.

"Did you come straight here to work after leaving Chippenham, Annie?"

"Heavens, no. I needed time to heal. My elder sister lives in Brentwood and works in the Housing Department of the Borough Council. She spotted a vacancy in the Safeguarding Department that appealed to me. I was prepared to do anything to get away from Wiltshire. I threw myself in at the deep end and covered every issue under the sun—the abuse and exploitation of children, vulnerable adults, and the elderly. The cases kept coming, and as the years passed, I seemed to have fewer colleagues around me to manage the workload. Something had to give. A domestic abuse case that received a lot of publicity led to me moving back west. A woman's estranged husband forced his way into her home before launching an attack. I'd been handling her case for several months, and she called me moments before her husband got inside and started punching her. I heard her screaming, and then everything went quiet. I realised she'd lost consciousness. I dialled 999 and raised the alarm. The police were at her flat in four minutes. They dragged the husband off the woman's body, and she was taken someplace safe. Like the woman I told you about earlier, she suffered several facial injuries. This wasn't something that happened out of thin air; there had been abuse in the relationship before, but it wasn't things she had reported. She told me it was fear that stopped her from reporting it. She didn't think people would believe her. She stayed in that situation thinking it would get better, but, in the end, it nearly got her killed."

"A situation you had experienced yourself," said Gus.

"The husband was charged with actual bodily harm and went to prison for two years," said Annie. "He breached the five-year restraining order within a week of leaving jail. Men like him have this sense of entitlement that surrounds them."

"That woman showed tremendous bravery to follow through the process," said Alex. "Too few victims are prepared to sit in the courtroom to see their attacker put behind bars."

"Reporting crimes of that nature can be tough for a victim," said Gus, "given the sensitive nature. We encourage anyone in a similar abuse situation to come forward and speak to the police, but I'm not sure we're getting the message across."

"The detective who handled the investigation told the press after the trial ended that I undoubtedly saved that woman from further harm because I stayed on the line to guide the attending officers to the scene. It may have saved her life. A week later, I was on a train to Bath for an interview."

"You had a phone call?" asked Gus.

"Mr Wood called me at work and asked if I could run my own office. I would handle similar cases to those in Essex, but there was no lack of resources and a greater success rate in punishing criminals. Penny, my sister, said I had nothing to lose by taking a look. So, I did."

"When was this?" asked Gus.

"June 2015," said Annie. "Mr Wood met me at Bath Spa station and brought me here. Someone had started converting the existing office into a nail bar. He said the charity he worked for thought it a waste of good office space and offered the nail bar owner money that convinced them to look elsewhere. So after I worked my notice in Brentwood, I moved to a place in Newton St Loe, which I rent from the charity. In the weeks between my coming for the interview and finally starting work, Mr Wood found two former employees of the previous firm and offered them their jobs back. Mrs Wood used to be a police officer too, and she's my third staff member."

"The mists are clearing," said Gus.

Alex frowned but then nodded. He'd been in the car with Gus and the others when Callum Wood had politely asked them to drive away from Larcombe Manor.

"Have I missed something?" asked Annie.

"You've told us much more than we ever expected to hear," Gus said.

"I wish I could have offered new information to help you find Mark Fennell's killer," said Annie Drew. "Those few conversations I had with Helen Roker were the only contact I had with the case."

"Never mind," said Gus. "We need to make a call before we return to the office. One of our colleagues will benefit from hearing what you had to say about DI Francis. Fore-warned is forearmed."

Annie Drew stood up and followed Gus and Alex to the door.

"I wish you luck with your investigation, Mr Freeman," she said.

"Hold tight to those thoughts of a better world, Annie," said Gus.

When they reached the Manvers Street car park, Alex called the Old Police Station office.

"DS Neil Davis speaking. How may I help you?"

"Neil, it's Alex. Any sign of Grace and Blessing yet?"

"No, mate. Why, what's occurring?"

"No wonder we heard Jim Francis might be an awkward customer. Grace needs to hear what Gus has to say before she rings him later."

"Okay, mate," said Neil. "I'll pass on the message."

Alex ended the call, and they exited the car park and headed for the Cleveland Bridge and the fastest route back to base.

"What did you make of what Annie had to say, guv?" asked Alex

"Jim Francis sounds like a piece of work. I never heard a whisper of inappropriate behaviour in Chippenham while working in Salisbury. But, no big surprise, we had our share of Neanderthals at Bourne Hill without looking elsewhere. Kenneth Truelove wouldn't stand for it at London Road. The first hint of any shenanigans like Annie Drew had to deal with, and the culprit would be out on his ear."

"We got nothing of use on the Fennell case," said Alex. "When do you want to visit Burnham-on-Sea?"

"Every conversation we've had so far suggests that's where the answers lie, doesn't it?" said Gus. "Our priority, for now, is to warn Grace."

"DO you know where we're going, Blessing?" asked Grace.

"Calne," said Blessing. "I've driven through it with Gus. He showed me the bronze artwork of two pigs in the town centre. He reckoned it had something to do with a company that operated there years ago. So I looked it up when I got home. The first record of a bacon factory on the site was in

1770, but the vacant buildings demolished in the mid-Eighties were only fifty years old."

"I'm a vegan," said Grace.

"Never mind," said Blessing.

Grace glanced at Blessing crouched over the steering wheel, eyes fixed on the road ahead. She wasn't sure whether she was being serious or not.

"It's left at the next junction," said Grace. "We'll pass the Town Hall on our left and then stay on Curzon Street until you can turn right onto North Road. That will takes us to Lickhill Road in three minutes. Perhaps you could drive a little faster on the return journey? I don't want to be late calling Jim Francis in Spain."

"My father says I'll never get stopped for speeding," said Blessing. "I inherited his lousy sense of direction, which makes me wary of missing a road name, or a signpost, that I try to commit to memory before starting my journey. As a result, I endured several detours during my first few days with Gus and the team, finding my way to the office from Worton."

"If you followed your usual routine before we left the office, you'll know the turning to North Road we want is twenty yards ahead. Don't miss it."

Blessing giggled.

"What's so funny?" asked Grace.

"I've just realised. You said vegan," said Blessing. "I thought you hadn't been with anyone."

"That's not something I would share with my work colleagues," said Grace.

"Surely, you have conversations with good friends on such matters?"

"Not really," said Grace.

I might if I had any friends, thought Grace.

Blessing slowed even further as they drove along Lickhill Road.

"There it is," said Blessing. "We've arrived safe and sound."

Grace was out of the car and marching purposefully up the short path to the front door before Blessing switched off her engine. Blessing trotted up the pathway with her notepad, wondering what the difference was between a Mandy and an Amanda Jane.

Amanda Jane Moth answered the door. Blessing tried to remember what Mark Fennell had looked like before he died. But unfortunately, the crime scene photos weren't a fair representation. Was he a handsome individual? Was that why so many women seemed to throw themselves at him? Or did he have a great personality? Perhaps the last forty years hadn't been kind to his ex-wife, but the sixty-year-old version of Mandy standing on the doorstep didn't look the sort of woman he'd have given a second glance.

"Amanda Jane Moth?" asked Grace.

"I am she," replied Ms Moth.

"This is Detective Constable Umeh, and I'm Detective Inspector Packenham from Wiltshire Police. We're here to interview you about a murder in 2005."

"I know why you're here, girlie," said Amanda Jane. "One of your lot rang to ask me to be in when you called. So you'd better come in."

Blessing could see nothing wrong with the outside of the property. There were no loose roof tiles or dodgy guttering. Amanda Jane had decided that cutting lawns, pruning hedges, and gardening weren't for her. The approach to the house looked bland, with paving stones and gravel as far as the eye could see.

When they stepped into the hallway, Amanda Jane

insisted they remove their shoes and leave them on the doormat. She then showed them into the lounge, and Blessing had to stop herself from gasping aloud. Her mother would love a room like this.

The lounge was bright, spotlessly clean, and reminded Blessing of images from an Ideal Homes exhibition. Amanda Jane perched on the edge of an armchair and invited Grace and Blessing to occupy the two-seater sofa by the window.

"Can we start from the beginning, Ms Moth?" asked Grace. "How did you meet Mark Fennell?"

"I worked at the EKCO factory in Malmesbury after leaving school. I didn't aspire to do much beyond a menial job in those days. My parents thought it wasn't worth following a career of any sort. I'd get married soon enough, so why bother? The work was boring and repetitive, but the people I worked with made it bearable. The company had a popular social club where something was always going on six nights a week when I started. It wasn't long before treating Sundays as a day of rest became a thing of the past, and they only closed on Christmas Day after that. I'd been with EKCO for almost four years when I met Mark. A crowd of younger girls and boys met at the club on Saturday nights. They usually had a local group playing all the latest hits. Then, they splashed out on a well-known band from Bristol or Swindon once a month. I hadn't seen Mark there before. Someone who worked at EKCO must have invited him, I suppose. Anyway, he was with another lad, Sam Webber. He came from Chippenham too."

"Sam Webber visited Mark's home in Kington Langley two weeks before the shooting," said Blessing. "So, they had known one another for a long time then?"

"Mark and Sam grew up on the same estate," said

Amanda Jane. "They were joined at the hip, and one never went anywhere without the other. Neither of you is wearing a wedding ring, but you're old enough to know how things play out. Mark chatted me up, asked me to dance, and we left Sam trying to get off with one of my friends."

"Have you had other relationships in the past?" asked Grace.

"I had my first boyfriend at fifteen," said Amanda Jane. "Nothing serious, just kissing in the back row of the cinema. So let's say I wasn't inexperienced when I met Mark Fennell. I'd played the field but never met anyone with whom I wanted to spend the rest of my life."

"I take it Mark Fennell changed that?" asked Grace. "You started seeing one another regularly from that night onwards and married the following year."

"A white wedding in the Abbey," said Amanda Jane. "My father walked me down the aisle, proud as punch, thinking his little girl had saved herself until the honeymoon."

"It wasn't a shotgun wedding," said Blessing. "Your daughter wasn't born until almost a year later."

"We were careful," said Amanda Jane.

"I presume Sam Webber was Mark's best man?" asked Grace.

"Of course, and Mary Holborn was one of my bridesmaids. She worked at EKCO too, but she was on holiday in Lanzarote when I met Mark. They didn't meet for ages because Mary was going out with another local lad, and Sam had the sense to make himself scarce when Mark came to visit from Chippenham. Sam and Mary started dating after the wedding, and it wasn't long before they followed suit and married. Sam was a different kettle of fish to Mark, so I'm not surprised he and Mary are still together today."

"Do you keep in touch?" asked Grace.

"With Mary, yes," said Amanda Jane. "Cards at Christmas and birthdays with a few words about our families and what we've been up to. You know the sort of thing,"

Grace wasn't sure she did, but they needed to dig deeper to find someone with a motive to kill Mark a quarter of a century after his first marriage.

"When did you first suspect Mark was cheating on you?"

"I was never certain whether Mark and I were exclusive all the time we knew one another. I know that sounds strange, but it's true. Unfortunately, I don't have any photographs from those days because I burned them after throwing Mark out. I'm a different person now. The girl Mark met at that social club dance was bright, bubbly, and pretty. I had no trouble attracting boys, but there was always a nagging suspicion things would change."

"The inside of your house is beautiful," said Blessing. "Yet, from the outside, it looks grey and lifeless."

"You're very perceptive, young lady," said Amanda Jane. "I always knew I would take after my mother. We were like those spring flowers that burst into life and brought glorious colour to the world for a brief period. Then an abrupt storm scatters those petals to the four winds. I was blind to what was going on around me for ages. Mark could have been seeing other girls in Chippenham while we were courting. How would I have known? I thought he loved me but always worried that I wouldn't be pretty enough for him any longer in five years or ten. After we married, we were perfectly happy, as far as I could tell. Mark had a decent job at Westinghouse, and we were able to start buying our own home. I continued to travel to Malmesbury to work at the factory, and then I fell pregnant with Philippa."

"When did you stop working?" asked Blessing.

"I was seven months gone when I left EKCO," said Amanda Jane. "Mark was away in Sweden that week. We'd not been having sex for a while, and Mark had a healthy appetite. We didn't argue, but I could tell the enforced wait was getting to him. Yet, when he flew home on Saturday morning, he was too attentive, if you can imagine. It wasn't like him. I wondered if something had happened while he was away. Then I tortured myself thinking back over other occasions when we'd spent time apart. Was this the first time he'd strayed, or had he been unfaithful all along? Normal service resumed soon after Philippa arrived, and I was expecting again in less than a year. I gave birth to Graham just before Christmas in 1981."

"How were things with Mark at that time?" asked Grace.

"He'd travelled to Germany and Sweden while I was pregnant," said Amanda Jane. "Mark also visited project sites in the UK over the previous nine months, so if he played away, there were numerous opportunities. But, as I said, how would I know?"

"So, you don't have the names of any of these women?" asked Blessing.

"Surely, Mark must have had relationships with women closer to home?" asked Grace.

"There was no way for me to discover the names of any women he had while overseas," said Amanda Jane. "It might have been possible to have him followed in this country if I could have afforded a private detective. But, instead, for years, I hid my head in the sand. I didn't want definitive proof he was a serial cheater."

"You went back to work after Graham was born," said Blessing.

"I decided to throw myself into a different line of work. A job with prospects that would fill my head with so much information I didn't have room to worry about what Mark might be doing."

"You became a local government officer," said Blessing.

"I loved it," said Amanda Jane. "Thirty-five years in Highways and Transport, and I retired earlier this year."

"What brought matters to a head? Why did you and Mark split up?" asked Grace.

"Maybe I'd missed the signs, and Mark had even had affairs with women in the same street. I don't know. While the kids were at school, we both had full-time jobs. Our weekends were too short, filled with tasks we had to shelve during the week. We were on a constantly moving treadmill like millions of other families."

"Work; eat; sleep; repeat," said Grace.

"It's the same for single people," said Amanda Jane. "We took the kids abroad on holiday for two weeks every summer. It's a routine you slip into without realising, and then one weekend, I decided to go into town to find a new outfit for work when I spotted Mark with another woman. They were walking by the shop, oblivious to anyone else. Mark had told me he was meeting Sam Webber for a few beers that afternoon, and he expected to get home by six."

"That was Jessie North, I presume?" asked Grace.

Amanda Jane shook her head.

"A terrific-looking girl with a great figure several years younger than Mark. When he got home that night, a lot later than he promised, I told him he should pack his bags and leave."

"Mark didn't deny he was seeing someone?" asked Blessing.

"He tried to make out it wasn't serious, but I told him I'd seen them together, and that was enough."

"How long had they been seeing one another?" asked Grace.

"Mark wouldn't say, but based on the last time he'd used Sam Webber as an excuse to have a few hours of freedom, six to eight weeks would be my guess."

"Did you ask Mark about other women in the past?" asked Blessing.

"I told him he may as well come clean. There was no way I was taking him back. Mark admitted having had one-night stands abroad and in the UK. However, he swore he never meant to hurt me, and there had never been anyone serious."

"It doesn't excuse what he did, does it?" said Blessing.

"Not one bit," said Grace. "So, when was it you threw him out?"

"The end of August in 2003," said Amanda Jane.

"So, whoever the girl you saw him with was, she was soon history. Because Mark met Jessie North, and they married on a beach in the Caribbean at Christmas," said Grace. "How did that make you feel?"

"I didn't want to kill him if that's what you mean. I shed my tears, burned my wedding photos, and explained things to the children. But, no, I'd just accepted a promotion at work, made sure the family had a great Christmas, and put my best foot forward to the New Year."

"That new suit you were looking for did the trick," said Blessing.

"I didn't buy anything that afternoon in the end, dear," said Amanda Jane. "My heart wasn't in it after what I'd seen."

"Did you ever see Mark again?" asked Grace.

"We had to grin and bear it through the divorce proceedings. Mark still visited the kids. They weren't living at home by then, anyway. The last occasion was in March 2004 when I visited Graham, and his Dad was there. It was awkward. We didn't have anything left to say."

"Nine months after that whirlwind wedding to Jessie North," said Blessing. "Mark was moving to Kington Langley to live with Helen Roker. What did you make of that?"

"I was surprised, to say the least. The girl I saw with him in Chippenham was a stunner. I never met Jessie North or Helen Roker, but their pictures made the newspapers. Neither woman could hold a candle to that girl as far as looks were concerned. That's not sour grapes. I'm just stating a fact. Perhaps they had other talents Mark enjoyed."

"The police will have asked you this at the time, Ms Moth," said Grace. "Where were you the night Mark died?"

"Sat in this room, alone, watching television," said Amanda Jane. "It wasn't quite as well furnished as it is today. But, on the other hand, I earned a decent salary and only had myself to spend my money on. So I took foreign holidays and bought myself a new car every three years."

"You were never tempted to find a new partner?" asked Grace.

"Never in a million years, dear," said Amanda Jane.

Grace closed her notebook. Blessing took her cue and did the same. They had filled in a few gaps in their under-standing of Mark Fennell's background but nothing that hinted at anyone with a motive to kill him.

"Is that it?" asked Amanda Jane. "Will you leave me alone to while away my days to Heaven now?"

Grace got up and made her way towards the front door. Blessing followed but turned to face Amanda Jane as they reached the doorstep. She had to take a step back to avoid bumping into her.

"Just one more thing, Ms Moth," said Blessing. "You never mentioned a caravan during the account of your marriage to Mark."

"I wouldn't be seen dead in one," snapped Amanda. "Sorry, not the best choice of words. I can't recall Mark ever mentioning having an interest in caravans, whether they were touring or static. Jessie North must have been the catalyst for that sudden interest."

"Thank you," said Blessing, and she and Grace headed for the car.

Grace glanced towards the house when they were sitting inside the Micra, but Amanda Jane Moth had already closed the door.

"What brought on that last question, Blessing? She wasn't expecting that, was she? Nothing seemed to phase her with our other questions, and suddenly she became defensive."

"I learned that tactic from Mr Freeman," said Blessing. "He got it from black and white television. He calls it a Columbo moment. The witness relaxes when you say you're leaving. If they had something to hide, and we haven't winkled it out of them, sometimes you can catch them unawares."

"I wonder whether we stumbled on something," said Grace. "I can't see how if Amanda Jane had nothing to do with Mark Fennell during the time he owned that caravan. This case makes no more sense now than when we started."

"I'll drive within the limit on the way back," said Blessing. "The school run is underway, and we don't want any accidents. But you're right about the case. I don't know how to solve it before Alex and Lydia fly off on holiday."

Chapter Eight

"DO ALEX AND LYDIA LIVE TOGETHER?" asked Grace as Blessing slowed for another set of traffic lights on the road out of Calne.

"Neil told me they started seeing one another soon after joining the team," said Blessing. "Alex was still using a wheelchair then, and Lydia offered to help. So how much do you know about Alex, anyway?"

"DS Mercer told me about his terrible motorcycle accident," said Grace. "Alex was lucky to survive."

"Gus told me Alex was desperate to return to his old job. Since he was a teenager, he has ridden motorcycles and travelled abroad, covering thousands of miles on a bike rather than wasting time on a beach holiday. I think that's how he managed to get to his late thirties without getting married. But, unfortunately, he never found the right girl to share his passion."

"What else is there to know about Alex?" asked Grace.

"Did DS Mercer tell you why Luke Sherman spent so much time with the team?"

"Not in any detail," said Grace. "I heard Alex was on sick leave. I assumed it was related to the injuries he suffered. So Luke transferred in to fill the gap while he was away."

"Alex couldn't handle the pain without medication," said Blessing. "He dispensed with the wheelchair, switched to crutches, and had regular physio sessions. Finally, it got too much for him. He was trying too hard to recover enough strength and mobility for the motorcycle pursuit section to give him another chance."

"He over-medicated," said Grace.

"Yes, and Alex needed treatment," said Blessing. "Lydia helped him through it. They were close before that setback, and they're closer than ever now."

"I'm surprised one hasn't transferred to another station," said Grace. "That's standard procedure when two officers are in a relationship."

"Gus has always been open with DS Mercer about the situation since I've known him," said Blessing. "DS Mercer was in Leamington Spa with Lydia when Suzie Ferris was kidnapped. That's where I met them. After that dreadful business was resolved, DS Mercer approached me and asked if I was interested in joining the team. Alex was in a clinic getting treatment, so Luke stayed on, and Gus told me I was needed too because Lydia would soon get promoted. Lydia's not an officer, anyway; she's a civilian. I thought you knew that. The Chief Constable pulled strings to get her on the team as a graduate intake. Lydia had just completed a forensic psychology degree. Gus said Kenneth Truelove would try to keep Lydia with us for as long as possible, but the PCC would eventually insist Lydia's future lay elsewhere."

"What's Lydia's story then?" asked Grace. "She can't have gone straight to university from school."

"Lydia studied Drama first because she had ambitions to be an actress," said Blessing. "After learning she'd been adopted, she traced her mother, Eleanor, to Edinburgh. Neil told me Lydia switched degree courses to enable her to join the police. She thought she could find her father quicker that way. Alex started helping her when they became an item, and next week they'll holiday in Dubai with Lydia's birth parents. I think it's wonderful that she can be so close to them after so long."

"So her mother was Eleanor Logan," said Grace.

"No," said Blessing, "Eleanor Scott. The couple who adopted her when she was only a few days old were so good that Lydia never wanted to change her name. Once Lydia discovered her father's name, the only concession she made was to become Lydia Logan Barre. Eleanor was eighteen when she gave birth to Lydia, and her family persuaded her to give the baby up for adoption. Lydia's father was a Nigerian sailor from Lagos named Chidozie Barre. Chidozie left Edinburgh within days of meeting Eleanor Scott and never learned he'd fathered a child."

"When did Lydia learn the truth about her father?" asked Grace.

"In June this year," said Blessing. "Her father had been a Chief Mate, a senior Merchant Navy position, but his seagoing days ended in May 2007 following a dreadful storm in the South China Sea. Alex and Lydia traced him to Rotterdam, where he owns a bar-restaurant called the 'Lady Eleanor' with his partner, Rosa De Vries."

"It must have been awkward coming face-to-face with her father after twenty-five years," said Grace.

"The awkwardness was only temporary," said Blessing.

"Her father told Lydia that Dubai was where he recuperated after his ordeal in the Far East. He bought an apartment by the Marina and returned there every autumn."

"An apartment in Dubai in 2007 when the place was only just growing?" said Grace. "Gosh, that must be worth an absolute fortune today."

"I'll say," said Blessing. "Since that trip to Rotterdam, Chidozie and Rosa have visited Eleanor in Scotland. Alex and Lydia travelled north a few weeks ago and persuaded Eleanor to accept the invitation to spend two weeks in Dubai."

"Happy families," sighed Grace.

"Where do your family come from?" asked Blessing.

"We're the poor relations of a family that traces its roots to a castle in Ireland," said Grace. "My parents live in a Jacobean hall in Lincolnshire, although I haven't visited the place since I left university. My father is a High Court judge, and I was destined to follow in the footsteps of five generations of family members who studied law and rose to the highest courts in the land. So my father was not best pleased when I came down from Cambridge and announced that I was joining the police force."

"Gosh," said Blessing. "You went to Cambridge. I left school with four A-Levels and joined the police. It was what I'd always wanted to do. My father wanted me to apply to Warwick, where he was a lecturer, but higher education never appealed to me."

"He moved to the University of Bath, didn't he?" asked Grace.

"As soon as he heard they were after him, my parents started asking whether I'd agree to move south with them. My father did not want me living alone in a bedsit, even in Royal Leamington Spa. So when Gus told me Mr and Mrs

Ferris had a room available, I persuaded my parents they could cut the apron strings. That didn't prevent them from paying a visit to check John and Jackie were suitable landlords."

"You're happy there, aren't you?" asked Grace.

"I've never felt lonely," said Blessing. "Jackie is lovely; she's warm and friendly and a wonderful cook. Anyway, since I met Jamie, I've always had a smile on my face."

"What does he do? Is he in the army?" asked Grace.

"Military police," said Blessing. "He's stationed on Salisbury Plain."

"You don't know how lucky you are," said Grace.

Blessing turned the Micra into Church Street and edged slowly into the vacant parking space.

"Where did you work when you left university?" asked Blessing.

"I spent four years in Lincoln, then transferred to Avon & Somerset Police at Portishead. I was promoted to Detective Inspector eighteen months before Geoff Mercer headhunted me."

"You must be the same age as Suzie Ferris," said Blessing as they made for the lift.

"I made DI just after my thirtieth birthday," said Grace. "Suzie got there at about the same age. So, yes, I suppose there can't be much between us. But I've only spoken to her a handful of times, so I can't be certain. The public thinks police officers are getting younger, but that's no longer true. If we don't reverse the trend, we're building future problems."

"Are you rushing off somewhere after work?" asked Blessing. "You said you didn't want to be late leaving when we were in the office earlier."

"I've got nowhere special to be. Why?" asked Grace.

"We're travelling in the same direction. So why don't we continue this conversation over coffee and a snack somewhere between here and home?"

"If you're sure," said Grace.

The lift doors opened, and Grace saw Gus had already stood up to meet them.

"We need to talk before your phone call to Jim Francis," he said.

"Sorry we're later than planned, Gus," she said.

"I'm not chastising your timekeeping," he said. "I wanted you to know what you're up against. Annie Drew painted a different picture than we'd heard so far."

Grace sat with Gus and listened to what he and Alex had learned.

Blessing went to her desk and started updating the Freeman Files from her notes.

"Did you uncover something worthwhile, Blessing?" asked Neil.

"Mandy Fennell, the downtrodden wife and mother, is long gone," said Blessing. "It's almost as if she created a new persona in Amanda Jane, the confident, successful administrator with a beautiful home."

"You got nothing then. Is that what you're saying?"

"There might be something," said Blessing. "Nobody ever mentioned a beautiful, younger woman Mark Fennell was in love with just before meeting Jessie North."

"Fennell was at it all the time wasn't he?" asked Neil.

"Maybe," said Blessing. "What made me think it more significant was that young girl was why Mandy threw Mark out."

"How can we be sure?" asked Neil. "Why couldn't that young girl have just been the final straw?"

"Amanda Jane told us she hid her head in the sand for

years as far as Mark's behaviour was concerned. I got the impression that she could live with it as long as she could believe Mark only had one-night stands, either overseas or in this country. He had a healthy appetite, according to Amanda Jane."

"I can't see me getting away with that one with Melody," said Neil. "So, what she saw made her think this was more than a one-night stand?"

"Can you check the murder file for the actual wording in the statement she gave to DI Francis and DS Gibbs? I want to finish my reports."

"Will do, Blessing," said Neil.

On the other side of the office, Grace was ringing Jim Francis.

"Hola."

"Good afternoon, Mr Francis," said Grace. "This is DI Grace Packenham from Wiltshire Police. I'm working with a Crime Review Team trying to solve the murder of Mark Fennell back in 2005. You were in charge of the original investigation centred on Kington Langley and the Chippenham area."

"So what? Water under the bridge, sweetheart. There was nothing that pointed to any clear motive. Fennell couldn't keep his hands off other women; that was the long and the short of it. We followed every lead we could, but my gaffer wasn't prepared for us to fly around Europe, knocking on doors and asking women whether they'd slept with the bloke. It was a lost cause. Fennell didn't keep a black book with names, addresses, phone numbers, and star ratings. Who dragged this one out of the ether, anyway, sweetheart?"

"Please call me Inspector, Mr Francis," said Grace.

"Oh, here we go. I didn't come down with the last

shower. I was a detective for longer than you've been breathing. Your accent tells me you were born in or near the East Midlands, and your education screams Oxford or Cambridge. You hadn't been in the job five minutes before they set you on an express route to the top. No doubt you have all the attributes they look for today, apart from being black, and no, I don't need a video call to ascertain that, *In-Spec-tor*. My hearing is still perfect. Your skin colour might hold you back in some regions, but they can't wait to get another man-hater among the Assistant Chief Constables or above in many parts of the country. It signals to the public the police no longer serve that you understand the meaning of the word diversity if nothing else."

"If you've finished, Mr Francis," said Grace. "You asked me a question. Wiltshire's Chief Constable, Kenneth Truelove, selected this case for review."

"Ken Truelove? Now that's a surprise. He's a straight arrow and one of only a few coppers I respected. The way things have gone since I retired, I expected Ken to have been shown the door ages ago. So how long's this team of yours been operating?"

"Six months," said Grace. "Their clean-up rate is impressive by anyone's standards. Now, can we get back to Mark Fennell, please? Why didn't you question anyone in Burnham-on-Sea? Fennell bought a caravan with his ex-wife, Jessie, and they spent time in the resort before he walked out on her. We know Fennell also visited the caravan site several times with Helen Roker in the months leading to his murder. Fennell also rented the van to friends like his best man, Sam Webber. How many other people used that caravan? What was going on at that site? What might Fennell have seen or heard while on a weekend break that resulted in the man in the BMW driving to Kington Langley to track him down?"

"Burnham-on-Sea was on Avon & Somerset's patch," said Francis.

"In a similar situation, we would ask London Road to make a courtesy call to Portishead, or Dorchester, to pave the way for any visit outside the county," said Grace. "It's never been refused. We're all working to the same end."

"You genuinely believe that?" scoffed Francis. "I'd had a few run-ins with Avon & Somerset. They weren't about to do me any favours. So we concentrated on Fennell's relationships because that had the best chance of success."

Neil slipped a piece of paper onto Grace's desk, and she glanced at its contents.

"When you spoke with Fennell's first wife, how did she describe those relationships?"

"Fennell's job with Westinghouse meant he visited several project sites on mainland Europe and the UK. He was like a sailor, with a girl in every port."

"Maybe, but Mandy didn't know who these women were or whether her husband had met them more than once, did she? There weren't letters, emails, or phone calls that suggested an ongoing affair, were there? I spoke to her this afternoon, and she didn't see these random dalliances as a genuine threat to their marriage."

"Fennell would have hidden that activity if he had any sense," said Francis.

"Well, you would understand how that might work, Mr Francis."

"What's that supposed to mean?"

"Come now, Mr Francis," said Grace. "I didn't come down with the last shower. We spoke to Henry Gibbs and Annie Drew before we contacted you. They were both accommodating. If we spoke to one of your contemporaries with Avon & Somerset Police at Portishead, would we learn that Annie wasn't the first female officer you seduced? Perhaps you chose not to follow up on the Burnham angle. It might have reopened old wounds. A female officer who moved to get away from you could have found the courage to join forces with Annie when she lodged her complaint."

"You're living in a dream world," said Francis. "I've still got friends who will back me against anyone you dredge up. Burnham's not bandit country, *sweetheart*. Fennell's killer was someone closer to home. You mark my words."

"You might be hearing from someone at London Road shortly," said Grace, "but I don't think there's anything more you can offer this team and our investigation. Good afternoon, Mr Francis."

Grace ended the call and sat back in her chair.

"What a horrid man," she said. "Thanks for the note, Neil."

"Blessing suggested I check the wording of Mandy Fennell's statement."

"I might have inadvertently started us off on the wrong foot," said Gus. "When the Chief Constable ran through the case headlines, he said Mandy had thrown Mark out of the house because of his affairs."

"A simplification that didn't match the way Amanda Jane described the liaisons when Blessing and I spoke with her this afternoon," said Grace. "Can I leave it to tomorrow morning to update my files, Gus?"

A glance at the clock revealed it was five minutes to five.

"No problem," said Gus. "You did well to keep your cool, Grace, and it was naughty of you not to warn Jim Francis he was on speakerphone. What made you think there might have been someone stationed at Burnham, or close by, that Jim Francis knew intimately?"

"Just a hunch," said Grace. "His reaction didn't suggest I was way off the mark, did it?"

"A hunch? Are we starting to rub off on you, ma'am?" said Neil.

"Some more than others, Neil," said Grace with a brief smile.

She tidied her desk, grabbed her handbag, and joined Blessing by the lift.

Gus wondered whether the day's work had brought them closer to finding their killer. They might still be in the dark, but Grace had shown she was learning to become a team player.

He travelled down in the lift with Neil. When they emerged in the car park, Grace and Blessing were leaving in convoy. Alex and Lydia had already disappeared.

"See you in the morning then, guv," said Neil.

"All downhill to the weekend, Neil," said Gus. "Do we have Jessie North scheduled for tomorrow? I can't remember."

"She's what you remember as being called a dinner lady, guv," said Neil. "Jessie told Alex she'd be available from two o'clock in the afternoon."

"You and I can visit her then, Neil. Keep an eye on the clock because we need to get out of there before Pavel, the boyfriend, gets home."

"Do you think he might cut up rough, guv?"

"No, but I want Jessie to speak freely about her relationship with Mark Fennell."

"Got it, guv," said Neil.

Gus followed Neil's car out of the car park into Church

Street. Another thirty minutes, and he'd still be some distance from the bungalow, thanks to those roadworks.

Half a mile ahead of Gus, the Smart car and the Micra had turned right towards the Kennet and Avon canal and into the Barge Inn car park.

"This looks nice," said Grace. "Have you been here before?"

"Jamie brought me here once," said Blessing. "We sat enjoying our meal and watched the barges as they passed. They were so close that we could reach out and touch them. It's a beautiful spot in the late summer. We haven't been here for a meal indoors yet, but it's all wooden floors and low ceilings, and the fireplaces promise a roaring log fire to fend off the cold in the winter."

They crossed the car park and entered the bar.

"I imagine we're too late for afternoon tea and too early for many evening diners," said Grace.

"They're open from noon to midnight," said Blessing with a shrug. "We can get coffee, cake, or a snack if you're hungry. Look, there's even a vegan sandwich on the menu."

"Things are looking up," said Grace.

"While we're waiting for our orders," said Blessing. "Why do you think you haven't made many friends since you moved here from Portishead?"

"You're assuming I had plenty when I lived there," said Grace.

"That's not an answer, and you know it," said Blessing. "I'm a shy person by nature, and I got bullied at school because of my skin colour and weight. However, I persevered, and I managed to find students I could relate to and trust. It was the same when I joined the police. As a raw recruit, I always got the flak, and it was far worse being a tongue-tied, nervous, chubby Nigerian. But, somehow, I found colleagues with whom I could get along, and my boss, DI Andy Carlton, was just what I needed to bring me out of my shell."

"Did you want to leave Leamington Spa?" asked Grace.

"I knew I could have stayed, and Andy would have encouraged me to put in for my sergeant's exam, but I don't think his superiors saw me as a potential high-flyer."

"You're going to tell me Gus has given you wings," said Grace. "I do believe that man could walk on water."

"I met Lydia in Leamington Spa, and she told Gus about me. He said Lydia thought I had potential and would be a good fit with the other team members."

"Did they accept you straight away?" asked Grace.

"Right from the start," said Blessing. "It helped when Gus found me such a great place to stay, but we get on socially and at work."

Their coffees arrived, and Blessing wondered whether Grace knew about the team's nights at the Waggon & Horses. Fortunately, another staff member delivered their sandwiches, which postponed the conversation.

"I needed that," said Grace after she'd eaten. "It was super."

"Neil told me you used to have lunch at London Road with Rhys Evans," said Blessing. "So you did make one friend."

"We were newbies and the same age," said Grace. "Rhys approached me, and I didn't know anyone else. I realised after a few weeks why he'd done it."

"That's okay," said Blessing. "I heard the story from a friend the other night. Rhys didn't want people at work to know he was gay, so he latched on to you for appearance's sake."

"Oh, I didn't know other people knew," said Grace, "That was bad enough, but Rhys thought I was gay too."

"Oh," said Blessing. "Jim Francis got that wrong, too, then?"

"I've had boyfriends in the past," said Grace, "at school and Cambridge. But once boys heard I'd received a first-class honours degree, they steered clear of me."

"You intimidated them," said Blessing. "I read in a magazine that the male ego is a tender creature."

Blessing only just managed to finish the sentence before laughing out loud. Grace joined in, and it was over a minute before they could resume talking.

"Do you mean you haven't been in a relationship since you left Cambridge?" asked Blessing.

"I told you my family all but disowned me after telling them what I planned," said Grace. "When I joined the police, I couldn't live at home, so I did what Luke Sherman is doing now. It wasn't ideal, but it was every bit as good as the digs I'd suffered at university. The trouble with Lincolnshire's police accommodation is that it's designed to be temporary, and people soon move on. I'd start seeing someone, and suddenly they were transferred two hundred miles away, or they found two or three mates that agreed to house-share, and I didn't fit into their plans. So when I got promoted to Detective Sergeant, I moved to Portishead, with over a thousand staff, both fire and police personnel, working in a modern building. I couldn't find digs in town, so I drove there every day from Clevedon, seven miles up the coast."

"Nothing to do there, I suppose?" said Blessing.

"I imagine its heyday was in Victorian times," said Grace. "There's a pier, a bandstand, and ornamental gardens. It's ideal for your parents if they fancy a trip to the coast in the summer. Unfortunately, the place was dead in the winter, and a single female police officer found it tough to find a boyfriend."

"You didn't fancy anyone at the Portishead HQ?" asked Blessing finishing the last of her coffee.

"I did see a couple of guys, but nothing serious," replied Grace.

"Just mindless sex?"

"A sad indictment on my life," said Grace. "I hoped Devizes would improve my fortunes."

"Can I be candid?" asked Blessing. "You need to let people in. I appreciate that you need to maintain a certain distance between yourself and those who report to you, but Jamie says that when troops see razor wire, they look for a way to bypass it rather than try ploughing through it."

"I suppose I do come across as prickly, don't I?" sighed Grace.

"You might have turned over a new leaf today," said Blessing. "Do you want to make a move?"

"Gosh, it's half-past six," said Grace. "Won't Jackie Ferris be worried where you are?"

"My evening meal will be ready when I am," giggled Blessing. "Jackie always cooks far too much. I'll call and ask her to set another place."

"Can she cope with a vegan diet?" asked Grace.

"Don't worry, Jackie will adapt. You like vegetables, and there are always too many varieties on my plate. You'll be doing me a favour. I might squeeze into the new dress I bought three months ago if you came to visit every week."

Friday, 5 October 2018

"RESTLESS?" asked Suzie.

"Not the best night's sleep I've ever had," said Gus. He rolled out of bed and padded towards the shower.

"I can discount a guilty conscience," said Suzie, following him on her way to the kitchen to start breakfast. "So. you must have been pondering your next move on the case."

Ten minutes later, Gus joined Suzie in the kitchen. His mug of black coffee was ready and waiting.

"Boiled egg and soldiers," said Suzie. "Any objections?"

Gus couldn't remember the last time that had been on the menu. He shook his head and took a sip from his coffee.

"I'll phone Geoff Mercer to ask for a contact in Burnham-on-Sea," said Gus. "He should be able to get someone keen for an early start on Monday morning. Today, we'll attempt to speak to as many people connected to Mark Fennell and Helen Roker that we haven't interviewed yet."

"You would prefer a clean sheet when you move your operation to the coast," said Suzie.

"Odd, isn't it? The team might spend a week at the seaside *before* their two-week holiday."

"Will you travel back and forth each day?" asked Suzie.

"I can't see Geoff Mercer splashing out for four nights at a Premier Inn. So we'll take three cars and suffer a ninety-minute commute."

"How's Grace fitting in?"

"Despite the ten-year age difference, Grace and Blessing have forged a good working relationship. They had a good day yesterday in Calne and the office."

"That's one pairing sorted for next week," said Suzie. "Who will work with you?"

"I'd rather put Neil with Grace," said Gus.

"Chalk and cheese come to mind," said Suzie.

"Exactly," said Gus. "That can often result in a good team."

"That leaves Alex and Blessing. Have they ever worked in the field together before?"

"If they have, the occasion escapes me," said Gus. "Those two get on fine in the office. Blessing has a knack of homing in on those tricky pieces of a jigsaw that don't seem to fit anywhere, and it will pay to develop more options."

"For the day when Kenneth decides it's time for Lydia to spread her wings," said Suzie.

She headed for the bathroom, and Gus was left to tackle his boiled egg and hope that day wouldn't come for a while.

Chapter Nine

"NEXT STOP, the first red traffic light," said Suzie.

She eased her Golf through the gateway and into the lane.

Gus followed her lead, and they took the Nursteed Road into town.

Variety is the spice of life. Gus peeled off the line of cars heading for the obstacle course on London Road and soon reached the brow of Caen Hill. What a grey day. Low clouds marred what was often a stunning view across the valley below.

This morning there was nothing for it but to concentrate on the handful of cars ahead and hope that one of them wasn't inclined to do something stupid. At the bottom of the hill, a well-established scrap yard exhibited hundreds of vehicles, piled ten feet high, that had suffered at the hands of idiot drivers.

Sadly, they weren't always vehicles that had belonged to the idiots.

After a thankfully uneventful drive through Seend, Gus

reached the outskirts of town and passed the junction to Crook's Way. The traffic volume had increased with the school run being in full flow; after all, Friday was the start of the weekend.

The queues at petrol stations and supermarkets were longer than on any other day of the week. Gus couldn't quite remember who decided the weekend should start at eight o'clock on Friday morning, but it had been that way every week since the CRT had moved into their office.

Gus heard the sound of angry car horns up ahead and spotted a Smart car and a Nissan Micra stopped by the side of the road. Those two small vehicles weren't causing the logjam; that was down to the thirty-eight-tonne truck blocking more than half the road and preventing traffic from entering or leaving Church Street.

Traffic was reduced to a crawl, but the cars ahead of him edged past the truck one by one. Finally, Gus parked his Focus behind Blessing's car and went to see what was happening.

His Detective Constable looked nervous. As for Amazing Grace, she was calmness personified. Perhaps it was because she didn't understand the Czech driver's words. Of course, Gus didn't understand him, but the branding on the cab door told him the company had depots in Prague, Brno, and Ostrava, which was good enough.

"I'm glad you're here, guv," said Blessing, moving position so that Gus was between her and the truck driver.

"What's going on?" asked Gus.

"Grace spotted he was on his mobile phone as we passed him half a mile back. Then she stopped and flagged him down as he drove into the town centre. He sounds furious, and look at the size of him."

"What was Grace thinking?" said Gus. "We can't ignore

people breaking the law, but investigating a murder case trumps everything else in my book."

Gus approached the side of the truck, where Grace was attempting to communicate with the man-mountain with the help of Google Translate.

"Have you got enough details for the appropriate department to charge him, Grace? If so, get this truck on its way right now, and make a phone call from the office. Traffic offences aren't our problem."

Blessing thought Gus should have turned to stone from the look Grace gave him.

The truck driver suddenly appeared to understand English and climbed back into his cab. He was pulling away and heading for the industrial estate on the other side of the river before Gus returned to his Focus.

Gus was waiting for the lift to return to the ground floor when Blessing and Grace joined him. They travelled to the first floor in silence.

"Morning, guv," said Neil. "Traffic problems this morning?"

Least said soonest mended, thought Gus.

"Nothing I couldn't handle, Neil. Can we speak with Sam and Mary Webber this morning?"

"Together, or separately, guv?" asked Alex.

"What do they do for a living?" asked Gus.

"They're retired, guv," said Lydia. "Sam was a car dealer, high-end Italian models for the most part. Mary stayed at home looking after their three kids, all boys."

"So they're in Chippenham, and unless they've left for a weekend trip to Burnham-on-Sea, we can visit them. Get that organised, will you, Alex?"

Alex checked the phone number in the murder file and dialled.

Gus grabbed his phone and called Geoff Mercer. The sooner they had that liaison officer from Avon & Somerset, the better. Vera Butler took the call as Geoff was in a meeting. She promised to pass on his request and agreed to call back as soon as she had confirmation of a name and contact details.

"Mary Webber said she's available any time this morning, guv," said Alex once Gus had ended the call. "Sam's on the golf course at Bowood with their three sons. He'll be home by lunchtime."

"We'll aim for eleven o'clock, Alex," said Gus. "Where are we going?"

"Black Bridge Road, guv. It's on the eastern outskirts of Chippenham. They lived just a ten-minute drive from Mark Fennell's house in Kington Langley."

"They were in each other's pockets from when they were at school, guv," said Neil. "I bet we'd find Mark and Mandy lived on that side of town when they were married."

"Jim Francis and his team don't appear to have recorded it in the murder file, guv," said Alex. "I don't suppose they thought it relevant."

"Amanda Jane told us Mark and Sam were joined at the hip and went everywhere together," said Blessing. "Sam was best man at their wedding. Mary must have been one of her best friends because she was one of her bridesmaids. We didn't ask whether she and Mark performed similar duties when Sam and Mary married."

"That firm friendship tends to continue through thick and thin," said Neil. "We know they were still close in 2005."

"One thing Amanda Jane was adamant about was her distaste for caravanning," said Blessing. "No way did Mark get involved with the Burnham-on-Sea site while they were together."

Gus looked to Amazing Grace for confirmation. She nodded. Gus wondered how long she would sulk; she'd made zero contribution so far.

"We'll discover when the caravan bug first bit Mark Fennell this afternoon when we speak to Jessie North," he said. "Who else is there we can catch this morning?"

"Joe Morgan?" asked Alex. "Is it worth a trip to Corsham?"

"Is he still a delivery driver?" asked Gus.

"Give me five minutes. I'll check, guv."

"It might pay us to chat to Joe about Sam and Mary Webber before meeting them. Joe was with Helen Roker at that New Year's Eve party in Chippenham not long before she died. I'd like to know what kind of people they are."

Gus's phone rang. Vera Butler had news already. He made a mental note to buy Geoff Mercer a pint.

"A DI Jill Crooks will drive over from Bridgwater on Monday morning, Gus," said Vera. "The station at Burnham isn't open around the clock these days, but she'll meet you there at ten o'clock."

"Happy days," said Gus. "I look forward to meeting DI Crooks. Does she have local knowledge?"

"Jill grew up in the seaside resort and worked in Burnham and Highbridge as a junior officer. She sounds to be my age and married to the job."

"Wonderful. Thanks, Vera. Have a good weekend."

Gus ended the call and saw Alex raise a hand.

"Joe Morgan is off work with a bad back, guv. He'll be happy to have visitors."

"I'll take Neil with me on this one," said Gus. "Grace, please meet us at the Webber household at eleven. Neil can be on standby to intercept the husband when he gets home from his round of golf. Then, you and I will tackle Mary."

"Was there anyone we could question, guv?" asked Lydia.

"Ian and Becky Hood are the only two names left on my list," said Alex.

"Becky was Helen's sister," said Lydia. "The link to the two murders is tenuous at best. The only connection to Burnham-on-Sea is that Sam and Mary Webber were at their New Year's Eve party. I wonder whether Ian and Becky used Mark's caravan too?"

"We can't lose anything by talking to them," said Gus. "I wonder what happened to that caravan, anyway? We must ask Jessie North what she did with it."

"For all we know, she's still using it, guv," said Neil.

He had tidied his desk and was ready to leave.

"Are we taking my car, guv?" he asked.

"My Focus has embarrassing memories of Corsham, Neil," said Gus as they entered the lift. "If memory serves, that was the last place where my windows got stuck halfway and wouldn't shift for love or money."

They headed across the river bridge two minutes later to join the Bath road. Gus scanned the industrial park for a thirty-eight-tonne truck, but the driver must have checked out. Gus could only hope the man-mountain had given Amazing Grace his correct home address.

The driver should get notified of the two hundred pounds penalty fine. Gus wasn't sure how the six points on his licence could be applied, but it wasn't something Gus had bothered with since he was a copper on the beat in Salisbury.

"Do you know where Dickens Avenue is, guv?" asked Neil.

"Not a clue. What's that place dead ahead at the cross-roads, Neil?"

"The Methuen Arms, guv, a Georgian coaching inn. They do a cracking meal. I took Melody there once on our wedding anniversary."

"We're not stopping, Neil," said Gus. "Joe Morgan's flat is supposed to be a two-minute drive from that inn, according to Alex."

"Got it, guv," said Neil.

After collaring an elderly gentleman pushing a shopping trolley, Neil discovered the way to Dickens Avenue. Joe Morgan's flat was on the second floor of a converted townhouse. Neil pressed a bell on the front door but couldn't tell whether anyone had heard it ring.

"Joe's got a bad back, Neil," said Gus. "Try the intercom."

"Never saw it amongst the grime, guv. Sorry."

Joe buzzed them in once communication had been established. Gus and Neil made their way up the narrow staircase.

"Hardly five-star accommodation, guv," said Neil. He knocked on the door to Flat 3.

"It's not locked. Come on in."

They found Joe Morgan propped in the corner of a high-backed settee in his lounge diner. He looked in some discomfort. The empty cans of Special Brew were the only signs of medication.

"Thanks for agreeing to see us at short notice. Mr Morgan," said Neil. "I'm DS Davis from Wiltshire Police. My colleague, Mr Freeman and I wanted to ask you questions about matters relating to the deaths of Mark Fennell and Helen Roker."

"I'll try," said Joe. "There's not a lot I can add to the

statement I gave the detectives in 2006, but anything that helps get justice for Helen has to be worth a punt."

"How old are you now, Joe?" asked Gus.

"Fifty-one," he replied.

"Where did you meet Helen Roker?" asked Neil.

"On the bus," said Joe. "She was travelling to Bath."

"You struck up a conversation with a stranger?" asked Gus.

"Not on the bus. I saw Helen again in the foyer at the Theatre Royal. We were there to see a matinee performance of a new play having a pre-West End run. We travelled back to Chippenham on the bus together. That was how it started."

"Was Helen already living in the flat on Foundry Lane when you moved in?" asked Gus.

"Yes, she'd been there several months."

"We don't want to labour the events of January 2006," said Gus. "I'm sure you've played them repeatedly in your head since then."

"It's not something I'm ever likely to forget. We made a good couple, Helen and me. That detective, Perry, I think his name was, gave me such a look when I said we were theatre lovers and had booked for Bristol Hippodrome the weekend after Helen died. It wasn't that he didn't believe me; I had the tickets. He seemed to have pigeon-holed us the same as the rest of that crowd."

"Did you ever look for someone else who shared the same interests, Joe?" asked Gus.

"I wouldn't have found anyone to replace Helen," he replied.

"Was the New Year's Eve party a noisy affair at Ian Hood's home?" asked Gus.

"No, we had a great evening. There was music, food,

and drink, but nothing to annoy the neighbours. I'd not met Ian before. Becky often dropped by the flat, and she and Helen spent the day shopping several times while we were together. That night was the only opportunity Helen and I ever had to socialise with the two of them."

"What did you make of Ian?" asked Neil.

"A good-looking bloke who had obviously done well for himself. Helen whispered to me that she hoped we'd have a home like that one day. Unfortunately, it would have cost much more than a delivery driver, and a care worker could afford. Ian could tell we were envious, and that seemed to please him. I found his tone a little brash."

"Rude, noisy, overbearing," said Gus.

"Not noisy, at least not that night," said Joe. "You're spot on with the other two observations. Becky thought the world of him, which is what mattered, I suppose."

"Do you know if they're still together?" asked Gus.

"If they are, you'll find them in The Tinings in Chippenham," said Joe. "I can't see why they'd want to move. They had a beautiful home."

"The Tinings rings a bell," said Neil. "Did I see that on the street map when I checked where we're going later this morning?"

"Black Bridge Road?" asked Gus.

"A stone's throw away," said Joe. "Depending on which end of the street you live."

"Becky hasn't kept in touch?" asked Gus.

"We haven't spoken since the funeral," said Joe.

"What line of business was Ian Hood in?" asked Gus.

"Import and export, that's all he was prepared to say when I chatted with him at the party."

"How many people did they invite?" asked Neil.

"Only us and Sam Webber and his wife."

"Did you know Sam Webber?" asked Gus.

"We hadn't met before that night. Helen knew Sam and Mary, of course. Almost everyone in Chippenham knows Sam Webber. He's cut from the same cloth as Ian Hood. Sam's full of himself and always the loudest voice in the room. He succeeded in his car business, and his three boys will carry on the franchise now he's retired. A few months ago, I saw an article in the Gazette and Herald with his cheesy grin plastered across the front page. I've no idea why Mary put up with him. I caught him ogling Helen and Becky throughout the evening. It's just his way, though. Sam thinks business success equates to being irresistible to women."

"Sam was great mates with Mark Fennell," said Neil. "They sound like two peas from the same pod."

"I never met Mark Fennell," said Joe. "I don't think we would have got on."

"Did you ever ask Helen what she saw in him?" asked Gus. "Did they share the same interests?"

"Mark wasn't interested in the theatre," said Joe. "He told Helen the only time he'd been near one was to have his appendix removed when he was fourteen."

"What did the six of you talk about during the evening?" asked Gus.

"It's hard to remember much from that long ago," said Joe. "I spoke to Ian without learning much about where he came from or what he did. Sam never let me get a word in edgewise while he bragged about a Ferrari he'd sold the day before. But, of course, Becky and Helen found plenty to talk about, and Mary sat quietly listening to what they said. We discussed the weather and what we'd done over Christmas, and Mary told us her boys had flown to Scotland, hoping to go skiing. They were twenty-two, twenty, and eighteen. That, I do remember."

"Did the subject of caravanning get raised at all?" asked Gus. "Was Burnham-on-Sea ever mentioned?"

"Ian was talking to Sam about something late on. It was well after midnight. I'd reached my limit regarding drinking, so I stayed in the lounge with Helen and the other women. Ian and Sam disappeared to the kitchen and returned ten minutes later. Ian handed Becky a set of keys."

"What was Helen's reaction?" asked Gus.

"Funny you should ask that question, Mr Freeman," said Joe. "Helen looked rather disturbed by it. It didn't make sense to me, but everyone soon talked about something else, and I never got to ask her. We left The Tinings at two in the morning. Helen had booked a taxi before we left Foundry Lane, and Sam asked the driver to take them and drop them on Black Bridge Road. It was in the opposite direction, but Sam jumped in the back, chucked a twenty-pound note over the driver's shoulder, and said nothing more. So we dropped them off, returned to the flat, and didn't surface until lunchtime the next day. It was a few days later I remembered the keys incident. When I asked Helen why she reacted the way she did, she refused to discuss it."

"Subsequent events meant you didn't get another chance to ask," said Gus.

Joe Morgan nodded.

"After Helen died, I hoped the police would discover who was responsible. I was positive she hadn't killed herself, but after hearing the inquest verdict, I sensed DI Perry and the girl he worked with lost interest."

"DS Frankie Price," said Neil.

"She was okay, sympathetic, and if she'd had some support, I think she would have kept searching for a killer.

But instead, Perry thought the coroner had been in the job too long, and his thinking was muddled. So, things drifted, and here we are twelve years later, and it's still unresolved."

"We've been reviewing both deaths for the past few days," said Gus. "I asked another coroner for a second opinion because I wasn't convinced the narrative verdict was helpful. Was there any change in Helen's behaviour after the New Year's Eve party that gave you concerns about her state of mind?"

"It was only a matter of days, Mr Freeman," said Joe. "As I told the detectives at the time, as far as I was concerned, the medication her doctor prescribed was doing her a power of good. From the day we met in Bath's Theatre Royal, I never thought Helen had suicidal thoughts. She had a lot of trauma to process, so her behaviour was bound to be highs and lows. I understood that and did what I could to help. But, of course, anyone can have an off week when they don't feel on top of their game. Perhaps Helen was less talkative than usual in the first week of January, but I didn't think anything of it."

"Joan Fisher, whose mother was one of Helen's clients, told police Helen thought she had a stalker," said Gus. "Did DI Perry mention that?"

"Frankie Price told me her boss thought Helen was paranoid. Helen was suffering from post-traumatic stress, taking tablets every day to deal with her demons, no wonder she saw things that weren't there. If she was drinking on top of that, nothing she said could be relied upon to be the truth. The only evidence was the empty bottles they found in the flat. I told them Helen was only a moderate drinker, but they ignored me."

"When I listened to the details of Helen's case, my first instinct was that suicide was the last thing on her mind that day," said Gus. "Nothing I've heard since has made me change my mind. Why finish the basket of ironing? Why book the theatre trip to Bristol at the weekend? You've just confirmed Helen was coping with life in the months leading up to the new year and looking forward to a future with you. I now believe we're looking at a double murder."

"But why would anyone want to kill Helen?" asked Joe.

"For the same reason they killed Mark Fennell," said Neil. "Which means we need to concentrate on the short period when Mark and Helen were a couple."

"Did Helen ever talk about that time in her life?" asked Gus.

"I didn't want to know, Mr Freeman," said Joe, "and when we first got together, Helen only ever spoke about the night Mark died and what happened afterwards. She tried to put the matter behind her, not chat about it over coffee every day. Helen told me she had wanted to stay in the house at Kington Langley, surrounded by memories of Mark and the good times they shared. But then, his ex-wife's solicitor turned up, telling her she had to leave. That didn't help with the healing process."

"We'll speak to Mark's friends about that period in his life in more detail," said Gus. "Can you keep the news about the double murder aspect to yourself for the time being, Joe? I want to inform Helen's sister in person. I think that's only right, don't you?"

"Oh, yes, I understand perfectly. You need to follow the proper procedure. I doubt I'll speak to Becky or her husband anytime soon, if ever."

"Good man," said Gus. "Our colleagues could be with Ian and Becky as we speak. So that embargo shouldn't last for too long. We'll contact them as soon as we leave here. That's all for now, Joe. Thanks for your time, and I hope your back improves and you can get back behind the wheel."

"So do I," said Joe. "I can't afford to be off work for too long. The bills still need paying, don't they?"

Neil and Gus left Joe Morgan, where they found him and closed the flat door behind them.

"Sometimes, the more you hear, the less you understand," said Gus as they reached Neil's car.

"Sorry, guv," said Neil. "You've lost me."

"According to everyone who offered information to detectives after his death, Mark Fennell was a womaniser. He had more girlfriends than I've had hot dinners. I haven't met all the women involved, but Mark Fennell's personality didn't change. By the sound of it, Sam Webber was capable of behaving similarly. However, DI Perry seemed confused because Joe didn't show the same character traits. Did you catch what Joe said? Perry thought it odd that he enjoyed going to the theatre."

"Yes, and that didn't gel with how the rest of the crowd behaved. Dave Perry meant people like Mark Fennell, Sam Webber, and Ian Hood."

"That's significant, Neil. I'm convinced of that," said Gus. "However, there's something else that's bothering me. I need to think about it while you drive us to Chippenham."

"Do you want to give Alex a ring first, guv?" asked Neil. "To see whether they've fixed up a time with Helen's sister and her husband?"

"Thanks for reminding me," said Gus. He called the office.

"DC Blessing Umeh. How may I help you today?"

"Did Alex and Lydia leave the office yet, Blessing?" asked Gus.

"Yes, guv," said Blessing. "I'm holding the fort. Grace has just left for Black Bridge Road as well."

"We'll see you after lunch, Blessing," said Gus. "I'll contact Lydia. I need her to inform Becky Hood that we now believe her sister was murdered. I want Alex and Lydia to gauge the couple's reaction to the news."

"I'm sure you'll explain what that means this afternoon, guv," said Blessing. "Good hunting."

"Lydia's Mini was in the car park when I arrived this morning," said Gus. "So, I'd better send a message to Alex. I don't want Lydia to answer her mobile if they're still driving to Chippenham."

"Why were you three late this morning, guv?" asked Neil. "I sensed an atmosphere."

"You'll make a good detective, Neil," said Gus. "Amazing Grace spotted a truck driver on his mobile phone and decided it was a good idea to haul him over. Blessing stopped to give moral support. The driver would have made mincemeat out of both of them."

"Around twenty-five percent of all drivers confess to making or receiving calls on a handheld phone while driving, guv," said Neil. "That figure is higher among young people."

"And you're four times more likely to be involved in a crash resulting in injuries," said Gus. "I'm aware of that, Neil, but Grace would be better served to highlight the lunacy of reducing the number of traffic cops to her superiors, not waving her warrant card at one errant trucker."

"You had words then, guv," said Neil.

"I don't think she'll do it again," said Gus. "Right, onwards to Black Bridge Road. Let's hear what Sam Webber and his wife have to say."

Chapter Ten

"WE HAVE another task added to our list," said Alex.

"Did Gus learn something important from Joe Morgan?" asked Lydia.

"He didn't say. We're almost at the end of Eastern Avenue. The turning to The Tinings will be on your right. Gus must have told Joe Morgan about his concerns over the narrative verdict Conrad Alderslade delivered. We have to tell Becky Hood we believe her sister was murdered. Gus wants us to gauge her response."

"We should leave that until we've covered the other questions we prepared," said Lydia. "Did she say why her husband couldn't return to the house until this afternoon?"

"A vague mention of a business meeting," said Alex. "Hang on, Gus has sent another message. Blimey, he's now given us a potted version of the whole conversation. You'll need to leave most of the supplementary questions to me. I'll have to read them from my phone."

Lydia parked the car at the side of the road, and they walked up the short pathway to the front door.

"When do you think these houses were built?" asked Lydia.

"The Seventies, perhaps," said Alex. "No expense spared in the garden. I caught a glimpse of a substantial amount of decking at the rear of the property when we rounded the bend back there."

Lydia rang the doorbell.

"Two cameras at the front of the house," she said.

"Joe Morgan told Gus that Ian and Becky had a beautiful home. I imagine they want to deter burglars."

The door opened, and one glance told Lydia this was Helen Roker's sister.

"Thank you for seeing us today, Mrs Hood," she said. "DS Hardy and I are from Wiltshire Police. We need to ask you some questions about your sister, Helen, and her relationship with Mark Fennell. My name is Lydia Logan Barre."

"You had better come inside," said Becky. "It's been so long since we heard from the police. I thought Mark's murder was ancient history."

"No unsolved murder file is ever closed, Mrs Hood," said Alex.

Becky led them through to the lounge from the hallway. Alex understood why Gus had mentioned the décor. Someone had spent a lot of money making this room and the hallway look picture-perfect. No doubt, the other rooms were equally impressive.

Whether anything remained from the furnishings Joe Morgan had seen at that New Year's Eve party was debatable. Perhaps only the photograph on the Welsh dresser of Ian and Becky's wedding.

"How did your sister meet Mark Fennell?" asked Lydia.

"They met in the Black Horse in Chippenham back in July 2004. She phoned me the following day."

"Did she know Mark Fennell was still married to his second wife, Jessie?"

"Mark didn't mention it that first night," said Becky. "A friend at work told me to warn her he had a roving eye, but Helen wasn't worried. She challenged Mark the next time they met, and he came clean. He said he and Mandy got married too young, and they had drifted apart when the kids were grown up. Mark said he hadn't realised how much the break-up had affected him. His wife had been the one to instigate divorce proceedings. Mark told Helen he'd married Jessie on the rebound and realised his mistake after a few months."

"Did Helen swallow that?" asked Alex.

"Love is blind, detective," said Becky.

"They moved in together in Kington Langley soon after meeting," said Alex. "Did you approve?"

"Not for me to say what my sister should do," said Becky. "I could tell Helen was in love with the guy. She thought he felt the same way, and while they were together, I never had cause to believe Mark was ever unfaithful."

"The house isn't far from here, is it?" asked Lydia.

"Kington Langley's not far from most places in Chippenham, so what?"

"We know Sam Webber lives in the next street over, and we suspect Mark Fennell lived close by during his first marriage. Did Ian grow up on this estate too?"

"Ian grew up on the other side of town, but they attended the same school and hung around together as teenagers. They used to drink in the Black Horse as young men. No different to hundreds of other young men in any town you want to mention. What's this in aid of, anyway?

"What line of work is your husband in?" asked Alex.

"Import and export," said Becky. "Ian's done well for himself ever since I've known him. After leaving Chippenham College at the beginning of the Eighties, he had some hard times, but he's never looked back since."

"How much older than Helen were you, Mrs Hood?" asked Lydia.

"Three years, I'm sixty-one now. I'm a lady of leisure these days. I haven't needed to work for years."

"It won't be long before Ian retires, too," said Alex.

"Ian's three years older than me, but he's not planning to retire just yet."

"How often would you say you and Ian visited Helen while she lived in Kington Langley?" asked Lydia.

"Ian drove over to see Mark once a month. They were mates and used to have a drink in the pub in the village, but I believe that's closed now. I went with Ian several times, and Helen and I stayed home for a catch-up while the boys went to the pub. I saw my sister more regularly in town because we used to meet for a coffee and arrange something for the weekend if she was available."

"For those weekends when she wasn't in Burnham-on-Sea at the caravan," said Alex.

"That blessed caravan," said Becky. "The seaside's lovely in the summer, but I couldn't see the attraction of going there in the dead of winter."

"You used it too?" asked Lydia.

"We all did. Not every weekend, but Mark, Ian, and Sam occupied the caravan as often as possible. Ian said it wasn't wise to leave it empty for too long. The local riff-raff might have decided to squat there. We would have had a devil of a job turfing them out so one of us could enjoy a rare sunny weekend in mid-July."

"Did you ever go there with Mark and Helen?" asked Alex.

"It wasn't big enough, not really. Of course, if you had young children, you could rough it, but that wasn't our style, as you can see."

"You have a beautiful home," said Lydia.

"Thank you. We've been here too long. I wanted to move to Spain," said Becky. "Especially after Helen died, but Ian put his foot down. He said we needed to stay here for the business."

"Import and export can cover a wide range," said Alex. "What more can you tell us about what's involved?"

"Ian told me it was far too complicated for me to understand when we got together," said Becky. "All I needed to know was that as long as he got more than it cost him for the stuff he bought, we'd be okay."

"I imagine he has a warehouse somewhere to hold the stock," said Alex.

"He hasn't got a warehouse or any big building I've ever heard him mention," said Becky.

Alex looked forward to meeting Ian Hood and asking him the same questions.

"When did you meet Ian?" asked Lydia.

"In the mid-Eighties," said Becky. "I must have been twenty-seven, and a group of girls I worked with were in town on a hen night. We went to Goldiggers, the nightclub they opened in an old cinema, up by the bus station. Everyone had too much to drink, and I woke up in a strange bed the next morning."

"You're still together," said Lydia.

"As I said, Ian has done well since he returned to Chippenham."

Alex made a note to check whether Ian Hood had a criminal record.

"What can you recall of the New Year's Eve party you held at the end of 2005?" asked Lydia.

"We invited Sam and Mary," said Becky. "I'd spoken to Mary on Boxing Day, and she said her sons were flying to Scotland for Hogmanay. So I told her that they should come along if they were on their own and didn't have anywhere better to be."

"Your sister came too, didn't she?" asked Alex.

"Yes, Helen had started seeing Joe Morgan. Ian didn't know Joe, and he wasn't keen on him being here, but Joe was the man my sister wanted to be with, so I invited them too."

"How did the evening pan out?" asked Lydia.

"Helen and I chatted easily enough. We were always comfortable in each other's company. It was no different when she lived with Mark. Mary's a quiet soul, but she joined in now and again. Joe did his best, bless him, but I could tell that Sam and Ian didn't rate him."

"They were Jack-the-Lads. Brash, cocky characters, and Joe didn't fit in," said Alex.

"Joe was a van driver," said Becky. "Ten a penny, according to Ian. So when Helen told us they enjoyed going to the theatre together and Joe listened to classical music in his van, they thought even less of him. It wasn't just that, though. Sam, Mark, and Ian had known one another for forty years. They were a tight unit."

"You're suggesting they didn't trust him," said Alex.

"Someone turned up at Mark's house with a double-barrelled shotgun and blasted him from a couple of feet away. I don't think they trusted anyone after that."

"Joe Morgan remembered Sam and Ian talking in the

kitchen after midnight. Joe was in this room with you, Helen, and Mary. Ian handed you a set of keys when he returned. What were those keys for?"

"It was such a long time ago," said Becky, "and I would have had a few drinks if it was that late."

"Don't mess us about, Becky," said Alex. "There's only one set of keys those three lads passed around. The keys to the caravan at Burnham-on-Sea."

"Then that's what they were, so what?" shrugged Becky.

"Joe Morgan told our boss that Helen looked rather disturbed when she saw that happen. It didn't make any sense to him, so a few days later, he asked Helen why she reacted the way she did, but she refused to discuss it. Helen was dead within a matter of days."

"Helen didn't kill herself, you know. No matter what the police thought. That coroner sat on the fence rather than deliver a clear verdict. Someone killed her. It had nothing to do with Ian, Sam, or those blessed keys."

Becky Hood was on the verge of tears. Outside, Alex heard the sound of a car pulling up.

"That will be Ian," said Becky. "He'll put a stop to this nonsense."

"Why don't we go to the kitchen, Mrs Hood?" said Lydia. "I'm sure everyone would appreciate a coffee. DS Hardy can chat with Ian, and then we'll get out of your hair."

Becky pulled herself together and led the way into the kitchen. Lydia wasn't disappointed. She'd been right about the high-spec finish continuing throughout the house.

"You have a superb entertaining area with that decking," she said. "If only we had the weather to make full use of it. Do you do much entertaining, Mrs Hood?"

"Call me Becky. Ian got this built three years ago. I'm

not sure why. We never had kids, Ian works every hour that God sends, and we don't have many friends to invite around. So it rarely gets used unless I sit outside for a coffee on a day like today."

"Make us a coffee, and we'll worry about the men later. You get the sun until late afternoon on this side of the street. Let's enjoy it while we can now the rain clouds have blown away."

Becky Hood poured two cups of coffee and looked at Lydia.

"Black, one sugar," said Lydia.

"Me too," said Becky.

They moved onto the verandah, where the rattan furniture looked brand-new. Lydia realised some serious money was coming into this house, whatever Ian was buying and selling. When they were seated, Lydia asked:- "Do you holiday abroad much, Becky?"

"The Caribbean in May and November. We used to fly to Spain for years when we first married, but it was always full of drunken Brits. Ian thought we deserved better and could afford it, so we treat ourselves."

"Our boss was interviewing Joe Morgan earlier. You might have realised that with some of the questions we asked. Now we're alone; there's something I need to tell you. You were on the verge of tears indoors when talking about Helen's death. We've studied the forensic evidence gathered at the flat in Foundry Lane, and we agree that the inquest verdict led the original police investigation along the wrong path. We now believe that Helen was murdered."

"I knew it," cried Becky. "Those detectives wouldn't listen to me, and that coroner was an old fool. What does it mean, though?"

"I'm afraid it means the person who killed Mark Fennell

also had to kill your sister. Can you think why that would be, Becky? What did they know so incriminating someone had to get rid of them?"

"How would I know?" asked Becky.

"Did they argue with someone they met in their few months together?"

"Ian and I didn't spend every waking minute with them," said Becky. "But I can't remember Mark and Helen going anywhere different to the rest of us."

"No, I suppose not," said Lydia. "Unless they were working or socialising in Chippenham, the only other place Mark, Sam, or Ian could have had a run-in with a new face would be in Burnham-on-Sea, wouldn't it?"

"I told you, we didn't go to the caravan site together. We always went alone, just the two of us, to use the caravan. I don't know how the others spent their weekends or midweek breaks. Each to their own."

"I believe you, Becky," said Lydia. "I can assure you we'll do our level best to discover who was responsible for the deaths of your sister and Mark Fennell. However, I think you need to ask yourself whether Mark, Sam, and Ian's close friendship over the decades was as innocent as you appear to believe. You claim not to know how your husband makes his money. Perhaps it is all above board, but you should start asking questions. You owe it to your sister, don't you think?"

Becky stood up and paced from one end of the verandah to another.

"Ian can't have been involved in Becky's murder," she said. "Sam's a loudmouth, but he's not a killer either."

"In that case, Mark must have crossed the wrong people," said Lydia.

"If Helen knew Mark was doing something that might

get him into trouble, she wouldn't have got involved with him," said Becky. "Not once did my sister say she wasn't sure whether she could trust Mark. They were getting married, for heaven's sake."

MEANWHILE, Ian Hood had burst through the front door and demanded to know what Alex was doing there. Alex produced his warrant card and suggested Ian calm down and take a seat.

"Where's my wife?" snapped Ian.

"My colleague is chatting to Becky in the kitchen. We called earlier this morning to tell her we're taking a fresh look into the deaths of Mark Fennell and Helen Roker. She agreed to answer our questions and said you were unavailable until lunchtime. A business meeting, I believe?"

"Something like that," said Ian. "Do we need our solicitor?"

"I can't see why, Mr Hood," said Alex. "We're having an informal chat in your home, not in an interview room at the station. You're not under caution. Of course, if you'd prefer a change of venue, we can oblige."

"What do you need to hear?" asked Ian.

"The truth would help," said Alex. "How long did you know Mark Fennell?"

"Ever since we were eleven," he replied. His mood was calming.

"You spent a lot of time with Mark and Sam Webber, both at school and as young men. Did you attend Mark's first wedding?"

"I wasn't around for that," said Ian. "I missed Sam's wedding too, but they both came when Becky and I married. So what?"

"Where did you serve your sentence?" asked Alex. "A Young Offenders prison, I presume?"

"Aylesbury, in Buckinghamshire. How did you know?"

"I didn't, just a hunch," said Alex. "Becky told us you had a hard time after leaving Chippenham College. My boss would say I'm developing a copper's nose. What was it?"

"Possession," Ian replied. "I got three years. After that, I learned my lesson."

"When did you set up in business?" asked Alex.

"Soon after the wedding. Thirty years ago almost."

"Importing and exporting what exactly?" asked Alex.

"I'm struggling to see how this impacts Mark's murder," said Ian. "I've dealt in all manner of goods, mostly from the Far East, and although I got my fingers burned a couple of times in the early days, I've earned a good living. Becky enjoys the better things in life, as do I, and we can do just that."

"My colleague will have informed your wife of our latest update on her sister's death. We've examined the evidence and are confident that Helen was murdered."

"You can't be serious. Why would anyone want to kill Helen?"

"I think that's obvious, Mr Hood, don't you?"

"Not to me," said Ian.

"Helen had to die for the same reason as your friend, Mark Fennell. We believe the man responsible for both deaths was seen in Kington Langley by Sam and Mary Webber two weeks before Mark died. Now, Sam and Mary told detectives they didn't recognise the driver of the BMW 3Series. I wonder whether the detectives showed you the same picture?"

"They did, as it happens, and I'd never seen the guy before. Neither had Becky."

"How often did you see Mark when he lived in Kington Langley?" asked Alex.

"Every three or four weeks. We were mates. I saw Sam Webber regularly too. All three of us didn't go out together like we did when we were younger. You know how it is. Work gets in the way."

"When did Mark start going to Burnham-on-Sea?" asked Alex,

"That was after Mandy had thrown him out. Mark couldn't decide what to do with himself. He'd worked at Westinghouse for so long that I thought he wouldn't leave until they gave him the gold watch. Instead, they were taken over, and the new company moved their operations to smaller premises seven miles away. Mark got fed up travelling back and forth. One day he decided to jack it in."

"Where were Mark and Jessie living?" asked Alex.

"Jessie? She wasn't on the scene at that point. Mark rented a flat in Chippenham after he left Mandy. He got fed up with people stopping him in the street and asking why he'd quit his job or saying how sorry they were that he and Mandy had split up. It was doing his head in. So. Mark drove to Burnham for a week's holiday on a whim, and when he returned on Friday, he couldn't stop talking about this great opportunity he'd discovered. On Saturday night, Sam joined us for a drink in the Black Horse, and Mark announced he was buying a caravan. We thought he was joking."

"What did he intend to do with it?" asked Alex.

"Live in the blessed thing, what do you think?" said Ian. "He had no job but could turn his hand to most things. His idea was to pitch the van on a residential site and scratch a living."

"Did you believe him?" asked Alex.

"If you've read about Mark in your files, you'll know a woman had to be involved. Sylvie, her name was, I only saw them together once, and she was a cracker. A few years younger than him too. Mark said he'd been in a Burnham-on-Sea pub on Monday night, and she'd been sitting at the bar alone. Sylvie looked across the bar and smiled. Mark never needed to be asked twice. He would have had his wallet out ordering drinks before she blinked. Sylvie was the person who convinced Mark a caravan was right up his street. She also assured him there was plenty of work on the four residential caravan sites in town to keep him in full-time occupation as a handyman. Moreover, she could get him an introduction to the site owners."

"What went wrong?" asked Alex.

"Nothing, as far as getting the caravan was concerned. Sylvie only came to Chippenham once to sort out the finances, as far as I could make out. Then, after that, she returned to Burnham and waited for Mark to move onto the site."

"Mark bumped into Jessie North, and the rest is history."

"Got it in one," said Ian. "If Mark had a weakness, it was women. But, then, he met Jessie, and Sam and I got invites to their wedding in the Caribbean before we knew it."

"When did the regular trips to Burnham start?" asked Alex.

"Before the wedding. Mark offered Sam the chance to use it first, and I drove down with Becky two weekends later."

"Any trouble?" asked Alex.

"None whatsoever," said Ian. "We weren't expecting any. The place was quiet at the end of October and the middle of November, but Becky said it was good to get away. I didn't have to dash off on business, and she had me to herself for a change,"

"Did you see Sylvie at all?" asked Alex.

"Sam said a woman knocked on the door when he and Mary spent the weekend there and asked for Mark Fennell. Sam said he wasn't around, and the girl disappeared. Of course, that could have been Sylvie, but nobody else bothered us while we were there."

The kitchen door opened, and Becky walked in with Lydia, carrying a tray.

"Sorry we took so long getting the coffee," said Becky. "All right, love?"

"This bloke reckons Becky was murdered," said Ian. "What do you make of that?"

"It doesn't make sense, Ian," said Becky. "I've never accepted it was suicide, but murder is something else. They think Mark and Helen must have crossed someone. I've racked my brain to think of the dates when everything changed. First, Mandy threw Mark out in the summer of 2003. Do I remember that right? Then he married Jessie North in December 2003. By October 2004, he'd left her to be with Helen. They lived in Kington Langley for six months, and then Mark was killed. So something happened between July 2003 and May 2005."

"The killer didn't realise Helen was inside the property in Kington Langley," said Alex. "If he had, she would have died alongside Mark that night. Instead, Helen found herself a flat in Chippenham. Joe Morgan moved in, but the killer had already traced Helen to the town and was stalking her. He killed her, trying to confuse the police and the forensic people into believing Helen drank two bottles of wine, swallowed thirty pills, and used the hot bath to render herself unconscious more quickly."

Becky sobbed as she listened to Alex describing how her sister died. Lydia sat on the arm of the chair beside her holding her hands.

"Why didn't the police realise this at the time?" asked Ian.

"The narrative verdict was unhelpful," said Alex. "Helen's doctor testified that the number of pills Helen took equated to how many should have remained from the latest prescription he'd provided. Joe Morgan maintained Helen never took more than the correct amount and confirmed they had paracetamol in a box in a kitchen cupboard, along with the usual odds and ends people keep on standby for cuts, bruises, and aches and pains."

"Joe was adamant having a couple of bottles of white wine wasn't unusual," said Lydia. "Neither was a big drinker, and those bottles would easily have lasted a week."

"The autopsy revealed various bruises difficult to explain accurately," said Alex. "Helen suffered bruising to the back of the head, which could have occurred if she slipped in the bath. The two empty wine bottles suggested she was intoxicated, and the pills would have made her movements less controlled. The skin wasn't broken, which supported the theory Helen banged her head rather than someone hitting her with a blunt object."

"Why did Helen drink all that wine, though?" asked Becky.

"Our boss suspects the blow to the back of the head could have occurred in the living room soon after the killer forced his way into the flat," said Lydia. "Perhaps Helen fell and struck her head. A blow that stunned and incapacitated her long enough for the killer to search the flat for what he needed to carry out his plan."

"Everything he needed was already there," said Ian Hood. "That makes sense now. Did he force Helen to drink the wine to help her swallow the pills?"

"That's what we believe happened, yes," said Alex. "The coroner found slight bruising around Helen's nose and mouth, but it wasn't possible to determine when those bruises occurred. The killer set the scene in the bathroom, so when Joe got home, he thought Helen had killed herself. The police and paramedics assumed the same thing once they arrived."

"I knew she hadn't done it," said Becky, "How awful. My poor sister."

"What made your boss take a closer look?" asked Ian.

"He looked at Becky and Joe's statements and saw that neither of you believed Helen was suicidal. Then he read how Joe had shed tears the following day when he found Helen had ironed his clothing and put it away neatly. It didn't feel right when he added that to the theatre tickets and a night booked in a hotel in Bristol at the weekend. So, he took the crime scene picture apart and tried to see how the pieces could have formed a different result. Helen's actions that afternoon and in the weeks leading up to it showed no sign she intended to harm herself. Therefore, someone else had to have caused her death."

"What now?" asked Becky.

"You defined the period we need to examine more closely, Becky," said Lydia. "The answer's there somewhere."

"What could they have done to have deserved to die like that?" asked Becky.

Ian Hood stared at the floor.

"It makes you think, doesn't it?" he said.

"What are you saying, Ian?" asked Becky. "You don't know anything about this, do you?"

"No way, love. How could you think I'd have anything to do with killing anyone?"

"It's the Burnham-on-Sea connection, isn't it, Mr Hood?" said Alex.

"I can't think of anyone in town or Kington Langley capable of doing something like that. So, it stands to reason the trouble started on the caravan site. Why didn't we notice anything while we were there? Sam never mentioned any bother, either."

"That blessed caravan was always more trouble than it was worth," said Becky.

"What happened to it, do you know?" asked Lydia.

"Jessie North would have got it in the will," said Ian. "We didn't go to Burnham again after Mark died."

"The solicitor told Helen she needed to move out, and she handed over all the keys," said Becky. "That would have included the house, Mark's car, and the caravan."

"That's good to know," said Alex. "We're speaking with Jessie North this afternoon. She also spent time at the caravan. Jessie could have information about our investigation into Mark and Helen's murders."

"Oh, my God," said Becky. "I've just had a dreadful thought."

"It might have been Jessie with Mark when this trouble started," said Ian.

"If the killer didn't realise Mark was with a different partner..." said Becky.

Chapter Eleven

WHILE ALEX and Lydia were peeling back yet another layer of the onion in The Tinings, Gus Freeman had already begun his conversation with Mary Webber.

He and Neil had driven to Black Bridge Road from Joe Morgan's home to find Amazing Grace's Smart car parked in front of the Webber house. She spotted Neil stop behind her and got out to greet them.

Gus wondered what the neighbours thought of three strangers gathering on the pavement outside of the home of one of Chippenham's leading lights.

"It's almost eleven o'clock, guv," said Neil.

"If you could make the introductions to Mrs Webber, Neil. I'll fill in the blanks with DI Packenham. We must be on the same page when talking to this couple."

"Got it, guv," said Neil. He walked to the front door and rang the bell.

Gus forwarded the message he'd sent Alex to Grace's mobile.

"Read, mark, and inwardly digest Grace," he said.

"That's what we learned from Joe Morgan. I haven't received anything from Alex at Ian Hood's home yet, but we'll start with what we know when we get inside. Then, if I learn of any new developments, use your common sense, and follow my line of questioning if it suddenly strays from what we agreed. Okay?"

"I'll do my best, Gus," she said. "I rue not taking tap-dancing when I was younger now."

Mary Webber had answered the door, and Neil nodded in their direction. Mary knew who they all were now. Once they got inside, they could start putting pressure on her because Gus thought Mary could be a weak link in the chain. According to Joe Morgan, Mary was a quiet soul and was undoubtedly bullied by her arrogant husband.

"There's plenty of room for you to sit down," said Mary when Gus and Grace joined Neil in the massive lounge. "With three sons who enjoyed lying on settees rather than sitting upright, we have far more furniture than we need now they've left home."

"I expect they still drop in to see their parents don't they," asked Neil. "Or has their father handed over the reins of the business altogether?"

"They don't often come to see us all at once these days," said Mary. "Now, what was it you wanted to ask? Perhaps it would be better to wait for Sam to get home. He won't be long."

"I think we can progress without Sam's help," Gus said. "DS Davis will meet your husband when he arrives. If he's in a good mood, Neil might even carry his golf clubs indoors."

"I don't want Sam to get mad," said Mary.

"This is just an informal chat, Mrs Webber," said Grace.

"We know so much already," said Gus. "Your contribution will simply clarify matters. Let's start with when you met Sam."

"At Mandy's wedding. I worked with her at EKCO," said Mary. "She asked me to be one of her bridesmaids when she married Mark. Sam was Mark's best friend, and of course, he was his best man. Sam asked me out soon after the wedding, and we've been together ever since."

"How did you get on with Mark?" asked Grace.

"Mark never tried it on with me," said Mary. "He was always polite and good company whenever we socialised with them. Of course, he spent a fair bit of time travelling with his job, so sometimes I met Mandy on her own, but I never had an issue with Mark."

"Do you know whether Mark tried it on with Becky?" asked Gus,

"I can't remember," said Mary.

"I'm surprised," said Gus. "Joe Morgan remembers your husband taking an interest in Becky and her sister, Helen, at that New Year's Eve party just before Helen died."

"Sam may have looked that night, but he never touched," said Mary.

"Were you surprised when Mandy threw Mark out?" asked Grace.

"We didn't discuss that type of thing," said Mary. "I imagine Mandy had a lot to put up with. But, if half what she claimed about him was true, then Mark deserved it."

"Where did Mark go after Mandy threw him out?" asked Gus.

"He found a place in Chippenham to rent for a few months while the divorce went through. After that, he went on holiday to the coast, and when he came home, Mark told Sam he'd bought a caravan, of all things. Everyone used it for a few days here and there, but Mark originally intended to move to North Somerset to live and work."

"With Jessie North," said Gus.

"Mark hadn't met Jessie when he made that decision," said Mary. "He bought the van and was preparing to move his stuff to the caravan when he met Jessie. We were the first couple to use it, then Ian and Becky. So it was a while before Mark took Jessie there."

"I've heard it described as a whirlwind romance," said Gus.

"That was Mark all over, zero to sixty miles an hour in three seconds. It wasn't a big wedding, just us six friends on a beach in the Caribbean, plus the chap performing the ceremony. Less than a year later, the marriage was over, and Mark was going out with Helen. I liked Helen. She was a good sort, like her sister."

"Is it fair to say you weren't as keen on Jessie North?" asked Gus.

"Hard as nails, that one," said Mary. "Pretty enough on the outside, but beneath the makeup lay a stone heart. Look at the way she treated Helen. Jessie had her solicitor on the doorstep with a copy of the will before Mark's body was cold."

"Did you suspect Jessie was behind Mark's murder?" asked Grace.

"They reckoned she had a bullet-proof alibi," said Mary. "I wouldn't put it past her to have paid someone to do it."

"The police checked Jessie's alibi," said Gus, "and found no evidence she paid anyone to murder Mark and Helen. Ah, I see that brought a response. You were surprised to hear Helen's death was now being treated as a murder?"

"Twelve years ago, the detectives stopped pursuing the

case once they received the coroner's verdict. Everything was left in the air."

"How often did you see Mark when he lived in Kington Langley?" asked Gus.

"Sam visited him every month," said Mary. "I went with him now and then. You have to remember how close those two were. Since Sam and I got together, he spoke to Mark on the phone every other day, and if Sam went out at the weekend, it was to meet Mark and Ian. Of course, they couldn't do that as often as the years passed, but they didn't mix with a different crowd or drift apart. They were as tight a unit as they had been when they met at school."

"The last time you visited Mark's together was two weeks before he died," said Grace. "You collected the keys to the caravan at Burnham-on-Sea."

"That's right," said Mary. "That was the night we saw that man sitting in his car. As soon as we passed him, I told Sam the bloke was up to no good. Of course, Sam laughed at me, but we mentioned it to Helen anyway."

"You described the man to the detectives," said Gus. "Other people in the village saw the same man, and their descriptions were very similar to yours. However, the man didn't appear familiar to you or your husband."

"No, and Ian said the police showed them a picture, too; based on what we'd all said, it didn't ring any bells with Ian and Becky either."

"Did you travel to Burnham the day after you collected the keys from Helen?" asked Gus.

"That's right. We collected the keys on Monday, and Sam drove us to Burnham on Tuesday evening. We slept there for two nights and drove home on Thursday. Sam needed to be in town on Friday for business."

"What was the purpose of your visit?" asked Gus.

"Just to get away for a day or two," said Mary.

"Did you make friends in Burnham?" asked Grace,

"Sam didn't encourage it," said Mary. "We kept to ourselves. He said our friends were in Chippenham. Of course, a residential site is different from a tourist site, but the way Mark used the caravan, our neighbours never knew who would answer the door if they knocked."

"Did you get visitors?" asked Gus.

"Not after the first weekend Sam and I stayed there. It was late at night, and we were ready for bed. Some woman hammered on the door, asking for Mark Fennell. Sam told her he wasn't there, and that was that."

"What did she look like?" asked Gus.

"I was half undressed, so I didn't go to the door," said Mary. "Sam only opened the door wide enough to see who it was, but if he recognised her, he never said."

"Was there any time you were using the caravan when you saw or heard something that caused you concern?" asked Grace.

"What an odd question," said Mary. "There was never any trouble. Sam didn't argue with anyone. As I said, we kept to ourselves. We would drive into town, enjoy the beach in the summer, find a café for a snack at lunchtime, and go to a restaurant for a meal in the evening. We did the normal things couples do when they're taking a couple of days away from the rat race."

"Would I be right in thinking that Tuesday to Thursday trip to the caravan was the last occasion you visited the site?" asked Grace.

"The last time for us, thanks to Jessie North," said Mary. "I don't think Ian and Becky used it, but you would need to check. Mark and Helen had just returned from Burnham on Sunday night when we saw that man in the car. I don't know whether Sam knows whether they went back again. Who else is there to ask?"

"You mean Mark and Helen may have been to the caravan from Friday evening until Sunday evening, getting home twenty-four hours before Mark was killed?" asked Gus.

"I couldn't say for sure," said Mary. "We never saw the keys again after Sam returned them. He drove to Kington Langley straight after closing the showroom doors on Saturday afternoon. Forty-eight hours after we returned to Chippenham."

"What happened to the caravan?" asked Gus.

"How would I know?" asked Mary. "Jessie had persuaded Mark to make a will. I don't think he'd bothered while married to Mandy, but that tells you what Jessie was like. Jessie led Mark around like he had a ring through his nose. She made sure she wouldn't lose out if the marriage went south. I expect people warned her Mark had a roving eye. Everything went to Jessie. Helen soon found that out. Sam didn't pay much attention to what she was getting out of it. He said the house in the village was rented. The gearbox in Mark's car was wrecked, and he'd never been clever with money. He spent it as soon as he got it."

"The only thing Jessie had with any value was the caravan," said Grace. "If it only slept two people in comfort, the depreciation after two and a half years would have meant it wasn't worth much."

"We can ask Jessie later," said Gus.

"A car has just pulled onto the drive, guv," said Neil.

Gus's mobile phone buzzed in his jacket pocket. He checked Alex's message and forwarded it to Grace.

"Tell Mr Webber who we are and why we're here, Neil.

Then perhaps you could take Mrs Webber into the kitchen while we speak to her husband."

"Got it, guv," said Neil.

"I'll keep Mrs Webber company until Neil gets back, Gus," said Grace.

"Thanks, Grace. Alex and Lydia have given us plenty to think about, haven't they?"

"Did you ever meet Sylvie, Mrs Webber?" asked Grace as she steered Mary gently into the kitchen next door.

"No, but Mandy phoned me one weekend to say she'd seen Mark in town with a younger woman," said Mary. "She didn't know her name, but Sam told me Sylvie was the woman who arranged the caravan sale. I couldn't quite work out what the relationship was between them. Mark's reputation meant he was probably besotted with her, and they were sleeping together. Mandy certainly thought so. She said how they looked at one another convinced her their marriage was over. People assumed Jessie caused the break-up, but young Sylvie proved the final straw."

"Mark was moving to Burnham to live in the caravan," said Grace. "Sylvie convinced him enough maintenance work was available on the caravan sites to earn a living. Mark returned to Chippenham, bumped into Jessie North, and fell in love again. I wonder why he didn't sell it?"

"Mark never did anything without reason," said Mary.

"He was lucky to have good friends, like Sam and Ian, who wanted to use the van to make it worthwhile keeping. When I spoke to Mandy, she told me she wouldn't go caravanning in a million years. By the way, she prefers to be known as Amanda Jane these days. So perhaps this Christmas, when you send her a card, you'll remember to use her proper name."

"She'll always be Mandy to me," said Mary. "I miss our

chats. Now the boys have left home, there's a lot of time when I'm alone or with just Sam keeping me company."

Neil Davis entered the kitchen and nodded to Grace. Gus was ready to start their conversation with Sam Webber.

"I don't suppose there's any chance of a cuppa, is there, Mrs Webber?" said Neil.

Mary tutted.

"You're just like my three boys, detective. They expect a woman to wait on them, hand, foot, and finger. Are you married?"

"Yes," said Neil. "We're expecting our first in two and a half months."

Grace could tell Neil would keep Mary occupied without any trouble. She joined Gus in the lounge. Sam Webber stood in front of the large fireplace, dominating the room.

"Welcome back, DI Packenham," said Gus. "I've told Mr Webber who we are and why we're here."

"Why did it need three of you?" asked Sam Webber. "My wife will have been terrified. I hope you haven't been harassing her. Surely, a simple phone call could have sufficed?"

"We're not happy we've heard the truth from everyone involved," said Gus. "The detectives investigating Mark's murder and Helen's death would have got much further if they'd learned facts you and your friends kept hidden."

"I don't know what you mean," said Sam.

"Sit down, Mr Webber," said Grace. "You'll give yourself a heart attack. We'll keep asking our questions until we're happy you've given us honest answers."

"I cooperated with the police in both investigations," said Sam. He didn't move from where he stood.

"Perhaps," said Gus, "but, for instance, you omitted to

tell the police about Ian Hood's conviction and prison sentence."

"Ian served his time, and as far as I was concerned, he should be allowed to move on with his life."

"What about the caravan?" asked Gus. "Why did everyone assume Mark and Jessie North were an item when Mark made that purchase? It's only now, thirteen years later, that we've learned about the mysterious Sylvie. We wouldn't have discovered her involvement if Mark's first wife hadn't mentioned seeing her with Mark. You and Ian Hood never volunteered that information."

"The detectives investigating Mark's murder thought Jessie was the reason for the breakdown of Mark's marriage," said Grace.

"Mark never missed an opportunity if a woman showed interest," said Sam. "Mandy could have thrown him out years before she did."

"But she didn't because as long as they were only one-night stands, Mandy turned a blind eye," said Grace. "She only saw Mark and Sylvie together for a few seconds as they passed a shop window and knew this was different."

"Different for who, though?" asked Gus.

"You're talking in riddles, mate," said Sam. "Sylvie couldn't have meant that much to Mark. He was seeing Jessie a couple of weeks later, and within months they were married."

"The marriage didn't last long, did it?" said Gus.

"Mark blamed that on Mandy," said Grace. "He seemed to believe his behaviour was acceptable. After all, Mark had married her, given her a good home, and had two children. He always had a steady job with a decent income. Why worry about the occasional indiscretion? One of your friends said that Mark claimed he married Jessie on the rebound because losing Mandy had devastated him. He realised what a fool he'd been within months of that Caribbean wedding."

"Who introduced Mark to Helen Roker?" asked Gus.

"They bumped into one another in a pub, as far as I can remember," said Sam.

"Oh, please, Mr Webber," said Grace. "How naïve do you think we are? It's more likely you and Ian got your heads together and decided what was best for your old friend."

"Where are you getting this from?" said Sam.

Grace could tell they were getting somewhere; Sam shifted from the fireplace and sank into a chair.

"Joe Morgan started me thinking about the wives and girlfriends," said Gus. "He remembered something DI Perry said while investigating Helen's death. Joe and Helen enjoyed things like theatre, cinema, and classical music. DI Perry sensed Joe wasn't like the rest of that crowd, and for some reason, that confused Perry. You, Mark, and Ian were like peas in a pod. Since school, you'd been mates, and nobody came between you, male or female. But Perry wasn't confused about the men involved; the women puzzled him. Then DI Packenham spoke to Mandy Fennell. Mark's ex-wife has changed since the marriage ended. Amanda Jane's a confident, strong woman who takes no nonsense from anyone. She found that strength when she saw Mark with Sylvie. Amanda Jane never believed she would remain attractive enough to keep Mark Fennell. She knew her looks would fade after reaching her mid-twenties; it was in her genes. There's a pattern emerging, isn't there? Mary is presentable but could never be described as a trophy wife. A prominent business owner like yourself, Sam. Seeing you with a younger model on your arm wouldn't be a surprise. Mary knows you have a roving eye, as Mark did. Maybe you've strayed too; there could be someone tucked away in an apartment in town if we looked hard enough. Who knows? But you needed someone you could control, someone who wouldn't question what the three of you were doing. Do you still think I'm on the wrong track? Let's look at Ian Hood and Becky. Becky replied import and export when asked what he did for a living. Ian told her not to worry her pretty little head about it when he started the business after they married. Becky and Mary are quiet, homely characters, not brash, loud, or constantly concerned with their appearance. I think DI Packenham was on the money with her question about Helen. If I were a betting man, I'd say you Three Amigos met in the Black Horse one Saturday night, and you and Ian persuaded Mark that Jessie North could rock the boat. Stick her nose in where it wasn't wanted. You suggested to Ian that Becky's younger sister, Helen, would be a better fit, and he engineered an introduction. With Mark's track record, it's easy to see Helen would have been flattered by the attention. With Jessie out of the picture, things felt safer for a while, didn't they? You had regained the status quo. You each had a malleable partner who knew better than to ask awkward questions."

"You're making this up as you go along," said Sam Webber. "I hope you haven't put ideas in my wife's head. Why is she being kept in the kitchen, anyway?"

"Calm yourself, Mr Webber," said Grace. "Your wife is perfectly safe. She's been very cooperative, as have Mr and Mrs Hood. However, we should tell you something else we've learned over the past few days. We are now investigating a double murder."

"What are you trying to say?" said Sam.

"The same man murdered Mark Fennell and Helen

Roker," said Gus. "We have yet to confirm whether Jessie North was the intended target, but something occurred on the caravan site at Burnham that forced the killer's hand. Mark was there with a female companion. They saw or heard something they shouldn't have, which meant they had to die."

"I don't know what that could have been," said Sam. "It had nothing to do with me."

"Everyone says the same thing about you three," said Gus. "You've been a tight unit since you went to school. Nobody comes between you. Of course, friendships do last a lifetime, but it's also true that some people have to stick together because they have something to hide."

"We find it hard to believe Ian Hood acted alone when he got into trouble after leaving Chippenham College," said Grace.

"The police caught Ian in possession of a Class A drug," said Sam. "They checked out Mark and me, but we were clean. Nothing to see here. Move on."

"Have you ever bought any imported goods from Ian Hood?" asked Gus.

"That Chinese stuff isn't my thing," said Sam.

"Where does it enter the country?" asked Gus.

"Bristol docks," said Sam. "The containers arrive in Avonmouth or Royal Portbury."

"Ian doesn't have a large warehouse to hold his stock," said Gus. "What was it Ian said about Joe Morgan? That's it. Delivery drivers were ten a penny. So, the stock is removed from the container, loaded into a fleet of vans, and delivered directly to the client."

"Why are you asking me?" shrugged Sam. "It's Ian's business. My Ferrari and Lamborghini arrive on the same docks. Are you going to ask him how I get my cars to the showroom?"

"Mark travelled a lot with Westinghouse," said Grace. "Sweden, Germany, and several UK cities. We know he found time for romantic liaisons. Perhaps he carried out other tasks while he was at it."

"Do you enjoy fishing, Detective Inspector?" asked Sam. "This is getting boring."

"I agree," said Gus. "We're seeing Jessie North this afternoon. That should tidy up a few loose ends. Next week, we will switch our focus to Burnham-on-Sea. We have a relatively short timeframe of eighteen months to two years on which to concentrate. We will find the killer, Mr Webber. If you wish to make a statement between now and early next week, we can arrange an appointment where your solicitor can be present. In these situations, it's always best to be the first to put your version on record. If you delay, you might find someone has dumped all the blame on your doorstep."

"I don't know what you're talking about, Mr Freeman," said Sam. "There's nothing in Burnham for you to find. Don't forget to take your rod with you. Fishing is all you'll do and never get a bite."

Grace tapped on the kitchen door and told Neil they had finished.

When they entered the lounge, Mary was chatting happily with Neil about her three boys.

"Is everything sorted, Sam?" asked Mary.

"Nothing to worry about, Mary," said Sam. "Unless you've been talking out of turn."

"I know better than that," said Mary. "What happens next, anyway?"

"We keep digging until we discover who killed Mark and Helen," said Grace.

"And why," said Gus.

Gus led the way to the front door, with Grace behind him. Mary and her new friend, Neil, brought up the rear. Sam Webber hovered by the lounge door.

As Gus stepped outside, Grace stopped and turned around.

"Can you remember what happened to the caravan, Mrs Webber?"

"We never went to Burnham after Mark died," she replied. "It wouldn't have felt right. That girl, Jessie, who was married to Mark, owned the caravan after that. You spoke to her about it, didn't you, Sam?"

"Interesting, " said Grace. "We'll be sure to ask Jessie about that conversation. Goodbye."

Mary closed the door, and as they walked to their cars, they could hear Sam Webber yelling at his long-suffering wife.

"What made you think to ask that, Grace?" asked Gus.

"Blessing told me it was one of your tricks, Gus," said Grace. "What she called a Columbo moment. Does it work every time?"

Gus stood by Neil's car with a hand on the door handle.

"When you ask the right questions," he replied with a grin.

"I'll see you back in the office," said Grace,

Neil turned the car around and left Black Bridge Road. Once they were on Eastern Avenue, he took twenty minutes to reach the Church Street car park.

Grace couldn't keep pace with Neil in her Smart car, so Gus and Neil were already discussing their progress with Alex and Lydia when she finally exited the lift.

"We don't have long," she said. "We're due in Corsham soon."

"Don't be in a rush, ma'am," said Neil. "You don't get anywhere by being too hasty."

"I'll remember that the next time we have three of us interviewing a witness," said Grace. "What did you talk about while Gus and I grilled Sam Webber?"

"Mary provided coffee and shortbread to keep me going while discussing happy families."

"That didn't take long in that house," said Grace. "Webber treats her like dirt."

"Mary didn't give much away," said Neil. "I never got the impression she knew whether Sam and the others were involved in anything dodgy."

"Do you think drugs were involved, guv?" asked Blessing.

"Ian Hood was done for possession in the mid-Eighties," said Gus. "He reckoned he learned his lesson."

"Not to get caught perhaps, guv?" said Alex.

"The detective who investigated that case would be long gone, guv," said Neil. "If we dug out the files, we might learn Ian Hood pleaded guilty and refused to give up the names of his accomplices."

"They were a tight unit back then and remained so, even after Mark's murder," said Lydia.

"What does that tell us?" asked Gus.

"Are you suggesting Mark acted alone, guv?" asked Neil. "He returned from Burnham after that week's holiday and claimed he had unearthed a great opportunity."

"If the three of them had got mixed up with a criminal gang in North Somerset, all three would be dead by now," said Alex. "Why would a gang draw more attention to the deaths by adding the wives to the body count?"

"Grace is right," said Gus. "We should drive to Corsham to speak to Jessie North. I want to be out of there before Pavel Dudek gets home. Once you've updated your digital files with your reports on our meetings this morning, you can get off home. Have a great weekend, and be back here ready to leave for Burnham at nine o'clock Monday morning.

"Got it, guv," said Alex.

"Are we nearly there, guv?" asked Blessing.

Gus knew they were closer than they had been yesterday. The trouble with being closer was that sometimes you couldn't see the wood for the trees.

"Ask me again on Monday morning, Blessing," he replied.

Chapter Twelve

"ARE you sure you want to take your car, Gus," said Grace.

"I'm not travelling in that," said Gus, pointing to the Smart car. "It reminds me of the bubble cars in the Sixties. They were fine if you were twenty years old and under five feet tall, but for a grown-up, forget it."

"You didn't define which Monday morning for Blessing," said Grace as they moved to the Focus.

"Can you blame me? We keep adding to our knowledge about the main characters in this drama, but I can't see the killer coming from Wiltshire. It had to be Burnham-on-Sea,"

"There's an inherent problem with investigating cold cases like this one," said Grace. "Criminals who were active thirteen years ago might not be around for us to interview for many reasons. That caravan site could have closed or changed out of all recognition. It might be impossible to identify the site where Mark Fennell and his female companion got themselves into trouble."

"We'll cross that bridge when we come to it," said Gus.

"As this week has progressed, I've asked myself why we left Jessie North to last."

Gus took the same route to Corsham as he had with Neil.

Swan Road was tucked away on a quiet estate close to Bath Road.

"A modest semi-detached building in a moderate state of repair," said Grace.

"I expect her electrics are in good nick, if nothing else," said Gus. "Let's see what Jessie has to say."

Gus and Grace approached the three-bedroomed dormer bungalow, home to Mark Fennell's ex-wife since 2005. Grace stepped forward to ring the doorbell. They didn't have long to wait for Jessie North to answer.

"Come in," she said.

Gus thought it sounded more like an order than a request. Yesterday, Jessie had been described as hard as nails by Mary Webber. It made sense. Sam Webber and Ian Hood would have been in Mark's ear as soon as they met her. She could be trouble, Mark. Please get rid of her.

Jessie led them into the kitchen at the rear of the property.

"I've only just got home from work," she explained. "I need a coffee and a sandwich to keep me going until Pavel gets home. He's working on a building site in Lansdown. They finish early on a Friday."

Gus and Grace sat on the only two chairs available. Jessie prepared her lunch but didn't offer to make them a drink.

"You wanted to ask about Mark," said Jessie.

"We understand you met soon after his marriage broke down," said Grace. "Were you a local girl? Your accent suggests you were born further east."

"I grew up in Reading and Didcot and moved to Chippenham six months before I bumped into Mark. He was fun to be with, I fell for him hard, and we didn't want to waste time waiting. Mark proposed after we'd known one another for just six weeks. We flew out to St Lucia just before Christmas with his friends and were married on the beach. You must know this. The detectives asked about the marriage after his murder."

"My colleague and I will ask questions the other detectives didn't," said Gus. "We asked whether you were a local girl for a reason. Mark Fennell was a serial womaniser whose marriage ended when his wife tired of his cheating. Most local girls might have run a mile rather than go out with him. But, as an outsider, you entered into a relationship doomed to end in tears. Then, within a year, Mark walked out on you to live with Helen Roker in Kington Langley. How did that make you feel?"

"I had suffered heartbreak in my life," said Jessie. "No way was Mark Fennell going to make me shed tears over what happened. So I made sure of that."

"We'll return to that in a minute," said Gus. "When was the first time you visited the caravan with Mark?"

"The last two weeks in July. The company I worked for had an annual shutdown, so I had no choice when I took a holiday."

"Mark wasn't working by then, was he?" asked Grace.

"He had some of his money from Westinghouse to tide us over. Mark told me he planned to live in the caravan and do odd jobs in Burnham. I told him flat out I wasn't living like a gipsy, so we carried on living in Chippenham, and he rented the caravan to friends."

"Was that Mark's only income?" asked Grace. "It's tough to see how he could afford a Caribbean wedding."

"Maybe his friends, Sam and Ian, helped him out," said Jessie. "They were always together or talking on the phone."

"Did you ever suspect Mark was involved in something illegal?" asked Grace.

"Never," said Jessie. "How would I know, anyway? Mark would disappear into town to meet Sam and Ian in the Black Horse. They contacted one another by text all the time. Mark told me he had password-protected his phone since he discovered his first wife had spied on him, checking his every move. I said I wouldn't do that, but Mark laughed and said he still wouldn't let me know his password. They could have been up to all sorts. I was in love with Mark. That was all that mattered."

"When did you realise he was cheating on you with Helen?" asked Grace.

"The summer after the wedding. I was eager to spend my two weeks' holiday with him, but after he drove us to the caravan, Mark said he needed to return home for a few days on business. He didn't explain why. So I spent the first week alone in Burnham. When he returned on Sunday evening, I could tell something had happened. We split up within three months. No big arguments. Mark just announced it was over, and he was leaving."

"That holiday was the last occasion you visited the caravan. Correct?" said Grace.

Jessie nodded.

"Did you ever meet Sylvie, the woman who sold the caravan to Mark?" asked Gus.

"Sylvie Tilson? Yeah, she hung around the site. I never trusted her or her husband, Gavin."

"You mentioned earlier that you made sure if something went wrong with the marriage, you wouldn't suffer," said Gus. "You persuaded Mark to make a will."

"When you're young, you don't think about death. I never imagined Mark would die as he did, but I knew what it was like to be in a relationship where my other half held all the aces. Then, not long after Mark and I got together, I heard whispers about what he was like. So I thought I should protect myself this time around."

"Mark was only renting the house in Kington Langley," said Gus. "His car had broken down, and he wasn't working. I don't suppose much was left in his bank account by that time. His only asset was that caravan. What did you get for that?"

"Sam Webber rang me and offered to buy it," said Jessie. "It was no use to me, and Sam was prepared to pay what it had cost Mark."

"You bought this house in 2005, didn't you?" asked Grace.

"That's right," said Jessie.

"My colleague in the office suggested I ask our forensic accountants at the Hub in Devizes to check whether there was a mortgage on this property. I told her we'd wait until we spoke to you this afternoon. What would we find if we asked them to go ahead?"

"It's none of your business," said Jessie. "I met Pavel eighteen months after Mark walked out on me. He's a good man, earning good money. We manage."

"Robert Rideout was your solicitor, wasn't he," asked Gus. "We haven't spoken to him yet. I think we'll call him first thing on Monday."

"He can't tell you anything. It's confidential," said Jessie.

"We're conducting a murder enquiry," said Gus. "If Mark Fennell's estate contained monies obtained through the proceeds of crime, confidentiality rules won't necessarily apply."

"Is it fair to say you received far more money than expected?" asked Grace.

Jessie nodded.

"What did Sylvie Tilson do at the caravan site?" asked Gus. "Did she live there or work there in some capacity?"

"Sylvie was the barmaid at the small clubhouse. I only saw Gavin when he dropped Sylvie off early in the evening and collected her after closing time."

"Who interviewed you about Mark's murder?" asked Gus.

"I think his name was Francis, a bit of a creep," said Jessie. "He had a Sergeant with him too, and they checked my alibi for the time of the murder. That was no hardship. Then they came back a few days later wanting to check my bank account to see whether I'd paid to have Mark killed."

"Probate hadn't been agreed, so that was no hardship either," said Grace. "A will takes an age to get settled, doesn't it?"

"I didn't do anything wrong," shrugged Jessie.

"Did DI Francis ask you about the people you met while using the caravan?" asked Gus.

"They wanted to know who might have wanted Mark dead. Francis was miffed because he couldn't connect me to the murder. He seemed confident one of Mark's ex-lovers had done it. We barely spoke about the caravan and Burnham-on-Sea. Why?"

"Several people saw a man in Kington Langley two weeks before Mark died," said Grace. "Police produced an artist's impression from their description. Didn't they ask you whether you recognised him?"

"I never saw anything like that," said Jessie.

"Do you have that picture, Grace?" asked Gus.

"It's on my phone," she replied. "It may be a little small for a positive ID."

Grace flicked through her photo gallery, enlarged the image, and held it for Jessie to see.

Jessie put her cup of tea on the worktop and walked toward Grace for a closer look.

"That's Gavin Tilson," she said. "He always wore that suit and grew his hair longer than most blokes of his age. I'd recognise his ugly mug anywhere."

"Another loose end dealt with," said Gus.

"Shall I ring the office, guv?" asked Grace. "DS Mercer can contact Portishead and arrange for Tilson to be arrested."

"Let's hang fire on that for a moment," said Gus. "I want Jessie to tell us about the occasions she spent in that caravan. Were you and Mark ever inside the caravan, or sat outside, under an awning, for example, and heard people talking? Did you see something change hands that didn't seem right? I know it's long ago, but it's important."

"You're frightening me now," said Jessie.

"We should tell you what we've told the others," said Gus. "Did you hear that Helen Roker was found dead in January 2006?"

"Of course. It was in the papers. Why? Do you believe there was more to it? It sounded like suicide, but the coroner didn't give a clear ruling, did he?"

"We're convinced it was murder," said Grace.

"There was one night I remember," said Jessie. "It was one of the few occasions when Mark drove me to Burnham for a midweek break. We left Chippenham on Tuesday night and stopped for a meal. Mark parked the car, and we walked towards the steps leading to the caravan. It was almost eleven o'clock, and the site was in darkness. The site stands on a hillside, so several sets of steps connect the different levels where the vans are parked. At the top, there's a terrace where you get a great view of the seafront. We stopped to listen to the sea, but it was dead calm, or the tide was that far out we couldn't hear anything. Below us, I could make out the occasional caravan roof where someone still had a light on. Most people were in bed, asleep. Then I caught the sound of whispering."

Gus sat up straighter in his chair.

"The voices were coming from somewhere below us," said Jessie.

"How many? Male or female?" asked Gus.

"I thought I saw two figures moving between the vans, but it was too dark to see properly. Later, when we chatted about it, Mark said someone might have lost their bearings and couldn't locate their caravan."

"You didn't think so," said Grace. "Why was that?"

"The few words I caught sounded as if the matter was urgent, and the female was afraid of getting caught. Does that make sense?"

"Can you remember what was said?" asked Gus. "That will help decide if it makes sense."

The woman said, 'Will it go ahead?' and the man replied, 'These things take time. Chill out, will you?' The woman asked, 'How long before they arrive?"

"Was that it?" asked Grace. "Didn't the man reply?"

"If he did, we didn't hear him. So perhaps they'd disturbed another caravanner, and he didn't reply until they were further away. So we went down to the caravan, opened up, and unpacked our things."

"Did you hear anything more that night?" asked Gus.

"Not a thing," said Jessie. "We discussed what I heard, and Mark reminded me we hardly knew anyone who lived there, so we were unlikely to recognise their voices. Especially from a whisper."

Grace and Gus shared a glance.

"What did it mean?" asked Jessie.

"On its own, very little," said Gus. "It might have been an innocent conversation."

"Gavin Tilson is the person we believe murdered Mark Fennell and Helen Roker," said Grace. "Our theory was they overheard something Tilson or an accomplice didn't want to be overheard."

"But Mark and I heard those whispers," said Jessie. "Does that mean…"

"There has to be more to it," said Gus. "One could interpret that brief conversation in several ways. First, we learned yesterday that Sylvie arranged the caravan sale to Mark. We think her husband may have been involved because a barmaid doesn't usually have that role in her job description. Then there are Sam Webber's actions to be considered. Why did he pay over the odds to retain control of the caravan after Mark's death? What was the ulterior motive for Mark purchasing the caravan in the first place? Finally, Mark returned from his week's holiday to say he'd uncovered a great opportunity. An opportunity to do what?"

Jessie North looked troubled.

"The news must have come as a shock," said Grace. "You mustn't blame yourself. Mark visited Burnham on numerous occasions with Helen Roker. They could easily have heard, or seen, something more suspicious than the few whispers you heard that night. Whoever it was threading their way through the caravans may not have realised you could hear them. When we discover why Mark wanted to buy that caravan, it might lead us to an incident where he and Helen angered people they were working with."

"Do you think Sam has continued to use the caravan?" asked Jessie.

"We spoke to Sam, Ian, and their wives this morning," said Gus. "They told us they hadn't returned to Burnham after Mark's death. Perhaps, they lied. We'll see."

"What will happen to me?" asked Jessie.

"That's not for us to decide," said Gus. "We were only ever interested in who killed Mark and Helen. When we report to our superiors, it will be up to them to decide what to do with matters we've uncovered that fall outside our remit."

"You'll need to attend the local police station with your solicitor to provide a written statement for the identification of the man seen driving the BMW in Kington Langley," said Grace. "That will count in your favour when the other matters are considered."

Jessie North leaned against the worktop and sighed.

"What a mess," she said. "What on earth did Mark get himself mixed up in?"

"It will all come out in the wash," said Gus. "We'll head back to the office, and you can decide how much you want to share with Pavel."

Gus and Grace left Jessie by the front door and returned to the Focus.

"Back to base," said Gus. "We weren't with Jessie as long as I expected. The others could still be beavering away on their reports. It would be good to bounce this around for a while."

"Hard as nails, my foot," said Grace.

"Pavel may have found her soft centre," said Gus.

"Thirteen years is a long time, and people can change, given the right stimulus."

"Do you think it was drugs, Gus, as Blessing suggested?"

"It seems the logical conclusion," said Gus. "You two get on well, don't you?"

"Blessing chatted a lot while driving back from Amanda Jane's house," said Grace. "Then we had a drink together after work. You'll hear about it over the weekend, but Blessing persuaded me to have dinner at the farm. John was working, but I met Jackie Ferris. Blessing wants me to make it a regular Thursday visit because I don't have many friends in Easterton. Jackie's in favour. She says my vegan diet will challenge her to try cooking something different."

Gus hoped he and Suzie never got an invite to the Thursday Club.

They arrived back in the car park behind the Old Police Station office at a quarter to four. None of the team's cars had left for home. So Gus and Grace took the lift to the first-floor office and delivered the good news.

"Have you alerted the Avon & Somerset people, guv?" asked Neil.

"Grace pointed out that thirteen years is a long time," said Gus. "Tilson could be dead or banged up in one of Her Majesty's prisons."

"Sylvie was younger than Mark Fennell, guv," said Lydia. "Marcus Weston told us the man was in his late thirties, early forties. Tilson would be mid-fifties now. But he could still be active."

"True," said Gus, "but arresting him for the murders before learning the truth about what they were up to might scupper Avon & Somerset's chances of identifying links to an entire drugs network."

"A network we won't get the opportunity to uncover," said Alex.

"That's life, Alex," said Gus. "Our job was to clear another cold case from the Chief Constable's list. However, I have no reason to doubt Jessie North. She says Tilson was a match for the image produced by several eyewitnesses, and let's face it; she must have seen him far more often."

"Gus is right," said Grace. "Tilson is our man, but whether he killed Helen Roker by mistake is still unknown. We don't understand where Tilson fitted into the scene in Burnham-on-Sea between 2003 and 2005. DI Crooks can help with that on Monday morning. If Tilson was part of a larger operation, they might have survived intact or moved on to a more lucrative scheme."

"We would have heard if a major drug ring had been exposed, ma'am," said Neil. "I can't recall too many major cases hitting the headlines from the North Somerset coast."

"Don't forget I worked at Portishead before coming to Wiltshire, Neil," said Grace. "We had our successes. I lived in Clevedon from 2013 to 2017, only twenty miles further up the coast and Burnham and Highbridge, the nearest town, have a crime rate that's twenty percent higher than elsewhere in the region. Drugs, anti-social behaviour, violence, and sexual offences are the big players in the area's crime statistics."

"The police station in Burnham ceased to be a twenty-four-hour concern in 2014," said Blessing. "It's staffed for a few hours each day, except weekends and Bank Holidays, but the threat of total closure remains."

"A false economy," said Gus. "However, we don't have a say in what our superiors do."

"What's the plan for Monday, guv?" asked Alex.

"We'll meet DI Crooks at the police station. Our unmarked cars shouldn't raise too much suspicion. I'm sure she'll want to keep us as far as possible from the caravan site even if Tilson and his crew are long gone. There could be another operation sanctioned by Portishead underway for all we know. God forbid Brendan Curran, and his National Crime Agency guys are on an organised crime outfit trail in the region. No, we need to be careful where we tread on his one. Kenneth Truelove won't thank us for blotting his copybook."

"Can we still go home if we've updated our files, guv?" asked Lydia.

"Grace and I can stay behind to get our latest information into the files," said Gus. "The rest of you can go when you're ready."

The team didn't need to be asked twice. Gus and Grace found themselves alone by twenty past-four.

"Updating the Freeman Files will take us beyond five o'clock, Gus," said Grace.

"You can't do too much for a good boss, Grace," said Gus. "Geoff Mercer won't forget your sacrifice."

Adding Jessie North's contribution to the files didn't take as long as Grace feared, and they returned to the ground floor before a quarter past five.

"Enjoy the weekend, Grace," said Gus. "Next week could be a busy one."

"You too," said Grace as she got into her Smart car. Two whole days with nothing to do and nobody to do it with. There was no point ringing Blessing; she was seeing Jamie on a rare weekend off duty. Grace decided to drive to Devizes and stop at the library on the way home. A good book would while away the hours.

Saturday, 6 October 2018

GUS AND SUZIE had risen at eight o'clock. They had no specific plans for the weekend. However, the weekly shop, a trip to Worton for Suzie to check on her horses, and a visit to the allotment for Gus to assess the volume of work required to make Bert Penman happy would make Monday morning arrive soon enough.

Gus prepared their breakfast, and as the clock in the hallway ticked to nine-thirty, Suzie thought they should stop lazing around and drive to the supermarket. Gus checked the list she'd prepared to ensure he knew which vegetables to harvest when he ventured along the lane later. As they strolled to the front door, the phone rang.

An unfamiliar female voice asked:- "Is that Gus Freeman?"

"Gus Freeman speaking. Who's this?"

"Jill Crooks. I got your home number from Geoff Mercer. Sorry to bother you, but we have a problem. A caravan on the Retreat site on Berrow Road burned to the ground last night. I'm on the scene now, but the fire officer won't let me get any closer."

"Was anyone sleeping in the caravan last night?" asked Gus.

"No persons reported is the phrase they use," said Jill. "They can't confirm anything until the debris has cooled and they can investigate thoroughly."

"Can we be sure that caravan was the one bought by Mark Fennell?" asked Gus.

"I've spoken to the site managers, Adam and Tina Watson," said Jill. "They confirmed the pitch now belonged to a Mr Webber. He hasn't visited the site for over a decade."

"That would be Sam Webber," said Gus. "Mark Fennell's ex-wife, Jessie, sold the caravan to Sam after Mark was murdered."

Suzie waved her car keys at Gus and left the bungalow. She had resigned herself to shopping alone. Gus told Jill Crooks everything they'd learned yesterday and his ideas on how they should approach matters from Monday morning.

"Gavin Tilson was known to us," said Jill. "He came back across the Bristol Channel to live in Burnham-on-Sea in the mid-Nineties. Sylvie, his wife, was sixteen when they got together. Tilson spent two years as the muscle man with a gang run by Shane Prosser in Cardiff. Prosser wanted to expand his horizons and sent Tilson to facilitate the distribution of drugs. But unfortunately, we could never pin anything on any of the gang's leaders. We could grab the low-level dealers, but they weren't who we wanted to catch."

"What happened to Prosser?" asked Gus.

"He died of cancer in 2006," said Jill.

"Was Tilson still active after Prosser died?" asked Gus.

"His position was precarious once he no longer had the protection of Prosser. However, it's possible whoever took control in Cardiff continued to trade with their contacts across the Bristol Channel," said Jill. "Two London criminals had arrived on the scene early in 2005. Paulie Atkinson, forty-three, and Johnny Newbold, fifty-one. They weren't as keen on drugs as Prosser. They wanted to smuggle people into the country and set them to work across the southwest. They envisaged supplying various enterprises, including prostitution, both male and female. Then they had nail bars and car valeting businesses that needed hard-working personnel. Whether those poor souls ever received the money they earned was another matter."

"I would have thought the south coast was the more likely entry point," said Gus.

"Too many Border Force personnel checking the coastline," said Jill. "It was easier to move people from mainland Europe to Cork in the Irish Republic. Then they used small fishing boats to ferry people from ports such as Kinsale and Cobh into the Bristol Channel. These boats anchored off the coast. We believe the organised crime group Atkinson and Newbold represented used boats capable of carrying three to five people, charging them around four thousand pounds for the journey. We look to target and disrupt groups involved in people smuggling at every step of the route. Much of this criminality lies outside the UK, so we need to share intelligence with law enforcement partners in the Republic of Ireland and beyond."

"Surely, someone must have seen these fishing boats lingering in areas of coastline where they shouldn't be?" asked Gus.

"The UK maritime industry was alerted to the problem," said Jill. "People higher up the tree than me talk to their partners in Europe to intercept these travellers before they leave mainland Europe. You will appreciate that it's been a constant battle."

"So, since 2005, people have been smuggled ashore somewhere on the North Somerset coast, and you've never caught any of them. Am I right?"

"Not quite, Gus," said Jill. "We catch plenty of them inland. We raid houses where we've received intelligence the place is operating as a brothel. A regular check is done on restaurants, hotels, beauty parlours, and the like for people working in the country illegally. The problem is Atkinson and Newbold warned these people about what would happen to them and their families if they spoke out about how they got here. So there has to be a transit point where these immigrants were being kept before getting transferred to wherever they were headed."

"Did you ever receive intelligence about the caravan site on Berrow Road?" asked Gus.

"Not a word," said Jill. "We've never found an illegal that admitted to coming ashore via that route."

"That begs another question, Jill," said Gus. "We wondered whether drugs were behind the purchase of the caravan Mark Fennell and his closest friends frequented."

"We have enough drugs swilling around in Burnham and Highbridge without importing more, thank you very much," said Jill.

"There you are then," said Gus.

"I see where you're going, Gus. That van was the transit point for Tilson. His supplies came from Prosser prepped and ready for the dealers. Tilson stashed them in the caravan. Easy enough to have a spare set of keys cut."

"They wouldn't have needed to," said Gus. "It was Sylvie Tilson who targeted Mark Fennell and persuaded him to buy the caravan. She gave Fennell her spare set of keys. When Mark holidayed in Burnham in the summer of 2003, he returned to Chippenham full of the joys of spring. Sylvie may have played a part in that, encouraged by her husband, but Mark told his friends he'd found a great opportunity."

"I take it you suspected Mark and his accomplices already had a supplier?"

"It's possible they brought drugs in through Bristol docks. Ian Hook claimed his business was import and export, which raised our suspicions."

"Perhaps Sylvie Tilson promised Mark Fennell better quality and larger product quantities, with less chance of a sniffer dog finding them out."

"Mark intended to leave Chippenham to move to Berrow Road permanently," said Gus. "Sylvie promised to find work in the resort. Enough to deflect attention from his true line of work, which would be moving supplies to Chippenham regularly."

"Why didn't he move to Burnham?" asked Jill.

"His future wife, Jessie, wasn't keen, but it could also be that Mark suddenly realised Sylvie wasn't as available as he thought. Mark Fennell, Sam Webber and Ian Hook were a brotherhood since schooldays. Mark asked them to share the load. They took turns using the caravan during the week and at weekends. The frequency was enough to keep a supply in Chippenham that satisfied demand. The wives had been hand-picked to look nice and not ask too many questions."

"What went wrong?" asked Jill.

"Jessie mentioned hearing a whispered conversation. Will it go ahead? The reply to this was these things take time. She asked when they would arrive. That could have been Gavin Tilson telling Sylvie to relax; their new venture would start when all the links in the chain were in place. If Gavin was joining forces with Atkinson and Newbold, he had access to something useful. They needed a place to keep people, perhaps for twenty-four hours, maybe more. The caravan was small, but these people had already suffered privations travelling across Europe, perhaps smuggled into the Republic in a container, and then a fifteen-hour journey in a fishing boat."

"Many of them have endured far worse, thinking they were about to reach the Promised Land," said Jill. "I imagine Sylvie, or Gavin, approached Mark and told him they were changing the business model. No more drugs, People smuggling was a bigger earner."

"That wouldn't fit with what Sam Webber did, Jill," said Gus. "He was on the phone with Jessie as soon as the police had finished with the house in Kington Langley. They'd interviewed Jessie twice, and she was in the clear. So Sam offered to buy the caravan. Jim Francis and Henry Gibbs would have been interested to hear that, but they never did."

"OK," said Jill, "You think Mark resisted letting the London gang use the caravan? Atkinson and Newbold were getting a firmer grip on Tilson and his set-up. Shane Prosser wasn't a well man, even in 2005, and couldn't prevent part of his empire from falling into their hands."

"Sam Webber hasn't visited the caravan for over a decade, according to the current managers," said Gus. "Tilson was the muscle-man, you said?"

"We've never tagged Gavin Tilson as a killer, Gus. He hurt people if Prosser told him they needed to learn a lesson, but that was its extent."

"Atkinson and Newbold were a different kettle of fish, I imagine?"

"Violent in the extreme, allegedly," said Jill. "It's impossible to get anyone to talk to us about them, though."

"They put the frighteners on Tilson," said Gus, "Told him to get rid of Mark if he wasn't happy to play ball on the people smuggling."

"Why murder Mark's girlfriend, though?" asked Jill.

"Either Tilson thought Helen might have seen him that night, or, more likely, it was to keep Webber and Hook from doing anything stupid," said Gus. "We'll pass everything we've got to you on Monday. There's enough to arrest

Tilson on a murder charge. It might take longer to prove he also killed Helen Roker."

"Just one problem, Gus," said Jill. "Gavin and Sylvie Tilson haven't been seen in Burnham-on-Sea since July 2006."

Epilogue

"WERE you working in Burnham in 2006, Jill?" asked Gus. "Did Avon & Somerset search for them? Maybe Tilson returned to Cardiff to meet up with Prosser's old gang."

"I left my home town twenty years ago, Gus," said Jill. "It's taken me a long time to reach the rank I hold today. I'm not one of the fast-tracked graduate intakes. Most of my career has been spent in Taunton and Bridgwater. As I said earlier, Portishead could never pin anything on Tilson. I think the top brass breathed a sigh of relief and assumed he was now someone else's problem. I'll check, but I guess they circulated photos and details to other forces advising them of the sort of nonsense they would be involved in if they surfaced on their patch."

"There were no live warrants for them, so they were free to leave," said Gus. "I think we both know what happened."

"Atkinson and Newbold had no further use for them," said Jill.

"That changed things for the people in Chippenham," said Gus. "Webber had kept the van so Tilson could keep the drug supply coming. Webber and Hood probably agreed the van would never be occupied, leaving it free for Atkinson and Newbold to hide illegals there for as long as they wished."

"Our intelligence back in 2006 indicated that Atkinson and Newbold were more interested in the people smuggling. I wonder what arrangement they came to with Sam Webber. Why didn't they simply buy the caravan from him?"

"Greed, I expect," said Gus. "Why not cut a deal with the Cardiff connection, and continue receiving supplies for Webber and Hood? You scratch my back, and I'll scratch yours. It was a win-win for all concerned."

"If Webber and Hood hadn't visited the caravan for a decade, how did the drugs reach Chippenham?" asked Jill.

Gus pondered that problem for a second.

"Delivery drivers are ten a penny," he said, "according to Ian Hood. He could have found a man with a van who needed the cash and wasn't fussy about where it came from and sent him to collect the goods. They got the keys from Jessie North. We haven't established the amounts involved, but my gut tells me London Road would have stumbled on an outfit supplying large swathes of the West Country. So, this was a relatively small concern."

"It's still worth getting it from one side of the Bristol Channel to the other," said Jill. "Street prices and purity levels are higher today than a decade ago."

"There's plenty for Portishead to get their teeth into," said Gus. "Atkinson and Newbold no longer have a transit point for their illegals after last night. I'd be keeping a closer watch on those beaches where the next batch might come ashore. Your colleagues can scupper this gang's operations at last."

"I'll pass the information up the line," said Jill. "I look forward to meeting you and your team on Monday. We'll know more about the fire by then. What are your plans for the rest of the day?"

"I'm about to spoil someone's Saturday morning. I want to check whether Sam Webber or Ian Hood visited Berrow Road last night. Our conversations yesterday could have stirred them into action to eliminate any evidence that might lead back to them."

Jill Crooks wished Gus luck and ended the call.

Gus dialled a number that had come through to the bungalow's landline last Friday.

"Grace? It's Gus here. Someone torched the caravan last night. Can you do me a favour?"

"Golly. I'm not doing anything that can't wait," said Grace. She cast aside the book she'd borrowed from the library last night. It wasn't holding her attention anyway.

"Can you drive to London Road, visit the Hub, and get them to check whether Sam Webber or Ian Hood drove to Burnham-on-Sea late last night?"

"You think we touched a raw nerve," said Grace. "Okay, leave it with me. Where will you be once I have an answer?"

"I'll be parked close to either The Tinings or Black Bridge Road, waiting for you to join me with your warrant card. If you draw a blank, I'll drive home and apologise to Suzie for not being available to carry the groceries indoors."

"How did you find out about the fire?" asked Grace.

"DI Crooks called me. She also informed me that Gavin and Sylvie Tilson went missing within six months of Helen Roker's death. Jill believes a pair of London thugs moved into the area in 2003 and slowly took over. Tilson murdered Fennell and Roker, and the new regime got rid of Gavin and his wife."

"No honour among thieves," said Grace.

"It's not personal; it's just business," said Gus.

"I'll call you later, Gus," said Grace and rang off.

Gus left a note for Suzie and set off towards Chippenham. He parked near John Coles Park, about a mile from his destination, and sat on a bench watching the world go by. There were worse places to spend a Saturday morning.

His mobile phone buzzed a few minutes after twelve.

"No sign of any vehicles registered to Sam Webber or Ian Hood, Gus," said Grace.

"Never mind, Grace. It was just a thought. DI Crooks will need to find the culprit in Burnham."

"I am coming to meet you, Gus," said Grace. "The Hub techies spotted a car on an M4 traffic camera at midnight. I've got a name and address for the registered owner."

Gus listened as Grace relayed the details. Finally, he told her he'd see her in thirty minutes.

Gus spotted Grace's car approaching along Eastern Avenue and eased into the line of midday traffic behind her. They arrived at the address and parked.

Grace led the way to the front door and rang the bell.

"Hello. I didn't expect you back so soon. Ian's not here, I'm afraid. He drove into town with Sam. They're having a liquid lunch."

"That caravan was more trouble than it was worth," said Gus. "That's what you said, wasn't it, Becky?"

Becky Hood's face fell.

"We know you drove to Berrow Road last night," said Grace. "After we spoke to each of you yesterday, you decided enough was enough. No matter how much money Sam and Ian made from the drugs they collected from the caravan, you wanted it to end."

"Alright, I did it, so what?" shrugged Becky. "That

caravan was old, no use to any of us, and unless I did something, they would have kept risking everything to keep Mark's memory alive. They thought they were the Three Musketeers. All for one, and one for all. You don't know what it's been like for us. Mark, Sam, and Ian always kept things from us, whisper, whisper, whisper. What good is money if you detest where it came from?"

Gus's mobile phone buzzed again. What now? It was Geoff Mercer.

"I can't imagine this is good news if you're ringing me on Saturday afternoon, Geoff."

"I've just heard from Jill Crooks. The fire officer has confirmed three people died in the fire. They believe two females and one male were locked inside the caravan."

"Thanks, Geoff. Grace can do the honours. Are uniforms on the way? Good."

Grace raised an eyebrow.

"The charge just escalated from arson to three crimes of homicide. There were illegal immigrants locked inside the caravan."

Grace caught hold of an arm as Becky collapsed to the floor. They had to wait several minutes before Grace could read Becky her rights. Finally, two uniformed officers arrived ten minutes later and led Becky to their car.

Gus and Grace followed the police car into Chippenham. The uniformed officers and their passenger headed for the custody suite on the edge of town. Gus turned towards Urchfont, and Grace carried on to Easterton.

Monday morning's schedule would require a reshuffle.

Next in The Freeman Files series

TED TAYLER

The perfect blend of detective mystery and everyday life with Gus Freeman, the Wiltshire Detective.

A MORNING MURDER

THE FREEMAN FILES SERIES

vinci-books.com/morningmurder

In Burnham-on-Sea, no secret stays buried forever.

Just as the team settles into a well-deserved break, a series of puzzling incidents in Burnham-on-Sea demands their immediate attention. As they dive headfirst into the investigation, they find themselves navigating a complex labyrinth of interconnected crimes that have remained unsolved for years.

Turn the page for a free preview…

A Morning Murder: Chapter One

BURNHAM-ON-SEA

Saturday, 6 October 2018

Gus reached home early on Saturday afternoon. He'd had a busy morning.

Amazing Grace had arrested Becky Hood for the murder of three illegal immigrants. But, despite never having set foot in Burnham-on-Sea, he and the team somehow solved the original case Kenneth Truelove had handed them.

Suzie had returned from the big shop and made a detour to the horses fifteen minutes before Gus wandered through the front door.

"I read your note," said Suzie, popping her head around the kitchen door before continuing to prepare a late lunch. "I hope you won't make a habit of dashing off with Amazing Grace on Saturday mornings. After all the things you've said about her, it's disconcerting. Don't worry. I've put everything I bought away safely."

"I would rather have braved the supermarket with you than have to deliver such dreadful news to Becky Hood."

"Oh dear," said Suzie. "What happened after I left here?"

Gus explained how drugs had been the dominant passion for the three Chippenham men in their late teens. They never used the evil stuff themselves but were happy to satisfy the demand among their peers if they could earn extra money. But, in the beginning, they weren't as security conscious as they later became, and Ian Hood got caught.

As Gus's team had thought, Ian had agreed to take the fall for his friends. When he returned to Chippenham, Ian found Sam and Mark were married to Mary and Mandy. Sam Webber was doing okay with his burgeoning car dealership, while Mark had an excellent job with a major local employer.

Ian married, too, once he found the right girl, Becky Roker, but he didn't fancy a career where he started at the bottom and worked his way up. So he imported goods from China that he hoped to sell at a handsome profit. However, most of the early items Ian purchased were cheap for a reason. The quality was shoddy, and Ian got his fingers burned. But, as always, he had the answer.

The cheap products he bought would need to make a brief stopover on their way to the UK. Drugs were hidden inside the items in the Middle East. The quantities involved weren't huge, and the system worked undetected for years.

"So, they smuggled small amounts destined for a select clientele," said Suzie. "A little and often. These products arrived in containers docking at Portbury or Avonmouth."

"Ian Hood arranged collection and transported the goods containing the raw material to a middleman," said Gus. "It was still profitable but risky. The middle man then cut and bagged the end product. Ian's transport system collected and delivered the finished article to their contacts in the Chippenham area."

"When Mark met Sylvie Tilson, he realised they could simplify the process," said Suzie.

"Shane Prosser's gang could get the finished product across the Bristol Channel to Burnham-on-Sea, stash it in Mark's caravan, and the three friends could transfer it to the end-user," said Gus. "The percentage profit rose steeply."

"Will you still need to go to the seaside next week?" asked Suzie.

"It would be rude not to," said Gus. "I'd like to delay meeting with Kenneth Truelove for as long as possible. We close the office on Friday, and I don't want him to have too long to bend my ear about uncovering more problems than I solved."

"Jim Francis?" asked Suzie.

"For one," said Gus. "Then there's Jessie North. Don't start me on Annie Drew and who she's working for these days."

"Plus, if this London gang bumped off Gavin and Sylvie Tilson, someone needs to start the search for their bodies."

"It looks like another two murders solved for which we can name a killer but never put them in front of a judge and jury."

"Never mind, Gus," said Suzie. "It's not as if you do it deliberately. Kenneth will understand."

"I hope you're right," sighed Gus. "How long before lunch is ready?"

"You've got time to change into your gardening clothes. I thought we'd make the most of this sunny spell and eat it on the patio."

Gus couldn't think of a better option, so he headed for the bedroom. When he joined Suzie in the back garden, he was surprised to see she'd poured him a glass of wine.

"A refreshing change," he said as he tucked into his BLT.

"My mother collared me while I was grooming my horse in the stable," said Suzie. "She reminded me it's been a while since we had Sunday lunch with them."

"That explains the wine," said Gus. "When are we dining in Worton?"

"Tomorrow," said Suzie. "Do you mind?"

"Not at all," said Gus. "I'll get as much done at the allotment this afternoon as I can. Whatever's left outstanding can wait until next weekend. If Bert Penman thinks otherwise, I'll give him cash to supplement his cider money."

"You shouldn't encourage Bert to overdo things," said Suzie.

"Gardening or drinking?" asked Gus.

After finishing their lunch, Suzie encouraged Gus to get out from under her feet and visit the allotment.

"The sooner you start, the sooner you'll finish," she said. "I'll wash these few things by hand, put them away, and then hoover around. We're booked in for a meal at the Fox & Hounds tonight, and we won't want anything to eat after Mum's finished with us tomorrow, so the dishwasher can rest until Monday. You can take your turn at the sink after breakfast in the morning."

"Will everything be so organised next April, do you think?" asked Gus, kissing Suzie before leaving the bungalow.

"We'll cope," said Suzie. "It's a case of having to."

Gus looked to the heavens as he strode along the lane

towards the church. The sun was still warm enough to allow him and Suzie to enjoy a pleasant lunch on their sheltered patio. With mature trees screening the rear of the property, it was a bit of a sun trap.

Once exposed to the elements, it was a different matter. He would have to keep working this afternoon. If he stopped to chat to Bert or the Reverend for any length of time, the cool breeze would play havoc with his back. That was the last thing he needed with two weeks' holiday around the corner.

He needn't have worried. Bert must have made an early start. Perhaps, when Irene returned from her sister's, she'd wanted him out of the house to get it shipshape. Gus doubted whether Bert was as keen on hoovering and dusting, especially after a session in The Lamb following his morning's labour.

Gus opened his shed door and consulted the oracle. The notebook he'd compiled from every lecture Bert had given him about what needed doing and when throughout the seasons. The oracle was a well-thumbed yet vital document.

"Things may be winding down in October, Mr Freeman," Bert had told Gus. "But there's still plenty to do, including harvesting late crops, planting for next year, and improving the soil."

Gus worked his way down the list; with runner beans, courgettes, and his main crop of potatoes to harvest, there was plenty to keep him occupied. As he gathered his produce by the shed door, he spotted someone waving a walking stick in the distance. Bert was leaving The Lamb after his liquid lunch and looked a little unsteady on his feet as he made his way up the lane towards home.

Gus redoubled his efforts. Suzie might be right. So, he sowed his broad beans, divided his rhubarb crowns, and then rooted around in the shed for his stock of canes. Bert reckoned they prevented the heavily-laden Brussels sprout plants from blowing over in the autumn winds.

"Why go to the effort of growing the darn things only to stand by and watch them rot on the ground?" Bert would say.

Gus made sure nothing was getting blown over anytime soon. He smiled at an item in the notebook he'd crossed through a couple of years ago. No way was he bothering with planting a variety of peas.

As the church clock prepared to strike the hour, Gus realised five o'clock had crept up on him already. Enough was enough. He hadn't managed to start improving the soil on his patch of land today, but manuring would have to wait until next weekend.

Gus was locking the shed when Suzie arrived in her Golf.

"Were you wondering where I'd got to?" he asked.

"No, but I did wonder whether you'd be able to carry everything home with you. So, just as well that I popped along based on what I can see."

They loaded the vegetables into the boot and drove home.

"You had the place to yourself by the looks of it," said Suzie.

"Bert worked this morning," said Gus. "No sign of Clemency today. I expect she's writing her sermon and getting ready for tonight."

"Are we giving them a lift to the pub?" asked Suzie.

"I didn't arrange anything with Brett on Wednesday night," said Gus. "Perhaps they'll cycle? It's only four miles."

"I can't tell if you're joking or not," said Suzie. "I'll

drive your car, and then you and Brett can have a drink. The Reverend rarely indulges these days. I think she has a soft drink to keep me company."

"We can blame Irene North and her homemade wine for Clemency not drinking," said Gus. "I'll call Brett and tell him we'll collect them from the vicarage just after half-past seven."

"Leave that to me," said Suzie. "You can shower and change while I make arrangements with the Reverend. We don't want her parishioners getting in a tizz if someone sees us dropping the couple at the Rectory close to midnight."

"Whatever you say, darling," said Gus.

"You're learning," said Suzie.

Gus was ready to leave within fifteen minutes but knew he had time on his hands. Suzie had spent several minutes rummaging through her clothes, lamenting the lack of something different to wear, before disappearing into the bathroom.

Gus went into the lounge and thumbed through a magazine Suzie had picked up while shopping that morning. The content was uninspiring, with news of offers any sensible shopper could identify on the shelves if they took their nose out of their phone while inside the store.

The colourful menu suggestions looked great, but why did every dish include so many exotic ingredients when we should encourage people to grow their own? First, the ingredients needed to be imported, and second the amount required for each dish was tiny. As a result, the customer would need to eat the dish five times a week to finish the packet, tube, or bottle before it went out of date.

Gus heard the bedroom door closing, which signified progress. He waited with bated breath. If Tess was anything to go by, he was in for a fashion parade. The decision on what to wear had been his responsibility. The trick was to pick the dress Tess had already chosen. Woe betide him if he got it wrong.

The bedroom door opened, and Suzie emerged barefoot in a floaty floral wrap dress.

"What do you think?" she asked.

"Give me a twirl," said Gus.

Suzie obliged.

"I like it, and I'm certain I've never seen it before," Gus said.

"More to the point, nor has Clemency," said Suzie.

She returned to the bedroom. Had he said the right thing? Gus was none the wiser.

When Suzie re-emerged, the only change was she now had flat shoes on her feet.

Gus found he could breathe more easily.

"Right, I'm ready," said Suzie. "Let's go."

Gus joined her in the hallway, dropped the magazine in the waste bin by the kitchen door, and handed over his car keys.

"Be gentle with her," he said.

"We need to have an urgent conversation about our transport needs," said Suzie. "I struggled to get the vegetables you harvested in the boot of my Golf earlier. Imagine trying to accommodate everything we'll need with the little one. As for your Focus, it's been on borrowed time for several years. What if it lets us down when I need to get to the hospital?"

"I'll make a mental note," said Gus. "We'll add it to the list of things that need sorting out while I'm on my so-called holiday."

Gus was impressed with how Suzie coaxed the Focus through the gateway without spraying tonnes of gravel toward the climbing roses. They arrived outside the Rectory at seven-thirty-five, where Brett and the Reverend were waiting on the pavement holding hands.

Once the couple was inside the car, Suzie drove just over the speed limit to the Fox & Hounds. The car park was almost full, but Suzie parked the Focus without adding to its war wounds.

"We've not been here before," said Clemency. "It's busy, which is always a good sign."

"You must book, especially on a Saturday night," Gus said. "We like its ambience and seasonal yet affordable menu."

"We like the Waggon & Horses for the same reason," said Suzie. "It's good to have somewhere that's not on your doorstep and gives you a chance to be alone. If you approve, perhaps you two can add it to your list of places to visit for a special occasion."

"Like tonight, do you mean?" asked the Reverend, brushing a loose lock of hair behind her ear.

Gus led the way into the pub, and they were shown to their table. The four friends ordered drinks and studied the starter menu.

"I'll be back in a minute," said Brett, heading towards the bar.

"What have you two been up to today?" asked Clemency.

"I was working this morning," said Gus. "Not a pleasant experience, but a positive outcome. Then, this afternoon I worked on my allotment. I saw Bert leaving the pub. I could tell he'd worked on his patch this morning."

" I know what you're going to say. I'm afraid I couldn't get there today," said Clemency.

"With Gus working on a case in Chippenham, I battled

the crowds alone doing the weekly shop," said Suzie. "Then, I drove to Worton before lunchtime to groom my horse, and I caught up with chores at the bungalow this afternoon. I imagine you had parish duties to perform, home visits, and a sermon to write?"

"All of the above," said the Reverend. "Although, I tackled the lion's share last night. Brett convinced me we must take a trip into Devizes this morning."

Brett returned to the table, followed by two staff members. One carried a tray with their drink order, and the other waiter delivered four flutes of champagne.

"Bubbly?" asked Gus. "What did I miss?"

"Call yourself a detective, darling?" said Suzie. "When I mentioned a special occasion in the car park, Clemency gave a big hint something was going on."

"Brett proposed last night," said Clemency, stretching her left hand across the table for Suzie to see the engagement ring more clearly.

"We were to blame for Bert having one or two more drinks than usual at lunchtime," said Brett. "We dropped in on him and Irene after returning from the jewellers in Maryport Street. Irene joined us in The Lamb for an hour, and then we took her home. She wanted to ring her sister to check she was okay."

"Congratulations, you two," said Gus. "I can't recall the last time anyone I know got engaged, let alone married."

"We don't plan on a long engagement," said Brett. "So you won't have long to wait."

Suzie and Gus raised a glass and wished the smiling couple every happiness.

"It's time we ordered food," said Suzie. "My bacon, lettuce, and tomato sandwich seems a lifetime ago."

When they finally made their way outside to the car

park when the pub closed, everyone agreed it had been a splendid evening. The food didn't disappoint, and on some occasions, alcohol wasn't required to get everyone in high spirits.

Suzie drove back towards Urchfont and slowed as they approached Brett's house.

"You can drop us at the Rectory, Suzie," said the Reverend.

"Gosh," said Suzie. "What will the Bishop say?"

Clemency giggled.

"Brett cycled to my place earlier," she said.

"I'll cycle home later," said Brett. "Honest."

When they reached the Rectory, Brett and Clemency got out of the Focus and waved as Suzie pulled away.

"I bet he won't leave until *much* later," said Gus.

"I'm happy for them," said Suzie.

"So am I," said Gus. "It was plain from the start they were meant for each other."

"I'm still happy with things the way they are if you were getting ideas."

"Me too. If it ain't broke, don't fix it," said Gus.

Suzie parked the Focus under the rambling roses, and they went indoors.

"Do you want a nightcap, darling?" asked Suzie.

"It's not the same when we can't enjoy it together," said Gus.

"We can't eat breakfast too late in the morning, or we'll never finish our roast dinner."

"I've just remembered something we *can* enjoy together," said Gus.

"Now you're talking," said Suzie heading for the bedroom.

Sunday, 7 October 2018

When Gus opened his eyes, he could hear Suzie already working in the kitchen. He rolled out of bed and strolled through to join her.

"Morning, sleepyhead," she said. "After last night's meal, I thought you deserved blueberries and Greek yoghurt for breakfast."

"Deserved is a stretch," said Gus. "Roll on when we can have bacon and eggs again. Oh well, a mug of coffee will ease the pain."

Suzie handed him a mug of black coffee.

"You were snoring well last night," she said, "so that's not why you're like a bear with a sore head this morning. What's the matter?"

"I had a weird dream," said Gus. "Brett had developed a refinement to those microchip cat flaps he was talking about the other night. So if anything other than the authorised moggie tried to enter the house, it got Tasered."

"That's dreadful," said Suzie.

"I couldn't agree more," said Gus. "Just before I woke up, Brett told me he'd sold a million units in the first year."

"You've never mentioned any of your dreams before."

"That's the first one I've been able to mention," said Gus as he poured himself another coffee.

"I'm off for a shower," said Suzie. "From the sound of things, you had better have a cold shower this morning."

"I can wash the breakfast things later," said Gus. "I'm coming with you."

"Incorrigible," said Suzie.

They left the bungalow ten minutes before noon, and Suzie delivered them to the Ferris farm in her Golf just as Jackie's kitchen clock struck the hour.

"They're here," she called.

Blessing Umeh came downstairs and hugged Jackie.

"Jamie will be here soon," she said. "We'll get out of your hair, and you can spend quality time with your family."

"John's somewhere on the other side of the farm," said Jackie. "I told him when to return, but the land and the animals control his time, not me."

"Good morning, guv," said Blessing as Gus entered the kitchen.

"Gus, when we're off-duty, Blessing," said Gus. "Have you got five minutes?"

"Jamie's picking me up," said Blessing. "So it will have to be quick."

"He followed us along the lane from the main road. Suzie's chatting to him outside. I wanted to update you on what happened yesterday morning."

"That's okay, Gus," said Blessing. "Grace phoned yesterday afternoon. She was too excited to wait until Monday."

"Oh, okay. Well, I'll tell the others when we get together in the morning."

Suzie came indoors and hugged her mother.

"Your young man can't wait to see you, Blessing," she said. "Enjoy your afternoon."

"We will," laughed Blessing as she dashed outside.

She bumped into John Ferris in the doorway.

"Sorry, Mr Ferris," she said.

"Don't worry, Blessing. It was a soft landing."

Gus could still hear Blessing laughing until Jamie's car roared out of the farmyard.

"That was a mad five minutes," said Jackie. "Now, let's eat, and you can tell us what you've been up to since we last got together."

"It's not been that long, mother," said Suzie.

"Humour her, Suzie," said John. "She's a grandmother-in-waiting. I tell her not to fret, but I might as well talk to that wall."

The delicious aroma of Jackie's cooking filled the kitchen as Suzie and Gus filled in the blanks on their daily lives over the past couple of weeks. Of course, Suzie's parents didn't expect to hear details of any cases Gus and the team worked on, but they were keen to learn what Gus might do during his vacation.

"Nothing has been decided yet," said Gus. "Although, at the weekends when Suzie is available, we've got a list of items that need both of us to thrash out."

"I won't ask whether you're planning any major projects at the farm," said Suzie. "Nothing ever changes."

"Everything will continue in the same pattern as it has for decades, Suzie," said her father. "Change is inevitable, but it happens slowly. If you think back to when you were leaving school, we didn't have the equipment we have in the barns now. There were more farmhands, and the materials we used were efficient but not good for the long-term future of the land."

"My brothers were still living here then, too," said Suzie. "You're right, there have been changes in the past fifteen years, but they were subtle."

"It's high time that roast beef was carved, John," said Jackie, busying herself on the other side of the kitchen. "Food first, and then we can put the world to rights later."

John Ferris winked at his daughter.

"Perhaps you were right. Nothing changes."

Sunday lunch was always a leisurely affair with Jackie in charge. After polishing off his second bowl of rhubarb and custard, Gus leaned back from the table and realised it was approaching four o'clock.

"That was fantastic, Jackie," he said, "I'm stuffed."

"Coffee?" she asked.

"Just the ticket," said Gus.

Suzie noticed her father didn't seem in a rush to get away. That was odd. He usually headed out to a remote corner of the farm to tend to something urgent.

"I'll just get these plates and dishes into the dishwasher," said Jackie. "The rest can wait."

"Okay," said Suzie. "What's going on? I should have known there was an ulterior motive for the sudden lunch invitation."

"We don't need a reason, sweetheart," said John. "Go on, Jackie, you'd better tell them."

"Blessing put the idea in my head," said Jackie. "Before she arrived, the two of us rattled around in this old farmhouse. You had moved in with Gus, and I suddenly realised how quiet the place was without young folk. The way things are going with Jamie, I can see we'll be losing Blessing too in time, so I thought we could rent out another bedroom."

"That makes sense," said Gus.

"On Thursday evening, Blessing brought a young lady home with her. She lives in Easterton, in one of Monty Jennings's properties."

"Amazing Grace," said Gus.

"The very same," said Jackie. "A polite girl, the same age as Suzie. I had prepared a meal for Blessing, and the three of us chatted while they shared the food between them."

"Grace is a vegan," said Gus. "That can't have been easy."

"Different rather than difficult," said Jackie. "After Grace drove home, Blessing told me how lonely Grace was in Easterton. She doesn't know anyone in the village and finds it tough to make new friends. So I thought as she works with Blessing, it would make sense for her to move here. They can take turns driving to the office. I'm sure they will appreciate the extra cash in their purse. As for me, I would welcome the company and the challenge of adapting my menus to suit their different requirements. I'm not too old to learn."

"Grace will only be with us until Christmas," said Gus. "Unless Kenneth and Geoff can't find a suitable replacement for Luke Sherman."

"Grace still needs to be close to London Road," said John. "Her and Blessing might not be able to car share for more than a couple of months, but every little helps. I'm happy to have Grace living here. Jackie reckons she and Blessing get on well."

"Grace did mention her visit here when we were in Chippenham on Saturday," said Gus. "Although, she spoke about a regular Thursday evening invite for an evening meal. I didn't realise things had moved so quickly."

"We haven't asked Grace yet whether she wants to move here," said Jackie. "I wanted to check you were happy with the arrangement first."

"What are you thinking, Gus?" asked Suzie.

"Any chance of a brandy to go with this coffee?"

"I'll join you, Gus," laughed John. "You two haven't always seen eye-to-eye, am I right? Blessing was explaining it to us yesterday evening."

"We sit in very different camps," said Gus. "I represent the old regime who those preaching the modern policing mantra want to disappear. While Grace was carrying out a special project at London Road for Geoff Mercer, we crossed swords on several occasions. I sensed trouble was just around the corner. When Luke left us, it would have been better if Geoff had conjured up a transfer for a bright, young detective sergeant. Someone I could educate properly before they were beyond help and brainwashed. Geoff insisted good candidates were thin on the ground, and DI Packenham was a rising star."

"How's it been so far, with her working in the CRT office?" asked Jackie.

"Grace is making progress," said Gus. "Teamwork wasn't in her vocabulary before she joined us. It worries me that she seems to be doing far better than I feared."

"Perhaps you misjudged her, darling," said Suzie.

"Time will tell," said Gus.

A Morning Murder: Chapter Two

Monday, 8 October 2018

"I'll expect you when I see you," said Suzie as they stood outside the bungalow beside their respective cars.

"There's no telling how long we'll be in Burnham-on-Sea," said Gus. "What will be, will be. But, either way, we need to wrap things up by Friday."

One slice of toast and honey was all either of them could manage this morning after yesterday's visit to Worton. They had left John and Jackie to return to Urchfont at eight o'clock, meeting Jamie's sports car on the long driveway. Blessing Umeh gave them a wave as they drove past.

Time would tell whether Grace and Blessing would soon be sleeping under the same roof.

"Think positive thoughts, Gus," said Suzie. "Grace could have rented a cottage in the village, like Brett."

Gus grunted and slipped into the driving seat of his Focus. He followed Suzie through the gateway, and they turned left. The start of another week and the now-familiar detour. Gus tapped the steering wheel to the lyrics of a song that entered his head. *I'll tip my hat to the new constitution, take a bow for the new revolution, smile and grin at the change all around....* He was sure that was The Who. Why did 'Won't Get Fooled Again' come out of the ether like that? Then the penny dropped. The Detours was the band's first name. It preceded The High Numbers, and the final name change gave the group the golden ticket to chart success. Somehow Gus felt The Detours would never have been as popular.

Gus arrived before nine despite the circuitous route to the Old Police Station office. The others were already there.

"Morning, guv," said Neil.

"Did you have a good weekend?" asked Lydia.

"Wonderful," said Gus. "What have you heard about Saturday morning?"

"Grace told us the gory details, guv," said Neil.

"Becky Hood torched the caravan," said Alex. "She didn't realise it wasn't merely somewhere for her husband and his mates to stash their drugs."

"We also know Gavin and Sylvie Tilson are missing, presumed dead, guv," said Lydia.

"There's not a lot to keep us here then, is there?" said Gus.

"We'll see you outside the Burnham nick, guv," said Lydia.

"We'll try not to keep you waiting too long," said Gus.

Alex and Lydia were soon inside her Mini, leaving the Church Street car park.

"Shall I go with Neil, guv?" asked Blessing.

"It looks like it's you and me, Gus," said Grace.

"Indeed," said Grace.

Gus returned to his car and waited while Grace fitted a

steering wheel lock to her Smart car. Why anyone would want to steal it, he couldn't imagine.

"Do you have a plan for today, Gus?" asked Grace when she joined him.

"We'll play it by ear," he replied. "Jill Crooks knows the terrain better than we do, even if she hasn't lived in the town for years. I know you were based in the area more recently, but most of your time in the county was either at the Avon & Somerset HQ or driving to and from Portishead."

"Fair comment," said Grace. "By the way, I had a phone call yesterday evening."

"From Jackie Ferris. Yes, I was aware she was calling you. Suzie and I had lunch with John and Jackie yesterday. They asked whether I thought you were house-trained."

"I have to give notice to my landlord, Mr Jennings," said Grace, ignoring Gus's remark. "So, I can't move in for at least twenty-eight days."

"You didn't accept the offer immediately?"

"I didn't want to appear too eager. But I'd be a fool not to make the switch. The rent is way lower than I'm paying for my current property, and Blessing and I can car share."

"The rental situation is straightforward enough," said Gus. "At the farm, you'll get bed and board. You will have seen how valuable that could be when you went to the farm with Blessing the other evening. Jackie's cooking is sensational. I suppose you need to weigh the reduced outgoings against the loss of independence."

"I've rented ever since I left university, Gus," said Grace. "I've no idea when I'll get my foot on the property ladder."

"What about the bank of Mum and Dad?" asked Gus. "Is there no possibility of help from that direction?"

"None whatsoever," said Grace. "No, I hope moving to Worton will give me more than a financial benefit."

"You've spoken to Blessing, I can tell," laughed Gus. "She calls the farm her home from home."

Grace didn't reply. She thought Blessing was lucky to have somewhere to call home in the first place.

Gus joined the M4 on the other side of Chippenham and headed for the Almondsbury interchange. Once they were on the M5 and heading west, he kept watching for Junction 22. They would be just two miles from the resort if he didn't miss it.

"We should reach the Burnham Police Station by a quarter to eleven," said Gus.

Grace was staring out of the window, watching the world go by.

"This must be the B3140," said Gus. "It's more like a country lane after travelling forty miles on the motorway. The first signs of life are up ahead. A holiday park on the outskirts of town."

"Don't you find it odd?" asked Grace. "Every coastal town I've visited has this style and mix of housing. They have bungalows and villas on the outskirts and rows of terraced housing near the town centre. Most have a Grand Hotel on the seafront. Yet, the weather in the UK is rubbish compared to the Spanish Costas, which have three hundred days of sunshine yearly. No resort on this coast can claim visitors are holidaying at the seaside. That's the Bristol Channel in the distance, not the Mediterranean. It's dirty and notoriously tidal. I don't see the attraction."

"Did your parents never take you to the seaside, Grace?" asked Gus.

"We visited Great Yarmouth for two weeks every summer. That's no better. The North Sea will have reclaimed most properties built on the cliffs in the next two decades. We were ecstatic if we had three sunny days during our fortnight's holiday. My mother prepared for four seasons daily, taking every scrap of clothing we possessed with us in our old Countryman."

"The Rolls Royce?" asked Gus.

"My father was a High Court judge. He wouldn't be seen dead in an Austin Seven."

"The Radford Countryman is as rare as hen's teeth. They sell for anything up to half a million depending on condition. Does he still own it?"

"No idea," said Grace. "Is that the police station on our right?"

"Not hard to spot, was it?" said Gus. "Lashings of red brick and zero character. Abandon hope all ye who enter here. That's for the staff's benefit, not the criminal's. We're the last to arrive. I don't recognise the lady speaking to Alex, but she fits the persona of the DI Jill Crooks I spoke with on Saturday."

Gus parked the Focus next to Lydia's Mini, and he and Grace joined the others.

"You made it then, guv," said Neil. "We were about to send out a search party."

"Good morning, Gus," said Jill Crooks. "I've met the team and your resident joker."

"I'm here all week," said Neil.

"The Berrow Road caravan site is a mile and a half north from here," said Jill, ignoring Neil. "It might be better if your team stays here while I show you around. Henry Gibbs suggested I bring DS Kurt Burgess with me from Bridgwater. He knows the Burnham and Highbridge crime map in all its grubby detail and can bring the team up to speed. We don't want to advertise that we have half a dozen

Wiltshire detectives on our patch. Kurt's inside, waiting for your people to join him."

"Fair enough," said Gus. "Grace, can you do the honours, make the introductions, update DS Burgess on our progress, and then listen to what he has to say about the main players operating in the area."

Grace nodded, and Gus and Jill were soon alone in the car park.

"My BMW's behind you," said Jill. "It has far too much power under the bonnet for my driving these days, but it looks the part."

Gus sat in the passenger seat, expecting a sarcastic comment about his vehicle.

"Did they offer you a car when you came out of retirement, Gus?" asked Jill as she drove out of the police station car park.

"The budget didn't stretch that far," scoffed Gus. "My partner and I are looking to buy a replacement in the next couple of months."

"I hope the Focus lasts that long," said Jill.

"I can't see the point of Suzie getting rid of her Golf," said Gus. "She'll return to work after she's had the baby, and if I'm still working with the Crime Review Team, we both need a car. So I expect I'll settle for a small family saloon."

"Don't sound so downhearted," laughed Jill. "You'll be a father. That's something to celebrate, even at your age."

"Do you have kids?" asked Gus.

"Never found the time," said Jill. "Didn't marry until my early thirties. That lasted three years before he left me for an Australian barmaid. I met my second husband at the Bridgwater carnival five years later. Pete Crooks was a lorry driver, and we had a great marriage, probably because our jobs often kept us apart. Sadly, Pete died of a heart attack at the wheel of his truck three years ago. The only godsend was he careered off the M5 and didn't take anyone else with him in the crash."

"What rotten luck," said Gus. "How do you keep going, Jill?"

"My faith and work get me through life one day at a time," she replied.

Gus spotted the sign for the caravan site up ahead. He thought once you'd seen one site layout, you'd seen the lot, but this did differ from the norm, as Jessie North had explained. Only a handful of caravans were visible on the top level. The main car park, clubhouse, and office building occupied the rest.

Jill Crooks parked her Beemer by the office building, and they went inside.

Adam and Tina Watson, the current site managers, sat at desks on either side of the office. Gus described them as being in their late thirties and early forties, overweight, and not welcoming any interruption to their well-ordered day.

The building reminded Gus of a 1930s flat-roofed cricket pavilion, the lower half brick-built and the upper half containing wooden-framed windows on three sides. Every inch of the office's solid back wall was covered in town maps, site diagrams, notices, brochures, bus timetables, and an array of helpful phone numbers for doctors, dentists, taxis, and takeaways. All were designed to give a visitor the answer to their question without the need to bother the management.

"I'm afraid I don't have any news for you about the caravan," Jill told the couple. "Forensics should finish with it today. Then we can arrange to remove the debris, and you can source a replacement."

"It's costing us money," moaned Adam Watson. "Even in October, we could expect to have a customer eager to find a residential pitch."

"I wish I had better news, but three people died," said Jill. "Your income is way down the list as far as priorities go. I have a colleague from Wiltshire Police with me today. He's arrested the person responsible for the fire, but his superiors have unanswered questions regarding Gavin and Sylvie Tilson."

"Josie Clift should be in the clubhouse getting ready for the lunchtime trade," said Tina Watson. "We weren't here when Sylvie worked in the bar, but Josie was, so perhaps you should speak to her?"

"We'll pop next door," said Jill. "I'll update you about the caravan as soon as I get the all-clear. We'll try not to delay Josie for too long."

Adam Watson wasn't listening.

Jill and Gus went outside and walked to the main door of the clubhouse.

"The far corner of the upper level is a good place to have the clubhouse," said Gus. "The bar windows look out over the caravans on the hillside below and out to the Bristol Channel. I spotted the opening and closing times on a notice on the back wall of the office. Midday to midnight in the summer season, but the residents prefer a quieter time after the August Bank Holiday. The clubhouse shuts at ten-thirty every night between September and the end of March."

"The fire officer thought the fire was set after midnight," said Jill.

"The M4 camera clocked Becky Hood's car heading this way at midnight, so that fits. But unfortunately, it also means the clubhouse was in darkness before she arrived. Zero chance of eyewitnesses."

Jill and Gus climbed the three steps into the building. They couldn't see anyone, but the chink of glass bottles suggested Josie Clift was somewhere to their left.

"The equivalent to a pub cellar must be over there," said Gus.

"Josie Clift?" shouted Jill. "Police. Can we have a word?"

A rosy-cheeked woman in her early thirties appeared in the doorway of the room at the far end of the building. She was carrying a crate of bottles.

"I'm Josie," she said, lifting the crate easily onto the bar counter. "I need to get on with bottling-up. Will this take long?"

"I saw you on Saturday morning when I attended the aftermath of the fire," said Jill. "You drove away before I had a chance to speak with you. Mr Freeman is with Wilt-shire Police and has some questions for you."

"Were you working on Friday night, Josie?" asked Gus.

"Not me; I cover lunchtimes only, five hours a day, seven days a week. Adam told me not to bother on Saturday. That's why I went home early."

"Who serves behind the bar in the evenings?"

"Adam and Tina," said Josie. "Then, casual staff from an agency cover the peak periods. The clubhouse doesn't warrant any extra permanent staff. Visitors to the holiday parks in town want entertainment after spending a day in the resort and are more likely to spend their evenings in a clubhouse. Here, the demand isn't as great. Many retired residents drink at home if they drink at all. Several owners rent their caravans out to friends and family, which means Adam never knows from one week to the next whether we'll be busy or quiet with a different crowd on site. It's easier to watch for unfamiliar car registrations in the car park and then make a phone call to the agency if there's likely to be an upturn in trade."

"What can you tell me about Sylvie Tilson?" asked Gus.

"Sylvie did this job before me," said Josie, "but the manager in those days wasn't married. So, Sylvie also worked behind the bar in the evenings every other day. Lennie, the manager, did the bottling-up before she arrived in the mornings to cope with the lunchtime bar trade."

"How did you come to get the job? It sounds as if Lennie had everything covered."

"Sylvie's husband wasn't keen on her working here. She didn't drive, so he had to make four trips a day in his BMW, and this place is open until midnight in the summer. He didn't appear to have a regular job, but somehow he always had plenty of money. If you ask me, Gavin Tilson was a nasty piece of work; I don't know why Sylvie stayed with him. I never trusted him. Lennie wanted a regular female face behind the bar because he reckoned the residents preferred it. So he advertised for someone to cover the lunchtime shifts, which suited me down to the ground. Sylvie showed me the ropes, and that was it. I rarely saw her after that."

"Did she ever mention anything about leaving Burnham?" asked Gus.

"Sylvie was too frightened of Gavin to go off on her own," said Josie. "Then, one morning, Lennie asked if I could work here that evening. Sylvie hadn't arrived at six the night before as planned. Lennie had rung her mobile but got no answer. Nobody knew where Sylvia and Gavin went; they just vanished. Lennie assumed whatever business Gavin was involved in must have failed, and they'd left town, leaving their creditors to whistle for their money. If that was the case, I never heard anyone mention it. Sylvie wasn't around to work here in the evenings. Life just moved on. We had agency staff help out when required."

"What happened then?" asked Gus.

"I agreed to work with Lennie for a week or two in the evenings. It was cheaper for him than employing someone from the agency. But it got too much for me. Lennie decided he'd had enough too, and it wasn't long before Adam and Tina took over. They leave me alone, saving them from having to do anything before six in the evening. That suits my home situation.

"What happened to Lennie?" asked Gus.

"He was getting on, a lot older than Adam. Lennie moved to a retirement village on the other side of Weston-super-Mare. I heard he died last year."

"You told us you rarely saw Sylvie after taking over this lunchtime job," said Jill. "Where did you bump into her?"

"We used to shop at the same supermarket in town on a Friday afternoon," said Josie. "Gavin didn't go with her, of course. That wasn't his style. So instead, we had a coffee and chatted while she waited for a bus to their place in Highbridge. The buses run every thirty minutes, so Sylvie took advantage of time away from him."

"Did Sylvie ever give you the impression she was afraid of anyone?" asked Gus.

"Apart from Gavin? There have been a few new faces in the area since I left school. People you would do best to steer clear of, you know?"

"People with a London accent?" asked Gus.

Josie nodded.

"Did they ever visit this clubhouse?" asked Jill.

"I wouldn't know whether they came here in the

evening," said Josie. "As I said earlier, it's quiet at lunchtime. So, no, I've never been bothered by them."

"Lennie would have been next door in the office," said Gus. "I don't suppose you would know whether he had visitors?"

"I'd have to leave the bar unattended and go outside to see," said Josie.

"On the other hand, when it's quiet, you could relax in the seating area on our right," said Jill. "Perhaps chat to the handful of customers in the bar. Lennie wouldn't mind. He told you the customers preferred someone friendly."

Gus walked to the large picture window at the end of the bar.

"From here, it's possible to keep an eye on the door and have an unrestricted view across the bay and most of the caravans. Anything to pass the time when you're not busy."

"Did you ever see any of those newcomers wandering through the caravans?" asked Jill.

"Hard to tell from that distance," said Josie.

"So, hypothetically," asked Gus. "If you had seen someone in the distance, would they have been close to the pitch where the fire broke out last Friday night?"

"I suppose so," said Josie.

"We believe Gavin Tilson was a regular visitor to that caravan," said Gus. "Sylvie sold it to a man called Mark Fennell. Before the London newcomers arrived on the scene, it suited Gavin for Sylvie to work here throughout the day. Nobody batted an eyelid when he dropped her off in the car park or sat outside in his BMW waiting for her to lock up late at night. He could visit the caravan, let himself in with a spare key, leave certain items for Mark Fennell, then lock the caravan behind him as he left."

"This is all news to me," said Josie. "Lennie never

mentioned that Sylvie used to own one of the vans. She didn't speak to me about it. What sort of items, anyway?"

"Drugs," said Gus. "That's how Gavin Tilson earned a living."

"I'm not surprised," said Josie. "Did Sylvie know?"

"We're positive she did," said Jill.

"Let me ask you again, Josie," said Jill. "Did you ever see any of those newcomers wandering through the site? Or another person that you know was associated with them?"

"I saw Ben Mulligan hanging around more than once. He was about twenty back then, a few years younger than me. The first time Ben was in trouble with the law, he would have been about ten."

"Kurt Burgess told me Ben Mulligan was a runner from the age of twelve, Gus," said Jill. "Ben moved drugs from one trap house to another and made deals on the streets. So it makes sense that Gavin Tilson had nurtured him. Perhaps Newbold and Atkinson persuaded him to work for them."

"When was the last time you saw Sylvie?" asked Gus.

"August Bank Holiday Monday, in 2006," said Josie.

"How can you be so certain?" asked Jill.

"My birthday is on the twenty-eighth of August. I finished work here, went into town, and met friends in a bar. Later that evening, as we moved to another pub, I saw Gavin arguing with someone on the other side of the road. The guy had his back to me, so I couldn't see who it was. Sylvie was standing five yards away. She looked across the road, and I'm sure she saw me waving, but she didn't respond."

"You couldn't hear what was being said?" asked Gus.

"We'd all had a few drinks, my mates were noisy, and the streets were full of holidaymakers. All I could see was two blokes shouting and pointing at one another. I spotted

Sylvie, waved, and then my friends dragged me through the door into the pub. I never saw either after that day, but people come and go, don't they? They don't have to ask anyone's permission if they fancy moving to a different town or city looking for a better life."

"Where might we find Ben Mulligan these days?" asked Gus.

"He was strung out on coke the last time I saw him," said Josie. "I can't remember when he was a regular in this part of town."

"We can ask Kurt when we get back to the station, Gus," said Jill.

"Will that be all?" asked Josie.

"For now," said Gus. "Thanks for your time."

Jill and Gus walked outside and made their way down the hillside to the remains of what had once been Mark Fennell's caravan. They stood in silence, studying the wreckage.

"Did the fire officer comment on how the fire spread?" asked Gus.

"He wasn't very forthcoming," said Jill. "Why?"

"Becky Hood is a mild-mannered suburban housewife. I can understand her losing her rag with her husband and Sam Webber. I can even imagine her attempting to damage the structure of the van to make it unusable. But, somehow, I couldn't see her capable of obliterating the van before the emergency services arrived. Would you know where best to start a fire and which accelerant to use?"

"I take your point, Gus," said Jill, "but Becky Hood admitted she drove here to do just that, and you've charged her."

"Becky didn't know there were three illegal immigrants locked inside," said Gus. "Someone else did, though."

"Newbold and Atkinson," said Jill.

"You told Adam Watson the forensic people hadn't finished with this pitch yet. Where is everyone? Perhaps we should get back to the station and follow up on that. The fire officer might have more he can offer us."

Gus and Jill walked up the steps to the top level and returned to her car. She drove them back to the police station, and once inside the building, they joined Kurt Burgess and the others in what had been the detective squad room.

Grace spotted the newcomers and came over to speak to Gus.

"DS Burgess has just ended his presentation, Gus. So we now have a complete picture of how things were in the Burnham and Highbridge district from the turn of the century until August 2006."

"Monday, the twenty-eighth," said Gus. "Bank Holiday Monday."

"Your trip to the caravan site was informative then?" said Grace. Gus thought she almost smiled.

"Josie Clift, the barmaid who took over from Sylvie Tilson, gave us that snippet of information," said Gus. "While Kurt, Jill, and the others grab a coffee, why don't you take me through the highlights of Kurt's presentation? Then, we can get a drink later."

"I'll see you in fifteen minutes, Gus," said Jill.

Within ten seconds, Grace and Gus had the room to themselves.

"You can see the wallboards," said Grace. "Kurt came in yesterday morning to prepare everything. The board in the centre shows Shane Prosser, the leader of the gang based in Cardiff. We know he died of cancer in 2006. Prosser was a career criminal who had been active for over three decades. South Wales Police had made dents in his organisation without ever reaching those at the top of the tree. All the other faces on that wallboard were based in Cardiff, Swansea, and various towns in the Rhondda Valley and the Brecon Beacons."

"We can ignore everyone on that board except the man on the extreme right, Gavin Tilson," said Gus.

"True," said Grace, "but DS Burgess had good news to pass on. I'll return to that. On the board to the left is the structure this side of the Bristol Channel around the time Mark Fennell holidayed in Burnham-on-Sea. The arrows on the main board indicate that Gavin Tilson reported directly to Shane Prosser. Tilson had met Sylvie after Prosser urged him to move from Cardiff to grow their business on the North Somerset coast. The names and faces on Tilson's board were locals he conscripted into his operation. Jack Carr, James Devine, and Gary Ellis were responsible for the distribution system. We already knew the drugs arrived by boat from Cardiff. Sylvie's details didn't appear on the wallboard because she was never deemed significant in the Prosser gang.

"A young tearaway named Ben Mulligan had the job of moving a small quantity of those drugs to the Berrow Road caravan site," said Gus. "Josie Clift saw him there, even after Gavin and Sylvie disappeared."

"Mulligan doesn't appear on the wallboard either," said Grace. "He was one of several youths the gang used that were expendable. Tilson could always find another feral teen to take their place. The picture changed dramatically after Paulie Atkinson and Jonny Newbold arrived. Kurt Burgess wasn't certain which London borough spewed them out, but in his words, they were different gravy from anything the local criminals had ever met. Within weeks of them moving to Highbridge, they targeted James Devine. Devine was from a fishing family. Although he had no intention of earning his living from fishing for mullet like his ancestors, he did have access to small craft that could put to sea and meet larger vessels further out in the deeper stretches of the Bristol Channel. That's where the transfer of illegal immigrants occurred at the dead of night. Devine brought them ashore and thus became the first link in the Tilson chain to break. Atkinson and Newbold convinced Devine that smuggling people into the country was a better prospect than handling a few kilos of cocaine."

"How did Tilson respond to that?" asked Gus.

"He recruited Adam Wilson from Bridgwater. Ellis and Carr continued to handle the drug imports from Cardiff. With Prosser's cancer making it tough to keep control of his operation, Tilson saw an opportunity to expand his empire by venturing further afield. Wilson had contacts in Taunton. Gavin Tilson wasn't prepared to take on the gangs in Easton or St Paul's in Bristol. However, he realised there was scope in the west of the county, avoiding the intergang warfare that undoubtedly would have been sparked if he'd ventured north-east."

"Jill Crooks told me on Saturday morning that Avon & Somerset weren't idle during this period. Of course, they had their successes, but it was mostly identifying illegals in whichever enterprise they'd been set to work and trying to repatriate them."

"The same old story, Gus," said Grace. "Low-hanging fruit, similar to the story from the Cardiff side of the water. The good news I hinted at earlier was down to a DI Williams."

"I know it's a long shot in Wales with that surname," said Gus, "but if it was Dai Williams, then I've met him."

"Dai Williams, that was the name Kurt mentioned. A bit of a character. Shane Prosser had died a few months before Tilson disappeared. South Wales Police had an undercover officer inside the Prosser gang who tipped off Dai Williams when a meeting was scheduled to arrange the break-up of the various parts of the organisation. Other gangs from Wales wanted a piece of the action. Williams led a raid of a meeting held in a Hells Angels' chapter club-house in Pembrokeshire. That raid resulted in a series of arrests."

"I remember things didn't go as smoothly as they would have wished," said Gus.

"Does it ever?" said Grace. "However, the Prosser organisation was destabilised to such an extent that Dai Williams and his colleagues could dismantle it over the next four years. As usual, other gangs moved in to fill the void."

Conversation in the corridor indicated that Jill Crooks and the others had returned from their coffee break.

"Just as we were getting to the interesting part," said Gus.

"What did you learn at the caravan site, guv?" asked Alex.

"We'll pick this up again in a minute, Grace," said Gus. "Well done. Right, what did we learn? Well, the barmaid who replaced Sylvie Tilson last saw her on the evening of Monday, the twenty-eighth of August 2006. Her husband, Gavin, was arguing with another man several yards away on the other side of the road. It appears to be the last occasion when anyone saw the couple."

"Did the barmaid describe the man talking to Gavin Tilson, guv?" asked Neil.

"He had his back to her, Neil. I thought it had to be either Atkinson or Newbold, but based on what Grace heard from DS Burgess, it could easily have been James Devine."

"Was this sighting in Burnham, sir?" asked Kurt Burgess.

"Yes," said Gus. "Josie Clift was celebrating her birthday with friends in various bars near the seafront."

"In that case, it couldn't have been Devine. He was in Highbridge that day. Traffic police stopped him for running a red light, and once he'd opened the car door, they smelled the cannabis. He was done for possession and driving under the influence. Devine was nowhere near Burnham that evening."

"I believe Gavin and Sylvie Tilson died within twenty-four hours of that last sighting," said Gus. "Atkinson and Newbold weren't strangers to using violence to achieve their ends. So where would they ditch the bodies, Kurt?"

"There's an awful lot of open ground within ten miles of the town in either direction," said Kurt. "Brent Knoll to Lympsham to the north and Sedgemoor to the south. When a criminal disappears from our patch, we tend to breathe a sigh of relief. It's rare for a friend or relative to report them missing, so we don't send out a search party."

"You rely on an elderly lady walking her dog in the countryside to find a bone," said Lydia.

"Pretty much," said Kurt. "Nobody has ever found anything in the past twelve years."

"There could be a good reason for that," said Jill. "If Atkinson and Newbold had two bodies to get rid of on Tuesday morning, they had other options."

"Devine would have returned from a night in the cells," said Neil. "He could have buried the bodies at sea."

"We'll never find them if that's the case," said Blessing.

"There could be a way to determine a possible location," said Kurt. "This station was operating twenty-four-seven in those days. My predecessors monitored activity between here and the Welsh coast. It was nigh on impossible to learn when and how the drugs reached these shores, but we did find instances where a small craft was in areas not generally used by the fishing fleets. GPS for a journey like the one you're describing might show an outward trace to an odd destination and a subsequent inward trace to Burnham marina."

"That could give us a general idea of where to look," said Alex.

"Better than that," said Kurt. "If we have the details on record, we can pinpoint the location of the bodies within five to ten yards. At seventy miles long and between five and forty-three miles wide, the Bristol Channel is the UK's largest natural inlet, with a depth of thirty to two hundred and forty feet. To avoid detection, they would have chosen deeper waters."

"Even if we found where the bodies were buried could we prove Atkinson or Newbold was responsible?" asked Grace.

"How does it help our case, guv?" asked Neil. "We're positive Gavin Tilson killed Mark Fennell and Helen Roker."

"True, but the conversation Jessie North overheard suggested that after Devine switched allegiance, Tilson soon realised he needed to do Atkinson and Newbold's bidding. He told Sylvie to relax. The switch to illegal immigrants becoming a major part of their business was just around the corner."

"You're suggesting that by August, with Prosser out of the picture, Tilson was working for Atkinson and Newbold."

"Although he liked to see himself as a leader, Tilson was

a follower," said Gus. "I don't reckon he had much choice if those two villains are as tough as Kurt makes out. The London crew were already in Highbridge by 2005. Devine jumped ship later that year. The newcomers started making noises about getting out of drugs and into people trafficking. Tilson drove to Kington Langley to dispose of Fennell. We can't know what happened over the previous weekend when Mark and Helen visited their caravan for the last time. It might have prompted Tilson to act alone. Prosser was a spent force, and Tilson was some way from throwing in his lot with Atkinson and Newbold. Helen Roker was a loose end. We may never know who decided she had to die. Perhaps, the London crew ordered the hit to incentivise Tilson's gang to follow their boss's lead and work for them. Whichever way it played out, Helen died in January, and although Sam Webber managed to maintain access to the caravan on Berrow Road, the balance of power had changed. Within six months, Atkinson and Newbold had removed Tilson and his wife and controlled everything in the region."

"What about between then and today?" asked Blessing.

"We've arrested dozens of people whose faces appear at the bottom of the other wallboard over there," said Kurt. "The senior members have the best defence lawyers in the country on speed-dial. We can never get evidence to connect them to any offences. They're untouchable."

"Find where they buried the bodies," said Lydia. "That will wipe the grin off their faces."

Grab your copy...
vinci-books.com/morningmurder